STIRRED UP BY A SEAL

A SMALL TOWN FRIENDS-WITH-BENEFITS
MILITARY ROMANCE

BAD BOY BAKERS
BOOK 3

KAIT NOLAN

TAKE THE LEAP PUBLISHING

A LETTER TO READERS

Dear Reader,

This book contains swearing and pre-marital sex between the lead couple, as those things are part of the realistic lives of characters of this generation, and of many of my readers.

If either of these things are not your cup of tea, please consider that you may not be the right audience for this book. There are scores of other books out there that are written with you in mind. In fact, I've got a list of some of my favorite authors who write on the sweeter side on my website at https://kaitnolan.com/on-the-sweeter-side/

If you choose to stick with me, I hope you enjoy!

Happy reading!

Kait

1

"What the hell is taking so long?" Jonah Ferguson paced another circuit of the hospital waiting room, no longer hearing the squeak of his dress shoes. He'd long since abandoned his tux jacket and tie, rolling up the sleeves of his button-down shirt as his only concession to comfort since he'd arrived straight from his best friend Brax's wedding reception last night. His very pregnant baby sister, Samantha, had thrown everyone for a loop when her water broke right on the dance floor.

Cayla Steele, wife of his other best pal and business partner, Holt, offered a tired shrug. "First babies can take a while. I was in labor with Maddie for fourteen hours."

Jonah fixed her with a frustrated glare. "It's been nearly twenty-four. Something has to be wrong."

His mother, Rebecca, pushed up from her chair and stepped into his path, forcing him to stop or run her over. She laid both hands on his considerably taller shoulders in a gesture she'd been using to soothe him since childhood. "Nothing's wrong. But if it makes you feel better, I'll go check on her again."

He jerked a nod. She patted his cheek and strode back down the hall to the birthing suite. Jonah resumed his pacing.

Holt shoved to his feet, holding out a hand for his wife. "Brother, I hate to do this to you, but we really need to be getting on home to Maddie. Donna has work tomorrow and technically, so do we."

Work. The bakery. Normal life. "Right. Of course."

Holt clapped him on the shoulder. "Listen, you stay here as long as it takes. Rachel and I can cover everything."

Rachel McCleary had completely rocked his world last night.

Jonah's mind slid to the party he'd left hours ago. His friend and business partner, Brax, had renewed his vows with his once-estranged wife, Mia. That was definitely cause for celebration. Jonah had stood in the shadows with Rachel—his *friend*, Rachel—watching the dance floor as everybody else got their groove on. He'd wanted to dance with her, wanted her in his arms with her scent surrounding him. Wanted to feel her body moving against his.

And that was exactly why he didn't ask her. He wished he hadn't finished the one beer he'd allowed himself. It would give him something to do with the hands that wanted to touch her.

He tuned back into their conversation. "Do you want to date?" Jonah told himself the answer didn't matter. He couldn't let it matter.

"I don't even know. John and I were high school sweethearts. I've never dated as an adult. And the whole idea of navigating that is... exhausting. I signed up for online dating and got so many dick pics in twenty-four hours, I deleted my account."

What the fuck is wrong with people? "Stay far, far away from the bottom feeders."

"Believe me, I intend to." Rachel spun the stem of her champagne flute between two fingers. "That said, I know John wouldn't have wanted me to be alone and grieving him the rest of my life. I'm working my way around to doing something about it." She took a bigger gulp of the sparkling wine and sucked in a deep breath. "I was hoping you could help me with that."

Everything inside him revolted. He'd looked out for her. He'd keep looking out for her. Of course he would. She was his teacher, the master baker who'd given him the skills to make a life for himself after the SEALs. And she was his friend, who'd helped pull him to the other side of the trauma of separating from the life he'd known. But helping her find a new love life? He wasn't sure he could do that. He worked to keep his face neutral. "You need me to screen some guys? Make sure they're worth your time? That they'll treat you right?"

"No, I've already done that. He is, and he does."

Jonah set his jaw. Who the hell was she talking about, and why hadn't she mentioned him before? Was this asshole good enough for her?

Rachel turned to him, blue eyes searching his face, her own full of something that looked an awful lot like hope and expectation. Except it couldn't possibly be that.

"Then how can I help?"

Those lovely, smooth shoulders straightened. She tipped back the last of the champagne and set the glass aside with a thump. "Maybe this will help clarify." And she curved those strong, slender fingers around his nape, closing the distance between them, to lay her lips over his.

Him. The asshole was him. Because apparently, in some past life, he'd done something incredible to deserve the attention of a woman like her.

On a sigh, he slid his arms around her, fitting that long, lean body to his as he angled his head to take the kiss deeper—

"Jonah?"

Blinking back to the present, he shoved aside the rest of the fantasy that had been playing on repeat for most of the last day and pulled Holt in for a back-thumping hug. "Thanks, man. I appreciate y'all sticking around this long."

"No problem."

When he stepped back, Cayla moved in, wrapping Jonah in a tight hug. "Sam's going to be just fine. And as soon as that little bundle of joy gets here, y'all will all forget about this stress."

"God, I hope so." Jonah squeezed her back. "Y'all go on. I'll keep you posted."

The two of them gathered up their things and headed for the elevator.

And then Jonah had nothing and no one left to distract him from the white elephant of The Kiss.

Surely the incident deserved capital letters. It had shocked the ever lovin' hell out of him. So much so that, in reality, he hadn't kissed her back.

He hadn't kissed her back.

It wasn't like he didn't want to. Hell, he'd been having fantasies about exactly that, almost from the day they'd met. But when she'd done it, he'd been struggling to analyze the ramifications of giving in to his own desires, when she might simply have been acting on a high of wedding nostalgia and too much champagne. A situation not at all helped by the reduced blood flow to his brain.

Then she'd pull back, and before he could do or say anything, his sister Sam had gone into labor.

Now here he was, almost a full day later, still at the hospital in Johnson City, waiting on the arrival of his new niece or nephew, and Jonah still didn't know what to do about it.

He'd spent the past two years telling himself to keep his hands off her. His inconvenient attraction didn't matter a damn. She'd been recovering from major emotional trauma, and he'd been working through his own trauma, physical and otherwise, along with coming to grips with the abrupt end of his career as a Navy SEAL. Neither of them had been in a place where anything more than friendship made sense. So it had been easy to tell himself that he wasn't what she needed. But now?

What exactly did she want? To date him? That was entirely impractical. His tiny hometown of Eden's Ridge was twelve hours from Syracuse. Rachel was only here for a few weeks.

Was she looking for a fling? Jonah couldn't imagine that. By her own admission, she'd never been with anyone else. Everything about Rachel screamed forever girl. And yet...

The echo of quick footsteps had him swinging toward the hall. His mom nodded at the nurses who'd become familiar faces over the hours they'd been here.

"Is the baby here?"

"Not yet."

"Damn, this kid is stubborn. Takes after both its parents."

"It shouldn't be too long now. She's finally fully dilated."

He really didn't want to think about what that meant.

Rebecca looped an arm through his. "Why don't you sit down before you wear a literal hole in the floor?" Without waiting for an answer, she tugged him toward a row of chairs.

"I'd rather swim fifteen miles than keep just sitting here." At this point, it felt like a year since Sam had gone into labor. He couldn't shake the knowledge that, despite modern medicine, women still died in childbirth. She was his sister. He'd spent his whole life protecting her. But this wasn't a battle he could fight, and the sense of impotence didn't sit well.

"You need a distraction."

"Yeah." He scrubbed a hand over his hair. "Yeah, I do."

"Okay. Then how about you tell me what's up with you and Rachel?"

It took all his considerable training not to tense at the question. "Nothing's up with me and Rachel."

"That wasn't what it looked like to me."

Jonah didn't even need to look to know she wore that bland, faintly amused mom expression that said *Busted*.

So she'd seen the kiss.

It wasn't like he had anything to be ashamed of. They were both single and unattached. But as he still had no idea what actually *was* going on with Rachel, he considered answering the question with his name, rank, and serial number.

Running footsteps from up the hall had Jonah shooting to his feet in time to see his brother-in-law, Griff Powell, racing into the waiting room, his face alight with joy, his dark red hair a wild halo around his head.

"It's a girl! It's a girl! Ten fingers, ten toes! I don't know what she weighs yet. They're putting her on the scale now. Come on!"

Relief loosened his limbs, and for a moment Jonah slumped against his mother, breathing a prayer of thanks. She squeezed his arm, then they both hurried after Griff. They arrived in time to see a tiny bundle swaddled in pink being laid in Sam's arms. Tendrils of his sister's dark hair were glued to her face with sweat, the rest of it pulled back into a messy braid. But despite the long hours, she looked wide awake and radiant.

"Eight pounds, twelve ounces. Eighteen inches long. And she got a full ten on the Apgar!" Sam announced the stats with all the pride she might've infused in saying the kid was valedictorian. Which she probably would be, with his sister as her mom. "You're gonna be tall, like your daddy."

Rebecca's "Oh!" sounded a tad watery as she moved to the opposite side of the bed to take her first look at her new grand-daughter. "She's beautiful."

Jonah's own throat went thick as he studied the baby. She was so very tiny. How could she be so freaking tiny? He swallowed. "What's her name?"

"Aurora Leigh." Griff eased a hip onto the bed, wrapping his arm around them both. "We're calling her Rory."

Rory. His brand new niece.

Cautiously, Jonah moved over toward Griff, laying a hand on his shoulder. "You did good, man. She's the prettiest little thing ever."

Sam nudged the pink hat up a little. "She got his red hair!"

"Your eyes." Griff pressed a kiss to her brow.

"Maybe. We'll see how they settle out in a few months. Either way, she's perfect." She beamed up at her husband.

As if sensing they were talking about her, Rory opened her eyes and seemed to look straight at Jonah. Those deep dark eyes just about took him out at the knees. She was new family. A new part of his circle to protect. And he vowed then and there that he'd do anything he had to in order to make sure nothing harmed this child or his sister's family.

Which meant that he had work to do.

~

RACHEL MADE another restless lap around the house. Jonah's house. Where she was meant to be staying for the next three weeks because he had two extra bedrooms, since Brax and Holt were now living with their wives.

It had seemed like a great idea when she'd accepted his invitation. She'd save a bundle on lodging while she was here, and it put her in close enough proximity to finally do something about this attraction. Except, after half a magnum of champagne, she'd misread everything.

Now she was dying in this awkward limbo, expecting him to get home any minute, not knowing what to say to him when he did. But it had been a full day since The Incident, and as far as she knew, he was still at the hospital, awaiting the birth of his sister's first child. Not that she'd dared text him to ask. Opening up any channel of communication seemed like the pinnacle of bad ideas under the circumstances. Instead, she'd paced the house like a lunatic, wrestling with the horror that came with reclaimed sobriety.

She was never drinking champagne again.

When her phone rang, she yelped, leaping away as if it were a poisonous snake. Calling herself an idiot, she edged closer to check the readout.

Audrey Graham.

On a shaky exhale, she scooped up the phone and answered the friend she'd put on a plane in Knoxville earlier today. "Hey."

"I just wanted to let you know I made it home to Syracuse."

"Oh, good." Her voice came out an octave higher than usual.

It didn't take Audrey's certified genius brain to figure out something was off. "Rach, what's wrong?"

She'd opted to say nothing to Audrey this morning, but after having the whole day alone with her thoughts, Rachel knew she had to spill or she'd explode. Dropping onto the sofa, she buried her face in her lap and groaned, "Everything. I kissed Jonah last night."

"Ah." The simple, one-syllable answer was so much Audrey's non-judgmental therapist response it had Rachel's temper sparking.

"What's that supposed to mean?"

"Nothing." Her tone was calm and placating, as ever. "I just wondered when that was going to come to a head."

"You knew?" What was she saying? Of course, Audrey knew. Even before all the graduate degrees, she'd been a natural observer. She saw everything. It was part of what made her a gifted clinician and researcher.

Instead of answering, Audrey came back with a question of her own. "How was it?"

Despite the fact that her friend couldn't see, Rachel covered her face with both hands. "Awful. He didn't kiss me back."

"Oh."

Audrey's legitimate surprise only compounded Rachel's mortification. "I just... We've gotten to be such good friends, and he's the first guy I've found really attractive since John died, and I thought it would be easier to take that leap with someone I care for and respect, just to get over the hump. But he didn't kiss me back, and then he was gone to the hospital with Sam. And of course he should have gone with her. But now I've had time to sober up, and, Audrey, what the hell am I going to do for the next three weeks? How can I face him? I'm staying in his house!" The words spilled out in a flood, laying out everything she'd been spinning over since last night.

"He's not home yet?"

"No."

"Hang on a sec." Her voice got muffled for a moment as she murmured to someone else. "I'll be off in a little while." A low, male voice answered, ending on a low chuckle. Because, of course, Audrey's husband, who happened to be Rachel's cousin, was right there.

There was a click that might have been the closing of a door.

"Okay, I'm back."

"Please, dear God, tell me Hudson's not listening in."

"Nope, I sent him to unpack and get the laundry started." Audrey sighed, and Rachel could picture her settling into the comfortable reading chair in her study, massaging the legs that had been rebuilt of pins and titanium after the catastrophic car accident years before that had first crossed her path with Hudson's. "Now, it seems to me you have two choices. You can either pretend it was a drunken mistake and laugh it off. Or you can talk to him about it while you're sober."

"If I could talk about it sober, I wouldn't have had to drink half a bottle of champagne to get up the guts to kiss him in the first place." Why, oh *why,* had she thought that was a good idea?

"You and Jonah talk about everything."

"Not everything." Not how she'd been having dreams about him. How his hands were the ones she was imagining on her body now. It was disconcerting. And it was thrilling to know that part of her hadn't died with John. Or it had been before she'd all but expired from mortification on the spot at the reception.

"What are you afraid of?"

"Are you seriously asking me that question?"

"Yes."

Rachel blew out an exasperated breath and tried to come up with a coherent answer. Fear had become so much a part of her life since John's accident. She'd gone from knowing who she was and where she stood, absolutely, to questioning almost everything in her life. It was why she'd sold her bakery. Why she'd spent the past couple of years as an instructor for Audrey's experimental baking therapy program for military veterans struggling with anxiety, depression, and PTSD, where she'd met Jonah and the other guys.

"I'm afraid of everything. Of ruining our friendship. Of being rejected. I'm terrified that the idea of a friends-with-benefits arrangement will insult him somehow. This seemed easy through the veil of champagne. It made sense. But now? I don't know." And the not knowing was killing her.

"Well, you can't undo the kiss. So you have to decide whether you want to make excuses, or whether to actually go for what you want. And you might want to make that decision soon, because Sam just texted. The baby's here, so Jonah will probably be on his way home shortly."

She so wasn't ready for that conversation.

"What did they have?"

"Girl. Aurora Leigh. They're calling her Rory."

As Audrey reeled off the rest of the expected information, Rachel smiled through the pinch around her heart. She and John had been trying for a baby the year he'd died, and a part of her had been devastated not to have a piece of him to carry on. But it didn't dim her legitimate joy for Sam and Griff. She didn't know Jonah's sister well, but she'd heard plenty about her through Audrey, as the two had taught at the same university for a while, before Audrey had reconnected with Hudson.

"I'm sure I'll be seeing lots of pictures. Thanks for listening."

"Any time. Do you know what you're going to do?"

"Not a damned clue. But I'll figure it out. I don't have any other choice."

She sat in silence for several minutes after hanging up the phone. Did she want to take the risk of talking to Jonah openly about what she wanted, or was it better to take the out of alcohol-impaired judgment and cling to the friendship they'd built? The answer wasn't simple. Neither option had a flashing neon sign saying, *Pick me!*

The truth was, he'd been up for something like forty hours by now. In all likelihood, he'd want to sleep in tomorrow. She needed to be up early anyway to get things rolling at the bakery so they could open on time at seven. The best option right now was to avoid him. Maybe after another night's sleep, she'd know what to do.

She scribbled a note and left it on the kitchen counter for him to find. Then, like the coward she was, she took herself to the guest room he'd given her and went to bed.

2

J onah shook a little as he slid out of his truck. The wake
of Rory's birth wasn't unlike the peculiar mix of exhaustion and adrenaline that hit him after a mission. A
healthy dose of anticipation pumped up the buzz as he
let himself into the house. Relieved of the worry over his sister
and the baby, his mind had been full of Rachel on the near
hour's drive home. He needed to see her. To set her at ease.
Because in all his ruminating, he remembered the distress in
her eyes when she'd pulled back. She'd probably imagined all
kinds of horrible reasons he hadn't responded, and none of
them would be the truth.

More than anything else, he just wanted another chance to
kiss her back. To satisfy this craving. Because now that he'd had
even the smallest taste of her, he couldn't turn it off as he'd
been doing for all these months.

The under-counter lights were on in the kitchen, along with
several lamps in the living room.

"Rachel?"

He moved through the house, automatically angling his

head to listen with his good ear. But he heard no reply. She wasn't curled up with a book or watching TV. Neither was she napping on the sofa. And why should she be? It was after ten. She'd probably gone to bed a while ago in anticipation of the early hour she'd be up for work in the morning.

Jonah found confirmation in the form of a note on the kitchen counter.

Headed to bed. Audrey told me the baby was here. Congrats, Uncle Jonah! You've been up forever and a day, so sleep in tomorrow. Holt and I have the bakery covered.

She'd signed her name in the familiar looping scrawl he'd memorized in the commercial kitchen where she'd trained him.

Before he could think better of it, Jonah found himself standing outside the door of her room, his hand inches from the panel. But he stopped himself before knocking. No matter what had happened last night, she was here to do them a favor. Waking her for this conversation wasn't smart or kind. Laying a hand against the door, he sighed with a mix of regret and resignation. It would keep. He just needed to wake up when she did to go in tomorrow morning. He'd set an alarm.

Too wired to sleep himself, and suddenly ravenous, Jonah retreated to the kitchen to scrounge up some food. The vending machine fare and hospital cafeteria options hadn't done much to hold him over. He found a container of leftover chicken noodle casserole Rachel must've made. Not wanting to risk waking her with the microwave, he shoveled in bites cold as he leaned against the counter.

The talons of a headache dug into his skull, squeezing just hard enough to remind him he'd pushed himself too far, too hard, and if he didn't get some proper rest, he'd be leveled with another of the debilitating migraines that were the bane of his existence. He'd had a lot fewer since he'd come home, but there were still regular enough aftereffects from the post-concussion syndrome he'd wrestled with for months after the accident that he couldn't feel fully normal. By rote, he lifted his hand and rubbed two fingers over the ridge of tissue on the back of his skull. His hair had grown back, covering the scar, but he'd never forget it was there, even if he couldn't clearly remember how he'd gotten it. Having read the mission report, that was probably a blessing.

Dropping his hand, his gaze fell on the clunky old radio shoved back into a corner beneath the upper cabinets. He didn't know why he kept the damned thing. A relic from the seventies, the sound quality was barely adequate, and it took up more than a reasonable amount of counter space. Maybe he hadn't tossed it because it was one of the few good memories he had of his dad. They'd taken the thing apart just to see how it worked. But it had been Jonah who'd put it back together. Because Lonnie Barker had not been a man who repaired things. He only broke them. It was what he'd done to their family, walking away when Jonah was eight years old, leaving him to take care of his mom and sister. It was a job he'd never shirked. Family was everything, and Jonah had spent his life trying to make up for the deficiencies of his deadbeat father. Living his life with honor.

Lonnie had died more than a year ago now and surprised the hell out of all of them when he'd left everything to Jonah and Sam, the kids he'd had nothing to do with in years. Not that everything had been much. The contents of his house and the decrepit bar he'd devoted his life to for the past twenty-odd years. They'd done the bare minimum. Jonah had boxed up the contents of the house, donating most of the furniture and putting the rest in storage until they felt like dealing with it. Sam would've been content burning it all, including the bar itself. But Jonah had looked at the building and seen possibilities. So much so that he'd dragged Holt and Brax down to

Tennessee to start their own bakery once they'd graduated from Dr. Graham's program.

It hadn't been all smooth sailing. The project had been plagued with problems from the beginning. Vandalism. Theft. An attack on Mia, who'd been their contractor for the renovation. Multiple crimes that they'd attributed to other things. But at this point, Jonah was pretty sure they'd been wrong about all of it. At the end of the day, he suspected that all the trouble that had come to their door could be laid at Lonnie's feet because of something he'd been involved with before he'd died. Jonah had always suspected his dad of something shady.

And before anyone else got hurt, he was determined to get to the bottom of what it was.

HAVING BEEN a professional baker all of her adult life, Rachel was accustomed to keeping early hours. Being up well before the sun suited her most of the time. But that was with coffee and the freedom to move around without having to worry about waking anyone. When not on shift at the firehouse, John had slept like the dead. Jonah's training as a SEAL meant he tended to be alert and awake at the slightest noise, so she hadn't even tried to start coffee, and she'd carried her shoes with her to the door, figuring she'd walk softer in bare feet. It felt like doing the walk of shame. As if she were sneaking out of his bed, instead of just his house.

His truck was in the drive when she eased down onto the front steps to put on her shoes. She hurried through the process, expecting the porch light to go on at any moment. When she made it to the car without interruption, she heaved a sigh of relief. Now if he'd only sleep through the starting of the engine, she'd be home free. At least for a few more hours. That'd be hit or miss, depending on whether his good or bad ear was aimed toward this side of the house. And that just sent her brain on a merry little trip wondering how he slept. On his back? On his side? On his stomach, with those long, strong limbs spread out like a starfish?

Focus, McCleary.

She cranked the engine and eased out of the driveway, keeping her eyes on the house in the rearview mirror as she slowly rolled down the street. No lights came on to indicate she'd woken him.

Finally relaxing, her mind shifted to recipes as she headed toward town. Though it had been more than a year, her brain clicked into planning mode automatically, mentally reviewing the contents of the walk-in cooler and storeroom she'd perused on Friday, and calculating what different things she could juggle to best maximize oven capacity and the time she had before the bakery opened. She realized she'd missed this, missed the anticipation of the work and the challenge of beating the clock. For the first time in a long time, she felt like doing things again. That was another little sign of healing. She'd finally reached a place where she could celebrate those small milestones instead of grieving them.

No one else was on the road. She enjoyed being awake when everyone was asleep. No one was giving her looks of pity or asking questions in that hesitant, careful way. No one was checking on how she was doing, eying her as if she were seconds away from falling apart. That had been the recurrent theme of her life since John died, and she was beyond tired of it. She'd loved her husband, and she'd grieved him. But her life wasn't over, and it was past time for her to start living it again. She just didn't think she could do it in Syracuse, where memories slapped her in the face on every corner.

That was part of what this stint in Tennessee was about. Testing out the small-town life, seeing if it was something she could be happy with. She liked the idea of it. Of becoming part of a smaller community. Somewhere she could learn the locals and where they could get to know her as her, not as that poor, young widow.

Eden's Ridge was a cute little town—emphasis on the little. Downtown consisted of about three blocks along Main Street, with a handful of other streets running crossways and parallel that hosted a variety of businesses. She drove past several on the way to the bakery, which was, itself, on the outskirts of town. The two-screen movie theater. The grocery store, Garden of Eden. Gift shops. Jonah's mom's salon. Crystal's Diner of the famed grilled mac and cheese sandwich, which she had yet to try. All shuttered and dark at this hour. But later on, the sidewalks would be filled with people moseying about their day. Her "Yankee sensibilities", as Jonah would say, couldn't consider the speed at which Southerners seemed to go about life as bustling. But she liked the slower speed. Liked the fact that people here felt as if they had the time to stop and talk to their neighbors and friends. It felt more personal. Not that she didn't have those connections back home. But she had them *because* it was home. Starting over somewhere entirely new seemed less intimidating to do in a small town.

She'd thought maybe of doing it here. Not because of Jonah —or, at least, not entirely because of him. But because of all the guys and their wives. Because she legitimately liked the town. But after The Incident, she'd probably screwed that up as a possibility. She didn't want to analyze the fresh surge of grief she felt at the idea that she'd taken that choice away from herself. Those were thoughts for after coffee. She'd brew a pot when she got inside, and start on dough for some cinnamon rolls.

Gravel crunched under her tires as she pulled into the bakery's driveway. She drove up the little hill and parked in front of the building. The original structure had been an uninspiring cinderblock rectangle. She hadn't seen it in person, but

Jonah had sent pictures when he'd asked for her opinion on converting it into a bakery. Brax's wife Mia had done the design, gutting the inside and covering the outside with siding now painted a rich forest green. A wide porch wrapped around three sides, and a bright tin roof accented the whole. It was woodsy and masculine and absolutely fit the three men who'd opened Bad Boy Bakers. The teacher in her was beyond proud of what her students had accomplished.

Mind on the coffee to be brewed, Rachel climbed out of the car and strode toward the rear entrance that led into the kitchen, one hand groping in her purse for keys. Okay, seriously, where the hell were they? She really had to clean out all the receipts and other garbage in here. No one who wasn't a mom should have a purse with this much crap in it.

A scraping sound had her head whipping up, her feet coming to a halt. Gooseflesh erupted along her arms, all the hair standing up.

I shouldn't be here.

The certainty of it was immediate and visceral, even before she spotted motion by the back dumpster. Was it an animal digging for food? Shit, they had bears here. But the shape she could make out against the dark blue of the dumpster wasn't an animal. It was very definitely human.

Holt's truck wasn't here, so it wasn't him. Lights weren't on inside, and he would've called out, anyway. Heart pounding, she began to back away. She needed to get to the car and call Jonah. Or 911. Something. But she had to get to the car first. Turning to run, she cursed when she bumped into one of the tables set outside for customers who wanted to enjoy the view.

Shit. Shit. Shit!

Footsteps sounded behind her, and the acrid taste of fear coated her mouth and throat as she stumbled on a chair, nearly going down. But she caught herself and lurched forward in an awkward run, digging for some more speed as she neared the corner of the building. Someone cursed and then a weight hit her square between the shoulders. She screamed as she lost her balance, flying forward toward the rail. Then the world exploded in a shock of white and pain before everything went dark.

3

Rachel had snuck out early. At least that was Jonah's assumption when he woke with his alarm to find her already gone. She had to be avoiding him. There was no other reason for her not to ride in with him. At least he'd have a chance to talk to her alone when he got to the bakery. He'd texted Holt last night, telling him to wait to come in until his usual time after getting his daughter off to the summer art camp she was doing this week. Or was it vacation Bible school? Jonah had lost track.

His brain felt like it was cotton soaked with Jell-O. The four hours of sleep he'd managed weren't nearly enough, and chances were, he'd be paying for it later. But he needed to clear the air with Rachel and set things back to rights. Whatever that was going to look like since The Kiss. That was largely going to depend on her and the specifics of what she wanted. Regardless of his own wants, he'd do what was best for her. But he needed more information to determine what that was, and that meant hauling his ass to the bakery.

According to the app on his phone, the security system still showed as set, so she couldn't be that far ahead of him. Dragging on jeans and one of the Bad Boy Bakers T-shirts that constituted their uniform, he grabbed his keys and stumbled out to his truck. At least there was no traffic at this hour, and nobody to bust him for breaking a few speed limits on the way.

Her car was parked out front, but the lights inside weren't on.

Maybe she was around the corner of the porch, unlocking the door.

Jonah slid out of the truck and went instantly on alert. Something wasn't right. He didn't know what tipped him off and didn't stop to analyze. His Glock 19 was in his hand without a second's thought as he edged toward the steps. With everything that had happened over the past six months, none of them were ever unarmed. He climbed the two steps to the porch, moving like the ghost he'd been trained to be. His eyes scanned the area for something amiss. Only having full hearing in one ear left him feeling at a stark disadvantage, and he'd yet to fully adapt. The damned ringing in his bad ear drowned out everything but the loudest of the night insects.

When he spotted the body sprawled facedown on the porch, his heart all but froze in absolute terror. He knew the dark wet stain on the porch boards was blood even before he dropped to his knees beside her. Fingers shaking, he checked her throat for a pulse, sending up a desperate prayer of thanks when he felt the flutter of it beneath his fingers. Training warred with instinct, but in the end, he rose and quickly checked the rest of the area for her assailant. Finding no one, he unlocked the door long enough to disarm the alarm and switch on the lights, and rushed back, cursing himself eight ways from Sunday as he stabilized her head, neck, and shoulders and carefully rolled her over.

"Rachel. Rachel, baby, wake up."

But she didn't rouse as he checked her over for other injuries. There didn't appear to be anything else, but the head injury was bad enough. Blood flowed freely from a gash on her temple. He carefully probed the edges, not feeling any obvious sign of skull fracture, but he didn't risk a more thorough examination. She needed medical attention, and she needed it now. The nearest ambulance would be nearly an hour out, and he didn't know how long it might take to rouse any EMTs from the volunteer fire department. He wasn't risking the wait. Clutching her carefully to his chest, he carried her to the truck, settling her in the front seat and buckling her in before leaning it back. Yanking the first aid kit from the center console, he dug for sterile gauze pads, gently pressing them to the wound. They soaked through in seconds. Swearing, he opened more, doing what he could with more gauze to secure them in place. Then he raced around the front and dove for the driver's seat.

His tires spit gravel as he reversed, heading for the road.

The moment his phone connected over Bluetooth, he dialed Holt.

The phone only rang once before Holt picked up, his voice rough but alert. "Yeah?"

"Get to the bakery. Rachel's been attacked."

"What?" There was a sound of bedsprings and then movement. "I'm on my way. Is she okay?"

"I don't—" Because panic was threatening to take over, Jonah curled his hands around the wheel until his knuckles went white. He took a breath. "She's alive, but unconscious. Head injury. I don't know if she was struck directly or if she got pushed into something and hit her head on the way down. There's a lot of blood." He sucked in another breath. "The scene was clear by the time I got there, and I locked the door back. I'm taking her to the hospital." It would be faster than waiting for an ambulance to come all the way from Johnson City.

"I'll deal with the police. Have you called them?"

"Not yet."

"Take care of Rachel. Let me know what the doctor says."

He didn't offer false platitudes, and Jonah appreciated it. Both of them knew that there were never guarantees that someone was going to be okay.

"Yeah. I will."

He hung up, and as soon as he hit the highway, he turned on his emergency flashers and put the pedal to the metal, flying toward help. He kept glancing over at Rachel, looking for any sign of consciousness. She looked so pale in the cold LED lights from his dash.

Unable to stop himself, he reached over to grip her hand. Her fingers were cold in his. Shifting his grip, he pressed his fingers to the pulse in her wrist. It continued to bump against his fingers, slow but steady.

"Don't you dare die on me. Don't you fucking dare. I can't lose you."

She groaned, shifting on the seat at the sound of his voice.

His heart leapt. "Rachel? Can you hear me?"

But she didn't respond again.

Keeping his fingers on her and talking the whole way, he made the usual forty-five minute drive in half that time, leaving a fair amount of burnt rubber on the pavement as he skidded to a stop outside the entrance to the Emergency Department. He'd already flung himself out of the truck when a security guard stepped out of the sliding doors.

"I need a wheelchair. A gurney. Something."

He ducked into the front passenger seat and unfastened the seatbelt, scooping Rachel's still limp form into his arms. Her color wasn't good, and she was motionless as a corpse, but for the shallow rise and fall of her chest. "Hang on, baby. Just hang on."

She groaned again, turning her face into his chest. "Jo—"

At the faint rasp of her voice, Jonah had to fight not to curl tight around her in relief. "Rachel. I'm here, baby."

He gently laid her on the gurney someone wheeled up and began reeling off details to the medical personnel who'd gathered around. "Victim is a thirty-two-year-old female with blunt force trauma to her right temple. She's been unconscious for about forty minutes since I found her, but seems to be rousing now. I don't know how long she was out before that."

The cluster of people rushed her through another interior set of double doors, where they'd doubtless be running tests.

A nurse stepped into his path. "What's her name?"

"Rachel McCleary."

"Someone will be out to get more information from you in a bit. We'll take it from here."

Jonah stopped, his hands curling into fists. But he nodded and watched as the doors closed behind them.

This was all his fault. She was here because of him. If he hadn't sat on his theory, hadn't kept quiet just so they could get through the vow renewal with no more interruptions or drama, they might have caught this son of a bitch already. But he hadn't done that, and she'd been hurt.

Self recriminations threatened to drown him. Lacing his hands behind his head, he paced a tight circuit.

Shut it down. You can kick your own ass later.

Right now, Rachel was alive, and he'd move heaven and earth to keep her that way.

∼

"Don't you dare die on me. Don't you fucking dare. I can't lose you."

They were her words—the charge she'd hurled at John in those first weeks after the accident, when he'd hovered between life and death, before it had become apparent he was never waking up. But it wasn't her voice. She slid away again before she could identify the speaker.

The familiar sharp scent of antiseptic and beep of machines interrupted the dark. Voices talked around her, but she couldn't focus on any of them. None were the deep one she'd heard before, and she retreated, not wanting a reminder of the hospital she'd come to hate.

A big, warm hand clutched hers. No, that wasn't right. She'd held his for hours every day. He'd never held hers back. Not until that one brief squeeze before the end.

Had she died? Was this John waiting for her on the other side?

Desperate to see his face again, she struggled toward the sensation, pulling out of the sticky black far enough to feel the pain and almost sinking down again. But she pushed on, fighting to open her eyes.

The first hint of light was blinding, setting off a shock wave of pain that seemed to echo through her whole body. She hissed, slamming her eyes closed. But the hand squeezed hers.

"Rachel."

Lured by that voice, she dared to open them again, confused when everything was blurry.

"Wha—?"

"Take it easy."

She tried to turn her head toward his voice and found she couldn't. The beep of a heart monitor sped up. She struggled to move.

"No, no. Don't move. It's okay."

A big form loomed over her, and his face finally resolved.

Not John. For a moment, the grief of that threatened to pull her under again before her sluggish brain offered up a name.

"Jonah."

His smile was full of a tremulous relief that was so at odds with the unshakable strength he usually projected, she almost reached up to touch him.

"Hey. You're awake. Thank God."

Why was she here? There was something she was supposed to do.

"What happened?" Her voice sounded weak and rusty.

"It can wait."

He hit the call button, and a minute later, a nurse walked into what Rachel now recognized as an emergency room bay.

The woman offered a kind smile. "It's good to see you awake." She checked the readout on the monitor. "I'll just go get the doctor. Be right back."

Rachel cut her eyes back toward Jonah. He looked so grim and haggard. She knew what it was to keep vigil after a head injury, knew the strain of wondering when or if someone would wake, and she wished she could reach out to smooth those lines in his face. How long had she been here?

A harried-looking woman in a lab coat with glossy black hair pulled into a low ponytail came through the door. The glasses she pushed up her nose magnified her big brown eyes. "I'm Dr. Choi. Let's see what we have here." She checked something on a chart. "Good news on both fronts. The CT scan shows no intracranial injury or skull fracture, and your spinal x-ray came back with no damage."

Jonah's hand flexed around hers.

"Let's get this cervical collar off, so you'll be more comfortable."

Cervical collar. So that's why she couldn't turn her head.

Jonah finally had to let her go so that the nurse could stabilize her head as the doctor undid the Velcro holding the collar in place. She slid the back piece from beneath Rachel's neck and lifted off the front. The air felt cool against her neck. The moment the nurse released her head, Rachel turned and searched out Jonah again.

He slid back into view, taking her hand again. "I'm right here."

She squeezed, as much for him as for her, because she didn't know what was coming.

Dr. Choi dropped onto a stool and rolled over to the side of the bed. "Okay, I'm going to ask you a few questions. Can you tell me your name?"

She licked her lips and croaked out, "Rachel McCleary. Water?"

Jonah instantly reached for a cup by the bedside.

"Just a sip," Dr. Choi cautioned. "You don't want to drink too much too fast, or you'll be sick."

Jonah helped raise the head of the bed up enough she could suck on the straw. The tepid water felt like mana from heaven against her parched mouth.

"Do you know what day it is?"

Did she? She had no idea how long she'd been out. "Monday? July the... something."

The doctor made a notion on a clipboard. "Do you remember what happened?"

"I..." Looking at Jonah, she tried to reach back to before. "I got to the bakery early. I wanted to let you sleep in since you'd been up so late waiting for Sam's baby to get here. Rory."

His lips curved a little. "Yeah, that's what they named her." The smile faded. "What happened when you got there?"

"Someone was there. In the back, by the dumpster."

"Did you see who it was?" he asked.

"No. Just an impression of movement. Dark clothes. I couldn't see his face. He must've been wearing a mask. I tried to run." Something had happened. There was something at the edge of her memory. She closed her eyes, trying to think past the dizziness and faint nausea. An impact. A fall. Then pain. The heart rate monitor shot up into a mad beat.

"I think he must have shoved me from behind. I crashed into something."

Jonah's fingers tightened on hers. "Porch rail probably, based on where I found you."

Dr. Choi's lips pressed together in a thin line. "Okay. I'm sure the police will want to speak to you. But let's get through the rest of this. What do you remember after you woke up?"

"Jonah. He was here. And then he got the nurse, and you came in."

"All right. No signs of amnesia. That's good." She went through the rest of her checklist, asking about symptoms and prior medical history. "Well, you have a concussion, but all in all, it could've been a lot worse. I'd like to keep you a few more hours for observation, just to be safe, but you should be able to go home later today. Once you do, you shouldn't be left alone for the first forty-eight hours."

"She won't be." Even in her hazy state, Rachel recognized Jonah was making a vow.

The doctor went over all the details of the aftercare with Jonah. He'd know all this already. He'd lived it himself. Rachel couldn't pay attention anymore. All the talking had exhausted her, and her head was pounding. She wanted the oblivion of sleep and must've drifted off again because the next thing she knew, she heard Jonah muttering, "This is all my fault."

That was sufficiently wrong that she struggled to open her eyes. "How is this your fault?"

His gaze flew to hers, full of an odd mix of grief and protective fury. "Doesn't matter right now. You need to rest. I'm going to take care of it."

There was some reason why this was a problem. "Jonah."

"Just rest, okay?" He folded his other hand over the one he hadn't let go. The contact was comforting, and somehow the gesture felt significant, but she was muzzy headed and couldn't properly think. Sleep was pulling at her again.

Before she went under, she looked up into those familiar green eyes. "Stay with me?"

"I'm not leaving your side."

And knowing he stood guard over her, she slid back into blessed unconsciousness.

4

"If you remember anything else, please let us know."

Jonah watched as Sheriff Xander Kincaid, one of his oldest friends, rose from the chair beside the sofa where Rachel was tucked into a nest of pillows, her cheeks pale, her eyes heavy with exhaustion.

Xander split a look between the two of them. "We're gonna find this guy."

"I'll see you out." Jonah followed his friend to the door.

Xander glanced back toward the living room. "This was a crime of opportunity, not a deliberate assault. My best read of the scene is that she surprised him, and he shoved her down to give himself a chance to get away. I don't think he set out to deliberately hurt her."

Frustration simmered, shortening the already fraying hold Jonah had on his temper. "Are you seriously trying to downplay this?"

"No. I'm just trying to give you some kind of context for what probably happened. Look, I know you're pissed. I know you're worried. But I need you to hear me when I say this, okay?

Don't take matters into your own hands with this. Let us do our jobs."

Jonah merely grunted. He wasn't about to make that promise. As much respect as he had for Xander and his capabilities, the Sheriff's Department hadn't gotten to the bottom of this in the six months since the trouble had started. Jonah wasn't leaving Rachel's safety or that of anyone else to chance. He'd do anything and everything necessary to stop this guy before anyone else got hurt.

Xander sighed. "Man, please don't do something I have to arrest you for."

"Then find this son of a bitch before I do."

A knock on the door interrupted whatever reply Xander might've made. Jonah pulled it open to find Holt and Cayla on the front porch.

Cayla lifted a casserole dish. "I come bearing food. I figured y'all would have your hands full and wouldn't want to cook."

"You figured right. Come on in. Xander was just leaving."

Was he being a bit of a dick to his friend? Maybe. But right at this moment, he didn't care about anything but protecting Rachel.

Xander leveled him with another long look. "I'll be in touch."

Jonah offered a short nod. "Thanks."

When he was gone, Jonah joined the others in the living room. Rachel was pushing herself into a seated position, her already pale face going white with the effort.

He leapt forward, not sure whether he was going to help her up or push her back down. "Shit. What are you doing?"

Rachel winced. "Cayla's going to help me get a shower so I can wash the blood out of my hair."

Jonah moved around the sofa, prepared to scoop her up. "I'll carry you."

She just batted his hand away, scowling. "I can walk."

Curling his hands in on themselves, he stepped back to let her, aware he was hovering like some kind of mother hen, but unable to stop himself.

She didn't slap at Cayla when she slid an arm around her waist to steady her. They made their slow, deliberate way to the bathroom down the hall, with Rachel weaving only a little. Jonah kept an eagle eye on her the whole way. He understood the frustration, understood the stubborn. He'd been so much worse when he'd been in that boat himself. But it didn't change a damned thing. He wanted to take care of her. Needed to make sure she didn't hurt anymore.

As soon as the door shut behind them, Holt nudged his shoulder. "Okay, man, how are you really?"

Jonah dropped the mask of calm civility he'd been wearing since Rachel woke up. "I'm ready to break some heads."

"I get it."

And Jonah knew he did. Cayla had been threatened by her ex-husband only a few months ago. It was what had led to their precipitous marriage in the first place.

"I'd say she was fairly lucky. It could've been a whole lot worse."

Jonah scrubbed both hands over his face, feeling every second of the hours he'd been awake. "This is my fault."

"How do you figure that?"

"I'm the one who asked her to come here."

"Brother, you didn't know this would happen. It's been quiet for months. We thought it was over."

"Except I didn't." And the guilt of that was gnawing at him. "You said months ago, when we had the last vandalism, that you didn't think this had anything to do with Mia, like we originally thought. I think you were right. I don't think the last round was anything to do with Cayla's ex, either. I think all of it has something to do with Lonnie."

"Your dad? How's that?"

"I always wondered whether he was involved in something shady. The Right Attitude was hardly a cash cow. But after he died, I didn't think anything about it. Even when all the shit started happening, we attributed it to other things. But the location—the bar—is the common denominator. I think Lonnie was into some shit, and his death left somebody mighty uncomfortable, worried about us finding whatever information is on that flash drive Abruzzi mentioned before Brax shot him."

Holt crossed his arms, considering. "Have you told the police?"

"Not yet. I will." He wanted to get a clearer handle on things before he brought it up to Xander, and to make sure his people were taken care of.

"Whatever you need. So let's talk about protection. You had both our backs when it was our women. It's our turn to have yours. Brax will help when he gets back."

Rachel wasn't his woman. Not in the way Holt was implying. But Jonah would protect her as if she was.

"I'm sending her home as soon as she's able to travel."

"Really? Why?"

"She needs to be where she's safe. And that's not here."

Holt's carefully blank expression told Jonah he didn't agree at all, but his friend didn't call him on it. Jonah would take the win.

"When are you going to tell her?"

"Not yet. I won't bring it up until she can handle the conversation." Because she'd fight it, and she needed to put her energy toward recovery.

"All right. Well, I know the first forty-eight hours are the most important. And beyond that, she won't be able to go anywhere for a week at least. I've got everything covered at the bakery. I spent all day baking and did a lot of pre-prep for stuff that will last and be fine tomorrow. I'll do the same when I get there in the morning."

Jonah felt another twinge of guilt. Bad Boy Bakers was a third his, and he was shirking his duty to the business. "Man, I hate leaving all this on you."

Holt waved off the protest. "Your priority should be taking care of Rachel. I've got no beef with that."

There was a significance to the statement Jonah chose not to address. He didn't have the bandwidth to explain to his friend how whatever he had with Rachel wasn't going to turn into the sort of connection Holt had with his wife. Their circumstances were entirely different. He'd just take the support and be grateful that his guys always had his back.

"What's the update on Sam and the baby?"

"They all went home with Mom about an hour before we left the hospital. She and Griff are staying here for a while before traveling home to Chattanooga." And Jonah's mom had all but ripped him a new one over not telling her immediately about Rachel's accident. But he hadn't been able to handle anyone else's concern at the beginning, and then he hadn't wanted to say anything that might upset the new mother.

The bathroom door opened, and the women emerged. Dressed in some kind of yoga pants and a loose T-shirt, Rachel seemed steadier on her feet and had a little more color in her cheeks. Some of the knots in Jonah's belly loosened a little. Her damp hair had been braided and hung over one shoulder.

"I really appreciate your help. I feel like a human-shaped thing again."

"Of course! Now, Holt and I are going to get out of your hair. I'm sure you'll want to eat and go on to bed."

"I feel like I slept most of the day away."

"And you'll probably sleep a big chunk of the next two," Jonah told her. "You'll be better for it. I speak from the voice of experience."

"Fair enough. Thank you for coming to check on me. And

for the casserole." She hugged Cayla before resuming her spot on the sofa.

Jonah walked his friends to the door, hugging them both. "I'll be in touch soon to set up a time to talk about the rest of this."

Holt nodded. "Just let us know. We'll be there."

Cayla's brows drew together. "The rest of what?"

"Holt will fill you in. Thanks again for everything."

Because he needed a few minutes to get himself locked down again, Jonah waited until they were backing out of the driveway to shut the door. By the time he made it back to the living room, Rachel had curled into a ball and fallen asleep again, her chest rising and falling in a slow, even rhythm. For long minutes, he watched that rise and fall, grateful she was resting easy and that her injuries hadn't been worse.

Knowing she'd likely be out for a while, he carefully scooped her up to transfer her to the bed. She stirred a little, snuggling against his chest. Jonah's heart stutter-stepped. Everything in him wanted to wrap her up, keep her safe. Swallowing hard, he carried her to the guest room and lowered her onto the bed. She made a little humming noise and curled onto her side. Jonah pulled up the covers, giving into the urge one last time to stroke his fingers over her cheek.

I'm going to keep you safe. I swear it.

With that silent vow, he left her to sleep.

FROM HER NEST of blankets on the sofa, Rachel listened to the smooth, deep cadence of Jonah's voice as he read.

"'Miss Dashwood,' cried Willoughby, 'you are now using me unkindly. You are endeavoring to disarm me by reason, and to convince me against my will. But it will not do, You shall find me as stubborn as you can be artful. I have three unanswerable reasons for disliking Colonel Brandon: he has threatened me with rain when I wanted it to be fine; he has found fault with the hanging of my curricle, and I cannot persuade him to buy my brown mare.'"

Jonah looked up from the copy of *Sense and Sensibility* his sister had sent over by way of his mom. "What the hell is a curricle?"

"It was a type of carriage, I think. In the movie version, Willoughby and Marianne are often seen tearing around the countryside in one."

"This Willoughby guy is clearly a tool. I don't know what she sees in him."

Rachel grinned at the affront in his tone, pleased when the motion didn't set her head to pounding again. "She's young and impetuous, and he's handsome and exciting. Passionate as she is. But don't worry, I'm totally Team Brandon."

Jonah scowled in disgust. "He's twice her age! What the hell is he doing looking at a seventeen-year-old-girl? She's a child. I mean, Jesus, that would be like me dating a junior in high school."

"You can't get hung up on the age difference. That was normal back then. Women were put on the marriage mart at seventeen or eighteen."

"Marriage mart? What is this? Brides R Us?"

She giggled. "A little. Upper-class women's value was entirely tied to their ability to marry well and produce heirs for the aristocracy."

Jonah shut the book with a decisive snap. "And y'all *like* these books?"

"I love a good historical romance."

"Why?"

"They take me out of the now and make me grateful to be a modern woman. And the really good ones are all about the heroines being subversive within the confines of a very restrictive social culture, finding and making their own happiness."

He laid the paperback on the coffee table and studied her. "If you can come up with a word like 'subversive', your brain is definitely on the mend. How are you feeling?"

They'd just passed the forty-eight hour mark since he'd brought her home from the hospital. She'd slept a ton. Jonah had been the consummate caretaker, making sure she had everything she needed and keeping an eagle eye on her symptoms. He hadn't been to work in three days. Rachel felt awful about that. She'd come down here to help, and now they were spread even more thinly, with Holt handling everything at the bakery so Jonah could play nursemaid. She didn't even know if Brax and Mia were aware anything had happened. She hoped not. She didn't want anything to dampen the celebration of their honeymoon.

"Better. Still tired. Still sore. But clearer." She wished she could see him more clearly in the low light. "Thank you for reading to me."

"It's no problem. I remember how bored I got when I couldn't watch anything or do anything."

His own recovery had taken months. Rachel was grateful hers would be much shorter.

"Are you hungry? There's more of that hash brown casserole Cayla brought. And Mom dropped by some poppyseed chicken this morning."

"Maybe in a little while." Bracing herself, Rachel eased herself upright. Her head swam with the motion, and she swayed.

Jonah was out of his seat in a flash, reaching toward her.

"No, it's okay. I'm okay." She regretted stopping him when his hand fell back to his side.

He hadn't touched her since they got home. Not past the bare minimum needed to assist her with whatever she needed.

After having him as an anchor through the whole ordeal, there was a new distance between them she hated, and she knew it was her fault. Knew too that he was blaming himself for what had happened to her. She hadn't forgotten what he'd said at the hospital. Now that she felt more like a human, she wanted to clear the air and accept the blame that rightly belonged on her own shoulders.

After a couple of deep breaths, the dizziness passed, and she patted the seat next to her. "Come sit with me."

He hesitated, but when she only continued to stare at him, he finally moved, lowering himself onto the other end of the sofa like he was afraid a bomb was set under the cushion. His posture stayed stiff, his hands flexing where they rested on his knees.

"Are you okay?" She searched his face, looking for some sign of what he was thinking.

"I'm fine."

At the curt, dismissive tone, Rachel laid a hand on his arm, feeling the tension coiled there. "Jonah. I'm not the 'I'm fine' friend. I know you're not fine."

His throat worked, but he didn't look at her. At last he bit out, "As soon as you're able, I want you to go home."

His words were a sucker punch, and she instinctively pulled back. For a long moment, she couldn't speak and had to close her eyes against the sudden threat of tears. "Did I screw things up that badly? I was more than half drunk, and I just thought... Well, it doesn't matter what I thought. I'm sorry. I won't ever mention it again. But I can still do what I came here to do and help out. I'll move to the inn—"

"No, you fucking won't. Look at me, Rachel."

She opened her eyes.

His own were blazing, and the line of his jaw was hard as granite. "You aren't going anywhere out of my sight so long as you're in town."

"I don't understand."

"I don't want you to go because of the kiss. I want you to go because it's not safe here. You got hurt because of me. You could have *died* because of me."

And she understood that the anger wasn't directed at her, it was at himself. "What are you talking about?"

He scrubbed a hand over his hair, making it stand up in spikes. "I haven't been completely honest with you. We've had a series of problems since we started renovating the building."

"What kind of problems?"

"It started with supply theft. There'd been a rash of them around the county, so we thought it had to do with that. Then there was vandalism. Then we found a bunch of surveillance equipment planted around the place."

"Surveillance equipment? What, like bugs?"

He jerked a nod. "Bugs. Cameras. There was some stuff related to Mia's past that made us think it was tied to her because she was the one doing the renovation. And that seemed confirmed when she was attacked on site one night."

"She was *attacked*?" How had he not mentioned that in all their conversations since he moved down here?

A muscle in his jaw ticked as he nodded again. "Yeah. The guy would've killed her, but Brax got to him first."

Did that mean a man had been *killed* in the bakery? Jesus. Rachel was kind of glad she hadn't known that part. "Who was he?"

"A hired thug."

"Hired by who?"

"That's the sixty-four thousand dollar question. We don't know. He was after information of some kind. The guy said something about a flash drive. We never found one, and after that, it went quiet for a while. Then we had some more vandalism right after we opened. We thought it had something to do with Cayla's ex-husband, who'd gotten out of prison, but more likely it was someone else looking for whatever it was the first guy didn't find." He fixed his tortured gaze on her. "Our best guess is that you interrupted the latest attempt. And it could've cost you everything."

She wanted desperately to soothe him, but couldn't quite bring herself to touch him again. "It wasn't your fault."

"If I'd told you about all this, you wouldn't have been there by yourself."

Rachel swallowed and decided her pride wasn't worth what he was putting himself through.

"Yeah, I probably would have."

5

J onah couldn't have heard her right. "What?"

Rachel knit her hands together, color rising to her cheeks. "I was trying to avoid you when I went in early."

"Why?"

"I was embarrassed."

The color in her cheeks and the twisting of her fingers made it clear she was still embarrassed.

"We're friends, and I shouldn't have tried to change that. You are not obligated to return the attraction."

Her gaze, which had been fixed somewhere around his left ear, dropped to her lap, and her shoulders rolled in on themselves. Jonah wanted to swear because he could tell she'd been imagining all kinds of awful things. That he didn't find her attractive. That he was upset she'd kissed him. That he was somehow repulsed by her offer. That he pitied her. He'd been all set to deal with this when he'd come home after Rory was born, but with everything that had happened in the last few days, it had been pushed way down his priority list. It rose back to the top as her flush deepened past embarrassment and into mortification.

He knew it was a terrible idea, but he couldn't let her keep thinking any of that. "Rachel."

Her voice rose half an octave. "Really, it's fine. We can just forget it."

With one finger, he tipped her chin up, forcing her to look at him. Her bluebonnet eyes were dark with distress, her breathing too fast and shallow. He couldn't stand it. Everything in him needed to make her stop hurting. "I don't want to forget it."

His fingers skimmed along her jaw. God, her skin was soft. He moved slowly, watching every nuance of her expression, giving her every opportunity to pull back. When she only watched him, those eyes full of a cautious, yearning hope, he closed the distance between them and gently, so very gently, laid his lips over hers. Jonah kissed her as he'd wanted to for months. Like she was precious to him. Like she mattered. Because she was and she did, whether he wanted her to or not.

After a beat of surprise, she sighed and melted into him, mirroring the way he cupped her face as she kissed him back with so much sweetness and warmth he wanted to drown in it. In her. He could lose himself in this, and he couldn't afford to. Couldn't afford to forget. Because he felt his control slipping, and he understood that there'd been no one since John, he made himself pull back instead of diving deeper, pushing for more.

Rachel's eyes were blurred, her expression full of surprise and relief. She weaved a little, and his focus sharpened.

"Are you dizzy?"

"Yeah. But the good kind."

Her fingers flexed on his jaw, and he instinctively turned into the touch.

Her thumb rasped over his beard. "After the other night, I thought... Well, I thought I had it all wrong."

"You surprised me." An understatement, but he didn't see

the point in getting into all the arguments he'd been having with himself since then.

One corner of her mouth quirked into a wry smile that had him wanting to taste her again. "I think I surprised myself by actually going through with it."

"What exactly were you angling for at the reception?" Jonah braced himself to let her down gently. The kiss and his attraction aside, he couldn't be her long-term anything, and she deserved another forever guy.

She sat back, color burning in her cheeks again, but she didn't look away this time. "I've never been with anyone but John. We were together from the time we were fourteen, and I can't imagine going there with someone I don't respect and trust. I'm not looking for forever. I don't expect to find that again. But you made me feel again, and I was hoping that, while I was down here, we could expand the parameters of our friendship."

That... was not at all what he'd expected. He'd thought she'd be looking for a true life partner. She was young enough to still have all the things she hadn't yet gotten to experience with John before he died. But maybe she wasn't ready to think about any of that. Maybe she was looking for a stepping stone of sorts.

"To clarify, you mean friends-with-benefits?"

She nodded with a little wince. "I hope you're not insulted by that. I don't want to use you. If it's not something you're interested in, that's fine. I'm not offended. I don't want to lose your friendship. Keeping that is more important to me than anything else."

She wasn't looking for a relationship. Wasn't looking for another husband. It was, in a sense, the next phase in her healing. And she thought he was a worthy candidate for that.

Jonah absorbed that fact, humbled by her trust in him. He had his own demons, his own healing to do. The idea of doing that with her was beyond appealing. They'd become each other's rocks. He loved the idea of becoming more, even if only for a little while. But under the current circumstances, it was a non-starter. Her safety was a bigger priority.

"I'm flattered. And if you weren't going home as soon as possible, I'd definitely be willing to explore that, but—"

Leaning in, she framed his face. "Jonah, I'm not going home."

That wasn't an option. He hadn't been clear enough. "But you're not—"

She interrupted him with another soft brush of her lips that had his brain short-circuiting. "I'll be perfectly safe with you. If you need me glued to your hip while I'm here, fine. That's not exactly a hardship. But I'm not going to leave you to handle all this alone. I can help you figure it out."

He sucked in a breath, about to tell her why that was basically the worst idea ever, but she just laid a finger over his lips.

"You can argue all you want, but I promised to stay until Mia and Brax get back, and that's what I'm doing, if for nothing else than to help at the bakery like I said I would. I'd rather stay with you, but that's your call. Just as the rest of this is your call."

If she truly refused to leave, she'd be safest with him, where he could keep an eye on her. And with her offer... He couldn't give her more than temporary, but if that was all she was looking for, he didn't see any more reason to fight it. She'd presented perhaps the only way he could actually be with her, and he definitely didn't want to see her pursuing this with anyone else.

Curling his hand around hers, he pulled it away from his mouth. "Yes."

Her eyes widened. "Yes? Really?"

Jonah uncurled her fingers and pressed a kiss to the center of her palm. "Yeah, really. It'll be a relief, actually. I've spent most of the last two years trying to keep my hands off you."

"You have?" She looked delighted at the prospect. "Why?"

"You needed a friend. Only a friend. And I wasn't exactly in a great headspace myself. You know. You were there."

Rachel laced her fingers with his. "We've both come a long way."

"Yeah."

"You've become so important to me, Jonah. Your friendship has meant so much. It's why I wanted to take these next steps with you. You know what I'm coming from. You know what it means to me."

He swallowed, feeling the weight of what he was agreeing to. "Yeah, I do. And I promise not to take that for granted. Not to take you for granted."

Her lips curved into a soft smile. "I know. You're far too noble and considerate for that."

Turning her hand over, he brushed another kiss to her knuckles. "I'll take care of you. For as long as this lasts." He had to say it. Had to remind himself that this was a time-limited thing.

She leaned in, wrapping her arms around him. "I'm counting on it."

He pulled her closer, glorying in the feel of her snugged up against him. "You've got more recovering to do first."

Her soft laugh vibrated against his throat. "Can't happen fast enough."

"Why is it that homemade mac and cheese made by a mom is inherently better?" Rachel asked the question of the group at large, gathered around Rebecca's kitchen table, as she scooped another half serving onto her plate.

Jonah's mom grinned, the green eyes she shared with her son sparkling. "The secret ingredient is in the handbook."

"My copy must've gotten lost in the mail. Or maybe it's waiting for me at home." Sam held out her plate. "Hook me up with some more of that while you're at it, Rachel."

Jonah arched a brow. "Taking advantage of eating for two?"

"You bet your ass I am. I'm riding this train as long as it lasts." She shoveled in another bite and hummed a long contented note. "She's totally right. Yours is so much better."

Rebecca's cheeks pinked. "Oh, now, you know I love seeing people enjoy my food. All the proposals were good for my ego."

Cayla straightened in her chair, attention sharpening like a dog on point. "Proposals?"

Holt took another spoonful of bacon-roasted Brussels sprouts. "Brax and I might've both asked her to marry us when we first got here. For me, it was the meatloaf. For him it was her apple pie." He pressed an exaggerated hand to his chest. "Sadly, she broke both our hearts."

"The better for me to pick up the pieces." Cayla pressed a grinning kiss to her husband's cheek.

Enjoying the family banter, Rachel finished the last of her pasta and set the fork aside. "I really appreciate you going to all this trouble. Everything's delicious." And as it was the first day she'd truly had an appetite back, she'd taken advantage.

"It was no trouble at all. I wish y'all had let us come to you at Jonah's. I don't know what he was thinking dragging you over here."

Not wanting him to get in trouble with his mom, Rachel intervened. "That was on me. I was rebelling against the bubble-wrap treatment and needed a change in scenery, so this has been great."

"I'm so glad you've enjoyed it, and that you're feeling up to getting out a little."

By tacit agreement, everyone pushed back from the table, gathering plates and serving dishes. Rachel set hers on the counter. "What can I do to help?"

"You can sit your butt down," Jonah informed her.

"The injured and the recently given birth are not allowed to do squat. I'm trying to enjoy it as long as possible." Sam crossed into the living room, where the baby was nestled into a bassinet. Her face fairly radiated joy as a tiny fist waved. "Hi, sweetpea. How's mama's little angel?" She started to reach for Rory, but Griff intervened.

"Nope, you sit. I'll bring her to you. You're not supposed to lift anything heavy."

With a bland look for her husband, Sam sat. "I don't think the baby counts."

"Not taking any chances." He carefully scooped up the little bundle, nuzzling her cheek. "Hey, baby girl. You hungry? Wanna go see Mama?"

Rachel's throat went thick as she watched the exchange, seeing their intimacy in the shared adoration over the new life they'd brought into the world. Her heart pinched at thoughts of what might have been. John had so wanted children, but she'd insisted they put it off while she got her business off the ground. And now she had none of the life she'd expected.

A warm hand pressed to the small of her back. "You okay?"

Jonah's low voice at her ear loosed the stranglehold of grief. Swallowing once, she nodded.

His eyes searched hers, as if trying to decide whether she was lying. Knowing he'd bundle her up and whisk her off home if he decided she was, she willed back the tears and dug up a smile. That big, broad palm lingered another beat or two before falling away. The moment it did, she missed his touch. But they hadn't discussed the idea of telling people they were anything more than the friends they'd always been, and Rachel wasn't exactly keen on announcing their new arrangement in front of his mother, no matter how awesome Rebecca seemed.

As everyone else began to file into the living room, Jonah squared his shoulders, obviously bracing himself to get to the meat of why he'd asked for this get-together. Rachel stayed where she was, needing to be near him to offer silent support. She knew he'd been dreading this conversation.

"You should sit," he urged.

She rolled her eyes. "You've had me horizontal for four days. I can stand up for a while."

At the collective choked laughter, she played her words back in her head and felt her face catch fire. "That came out wrong."

Jonah's lips twitched.

"What I *meant* was that I'm tired of being an invalid. I know when I'm overdoing. I'll sit down when I need to." She waved a hand in his general direction. "You keep your bubble wrap over there with you."

He blew out a breath. "Fine." Shifting gears, he faced the rest of the group. "Alright. Now that we're fed and happy, I'll admit that I had an ulterior motive for pulling everybody together tonight."

Rachel didn't miss the speculative looks Sam, Griff, and Rebecca shot between her and Jonah. Wait, did they think this was about the two of them?

"I want to bring everybody up to speed on what's actually going on with the bakery."

Rebecca blinked, her amusement fading into concern. "What's going on with the bakery? Is there a problem? I thought business was good."

"Business is good. That's not the problem. You're aware of the theft we had during the renovation. Of the bouts of vandalism. At first, we all thought it was connected to something from Mia's past. Then we blamed Cayla's ex. But at this point, I don't think any of it had to do with either of those things. I think it had to do with Lonnie."

A murmur of surprise swept the room.

Sam's brows drew together. "Why would this have something to do with Dad?"

"It was his bar for more than twenty years. We always kind of wondered how he was paying the bills, and I never saw any kind of accounting or books. I think he was involved in something shady. Before Brax shot the guy who went after Mia, he kept going on about a flash drive, looking for some kind of information he'd been hired to find. He clearly never found it, and things have just continued to happen. Another break-in, more vandalism. Likely would have been more of both if Rachel hadn't surprised whoever it was the other morning. Whoever is behind all this hasn't found whatever they're looking for, and I think it's just going to continue happening until we figure out who it is and what they want. Or what they're trying to hide. So, I wanted to loop everybody in. See what y'all's thoughts were on the matter."

Rebecca's cheeks had gone pale. "Why didn't you say anything?"

"Seriously, man. If this is to do with your dad, who's to say this asshole won't try to come after Sam? How could you just sit on this?" Griff's tone was hard.

"Everything that's happened has been around the bakery, so there's no reason to think any trouble would've spilled over on Sam since she hasn't been here. But you're right. I should've said something about all of this before. My only excuse is that I'm accustomed to running covert operations on a need-to-know basis, and I didn't think you needed to know. I was wrong. That said, as soon as you're comfortable traveling with the baby, I think you should head home. You'll be safe there. I'm not letting anybody else get hurt on my watch."

He wanted his people safe. Rachel got that and knew he was still annoyed that she'd refused to bend to his will and go home herself. She could also see he was falling back down the this-is-all-my-fault black hole again. His hands opened and closed at his sides. A muscle jumped in his jaw, and his breathing had gone just a little too shallow. If he didn't stop this spiral, he'd have a panic attack.

"Jonah, look at me."

At the sound of her voice, he turned to face her, his eyes zeroing in on the ugly yellowing purple blotch on her temple, as it had with increasing frequency over the past few days. His pupils shrank to pinpricks.

Reaching up, she cupped his cheek, tipping his face toward her. "Not at the bruise. At me."

When he finally met her gaze, she kept her voice very quiet, very serious. "I need you to actually hear me when I say this: I'm okay. You can stand down."

His nostrils flared, his eyes going glacial, as they had when she'd been in the hospital.

She cupped his other cheek, framing his face and willing him to listen. "Stop blaming yourself. You think because you've got these big monster shoulders, you have to take everything on them. You don't. I realize this is a lifetime habit of yours, but the first step in recovery is admitting you have a problem."

He blinked and some of the hardness left his eyes as he curled his hands around her wrists. "You don't pull punches, do you?"

"You wouldn't like me nearly as much if I did. Now take a breath."

She waited until those shoulders rose and fell.

"And another."

On his next exhale, the tension ebbed and his pupils dilated back to something more normal.

"Better?"

Jonah nodded once.

Rachel released his face, but he was much slower to let go of her wrists, as if he still needed the contact to settle himself. It wasn't until he stepped back and froze that she remembered they had an audience. Everybody stared at them with varying degrees of speculation. Rachel's cheeks heated, and she fought the urge to step behind Jonah to hide. Well, they hadn't discussed keeping things a secret any more than they'd talked about announcing the change in their relationship. There didn't seem to be much hiding it now.

Holt was the one who finally broke the silence. "So, what are we going to do about this? I'm all for anything that'll put a stop to all the disruption."

God bless him for pointing everyone back to the business at hand.

Jonah picked up the thread of conversation. "We're gonna try to find whatever Lonnie hid."

Cayla leaned forward, elbows on her knees. "How do you even know there's anything to find?"

"We don't. But obviously if there is something, it wasn't in the bar or we'd have found it. So the next step is going through all his stuff."

"But his stuff is gone," Sam protested. "You tossed it after the funeral."

"Actually no. It occurred to me neither of us was in any mood to deal with his shit at the time, but that there might be something important in there, so I hauled it all to Nanna's old house. Free storage. I figured we could just deal with it when we had time. Now's the time."

Rebecca's usually sunny face was sober. "I want to help."

Jonah tensed again, and Rachel instinctively laid a hand on his arm. "I don't want you anywhere near this, Mom."

"Come on. I was his wife. I knew him better than you. I knew him longer than you. I might recognize something you wouldn't."

He angled his head in grudging concession. "Nobody's going out there on their own. Apart from the fact that it's just smart, the house isn't in that great a shape, and it's a long-ass way from help if somebody were to fall through the floor or something. We can start sorting through on Sunday, when the bakery is closed. Any of you who wants to waste your weekend that way is welcome. In the meantime, I've gotta loop Xander in on the whole thing, in case there's some past charges we're not aware of or something."

Holt folded his arms. "He's gonna be pissed you didn't tell him sooner."

"He can get in line. Meanwhile, I'm calling curfew on Rachel. She needs her rest." His arm came around her, a comfort she didn't hesitate to lean into.

Because she really was exhausted, she didn't argue when he started herding her toward the door. Goodbyes were said and hugs were passed out. Rebecca retrieved the bag of leftovers she'd prepared and handed it off to Jonah so she could carefully fold Rachel into an embrace.

"You're good for him." The murmur was quiet.

Rachel had no idea what to say to that. In the end, it didn't seem like his mom was looking for a reply.

Rebecca just smiled and turned to give Jonah a squeeze. "Get some rest, son. You've been doing all the caretaking, and I can tell you're not sleeping enough."

He kissed her cheek. "Yes, ma'am."

She winked at Rachel. "I trust you'll keep him in line."

Was this approval? Rachel had no idea. With a quick glance at Jonah, she offered a tentative smile. "I can try."

6

Jonah wasn't a fan of admitting he was wrong. He figured most people weren't. But he knew he hadn't done right by Xander and had probably hampered his investigation by not passing on his suspicions sooner. So Saturday morning, he bearded the lion in his den—aka Xander's office at the Sheriff's Department, where his wife, Kennedy, had said he'd be.

"Why, Jonah Ferguson! Aren't you a sight for sore eyes? Come on around here and give me a hug."

Essie Vaughn, the dispatcher and admin for the department, who'd been around since God was a boy, was a long-time client of his mama's salon, so the familiar greeting didn't surprise him. This was one of the pieces of small-town life he'd grown to appreciate as an adult. Connection and caring. He was still getting used to being back in it.

Circling the desk, Jonah wrapped one arm around the tiny older lady. "How you doin' Miss Essie? Xander treatin' you right?"

"Oh, you know he is. That one's a lot less stuck in his ways than his daddy."

Xander's father, Buck, had been sheriff all the way back when they'd been teenagers. He'd been a tough man, with very clear ideas about how things should be done. A definite member of the good ol' boys' club, who'd made some questionable uses of his authority over the years, Buck had retired after a heart attack a few years back. Xander had slid into the job as interim sheriff, then won the election outright after that. There'd been little opposition to the change, and Xander had used his tenure to start upgrading and modernizing the department where time and budget constraints allowed.

"He in his office?"

"Grumbling over paperwork, as usual." Essie eyed the bakery box Jonah carried.

"Could be there's something in here that might sweeten his attitude. Might be something for you, too." He lifted the lid, revealing the assortment of pastries and muffins he'd brought from Bad Boy Bakers, where he'd left Rachel under Holt's watchful eye this morning.

"You charmer, you. You know the way to my heart is through orange raspberry scones." She plucked one from the box.

"A wise man remembers what the women in his life like to eat."

"That is the God's honest truth. Go on back."

Jonah went down the short hallway and knocked on the doorjamb.

"Come in."

Xander's sandy hair stood up on one side, as if he'd been tugging at it with one hand. His face brightened at the sight of Jonah. "Hey."

"You got a minute?"

"I'll make a few. You're preferable to dealing with this latest bullshit from the Fullers."

"The Feral as Fuck Fullers?"

Xander snorted. "Well, we don't call them that in an official capacity, but between you, me, and the wall, the moniker still fits. J.B. Fuller—you remember him? He was a year or two ahead of us in school. He got sent away a few years back for meth production. I'm pretty sure his baby sister took over his operation and moved it elsewhere in the county. I just haven't been able to prove it yet."

"Apples didn't fall far from the tree, I see."

"Nope."

There were stories about the Fuller family going back multiple decades in the Ridge. They were the family you didn't piss off because angering one Fuller was angering the entire clan, and they were way more about vigilante justice than allowing the legal system to take care of matters. They insulted easily and carried grudges like battle axes, passed down from one generation to the next.

"I don't envy you having to deal with that."

He shrugged. "It's the job. How's Rachel? I'm sorry I haven't been by to check on her."

Jonah waved that off. "She's okay. Browbeat me into letting her actually go into the bakery this morning. I didn't want to, but I knew she'd go on her own if I didn't handcuff her to me, so I dropped her off with Holt before I came here."

"Glad to hear she's on the mend. I don't have any updates on the case."

"That's not why I'm here. I came to apologize."

"Man, somebody you care about got hurt. I get it. I wasn't offended."

"I appreciate that, but I'm not here about that either." He set the box in front of Xander. "Have a pastry."

His friend shot him a healthy dose of side eye. "Why do a get the feeling you're trying to bribe me with sugar to not be pissed about whatever you're about to confess?"

"Because you've known me for more than twenty-five years. Eat a pastry anyway."

Jonah waited until Xander had picked out a muffin and grabbed another of the scones himself. "I haven't been completely honest with you."

"I'm listening."

He laid it out, as clear and concise as he could. By the time he was done, Xander was halfway through a blueberry danish, and his expression hadn't changed much.

"Why didn't you bring this up before?"

"I wasn't sure about it. I wanted time to think it through. And I had other priorities. Pick one." Jonah shrugged. "I realize, ultimately, none of them are good reasons."

"Mmm. Well, it's a damned good thing I thought of it right off the bat."

Jonah sat back in his chair. "You did?"

"Sure. I broke up dozens of bar fights when it was The Right Attitude. Made a few drug busts in the parking lot. Conducted surveillance on more than one lowlife that frequented the place. Never tied any of it to Lonnie, but it isn't a jump to think he could've been involved in some shit we didn't know about, and it's bleeding over to you now."

And here Jonah had thought he'd been so clever putting the pieces together. Perhaps his post-concussion brain wasn't back to being as sharp as he'd imagined. "Well, now I feel stupid."

"As you said, you've had other things on your mind. And with the trouble that was following Mia and Cayla, everything got muddied. But for what it's worth, I agree with your conclusions. Those threats were resolved, and something is still going on. After eliminating all the other possible explanations, Lonnie's the common denominator. What is it you think he might've been involved in?"

"That flash drive Abruzzi mentioned could hold anything. Blackmail material. Drug clients or supply chain shit.

Nobody'd be so het up about getting it back if it wasn't a secret they didn't want revealed. I don't know if it's something Lonnie was directly behind, or if he and the bar were somehow a go-between for something bigger. We're gonna start going through his stuff to see what we can find. I don't remember seeing a computer or anything like that, but I wasn't paying a hell of a lot of attention when Harley and I packed all his shit up after he died, and I sure as hell haven't gone through it yet."

"Harley Molina?" Xander scribbled the name on a notepad. "He was a bartender there for years. I assume he and Lonnie were friends."

"You'd know that better than I would." Jonah had been gone for years, and neither he nor Sam had kept up with their dad in more than broad strokes since they'd hit eighteen.

"How'd he react when you and Sam elected to shut down the bar?"

"I mean, he wasn't thrilled. I think he must've liked the job to have stuck around for so long. But he wasn't an asshole and didn't pitch a fit about it."

"Leanne spoke to him after all the break-ins during that first round of shit. He had alibis for everything, so we didn't think he was behind it, but I'll have a chat with him. See if he remembers anything useful about what Lonnie was up to. Do you know where the financial records for the bar were kept?"

"We didn't find any in the bar itself, so we'll definitely be looking for those to see if his bookkeeping gives any clues as to what he might have been involved in. And I swear I'll keep you in the loop this time."

"See that you do. If you can find them, that might be the best possible lead we've had."

Jonah rose, ready to get on to the bakery and back to Rachel. "Are we okay, man?"

Xander laughed. "Yeah. Believe it or not, you're not my first stubborn, bull-headed, former Special Forces officer to deal with." He pointed to the gray hair in his sideburns. "I'm pretty sure all this was entirely from when Ty's wife went missing."

"Not gonna blame Caroline and parenthood?"

Just the mention of his daughter had Xander's smile blooming. "I mean, the toddler years have been their own challenge, but her I can handle. And good thing, too, because we're thinking about having another."

"No shit?"

"Best decision we ever made."

Jonah had a hard time wrapping his brain around the idea of his buddy being so enamored of family life. The days when they ran wild around the county were long over, and it seemed like everybody was moving on, settling down. Strange as it felt, that was as it should be.

Xander sobered. "Look, I know you're capable, but man, please let me do my job."

"I will. And to be clear, it's not about my lack of faith in your capabilities. I'm just used to handling things on my own."

He came around the desk and clapped Jonah on the shoulder. "You're home now, brother. That means you're not alone."

There was truth to the statement. It was part of why he'd chosen to make his new life back where he'd grown up.

Jonah pulled him in for a back-slapping hug. "Thanks, man. I'll keep in touch."

"I'll do the same."

NOTHING ON EARTH was more comforting than butter, sugar, and flour. Rachel inhaled the familiar scents, and the tension she'd been carrying for the past week began to dissipate. They'd want some kind of savory option for the later Saturday morning crowd, but right now, she wanted sweet. There was puff pastry prepped in the walk-in cooler and fresh peaches that practically smelled of sunshine. She just had to decide if she wanted to make turnovers or peach and cream cheese danishes. Turnovers would transition to later in the day more easily, since they could be considered dessert, but they also took more chill time.

"Danishes it is." She set the oven to preheat and began to peel peaches to make the peach jelly that would be the base.

From the other side of the kitchen, Holt prepped a batch of raspberry streusel muffins that were a variation on the blueberry that had become one of the bakery staples. "Happy to be back in the kitchen?"

"Oh my God, yes. Jonah hasn't let me lift anything heavier than a spatula. He practically read me the riot act when he got home yesterday to find out I'd made oatmeal chocolate chip cookies. I was a good girl. I let the Kitchenaid do all the heavy lifting!"

Holt chuckled. "He's just looking out for you."

The bell out front jangled, and he pushed through the swinging doors to deal with the next spate of customers.

Rachel lost herself in the familiar rhythm and routine of baking, starting the jelly to simmer on the range before adding the flour-coated berries to the muffin batter Holt had begun.

She was half finished filling muffin cups when he came back through the door.

"Thanks. Those were getting away from me. We always have a pretty steady stream for the first part of Saturday."

"That's a good thing. The weekenders are often a different crowd than the weekday folks. People who might not have time to make it in during the week or who want a special kickoff to the weekend."

He took the scoop from her, and she retrieved the cream cheese from the cooler to let it soften for the next phase of the filling.

Holt's gaze followed her as she moved around the kitchen. "So, how are you feeling, really?"

"Good. I'm still a little sore, but that's more from inactivity. I'm not used to lolling around on a couch for days at a time unless I'm sick, and that doesn't happen too often. I'm more than ready to get back to normal."

Or some variation of normal, anyway.

Jonah had been cuddly. There'd been plenty of touching, casual, comfortable contact that made her feel closer to him, more at ease with the arrangement they'd agreed to. There'd even been a few more of those toe-curling kisses, but nothing more. He'd been treating her with kid gloves, and while Rachel appreciated his capacity for gentleness, she had needs that had been ignored for far too long. There wasn't a chance in hell that Jonah would act on the benefits side of their agreement until he was convinced she was fully recovered.

"Guess this wasn't quite what you signed on for when you took him on as a temporary roommate."

What was that supposed to mean? Rachel glanced at Holt, but all his focus was on filling the remaining muffin cups with fresh batter.

"He's been great. He's just driving me crazy because he wants to put me in a bubble. He's still blaming himself for something that absolutely was not his fault." She gave the jelly another stir and went to retrieve the puff pastry from the walk-in.

"That's his way. Which you absolutely figured out already. You handle him well, calling him on his shit without going so far as to piss him off. Most people don't manage that."

She heard the unasked question and shrugged. "I was with someone very much like him for seventeen years."

Holt paled. "I'm sorry. I didn't mean to bring up something that would make you sad."

"No, it's fine. In most respects, he's nothing like John, but in this... yeah, that overgrown sense of responsibility is very familiar." But it didn't make her ache as it had in the beginning. Jonah was his own man, not some kind of substitute. She never would've pursued him if he were.

The back door swung open and the man himself strode inside.

Holt slid the prepped pans of muffins into the waiting oven. "How did it go with Xander?"

"Told him everything. Turns out he'd already guessed."

"Huh. I suppose he had a good laugh at us trying to conduct our own investigation."

"Nah, he's not like that. And he didn't bust my balls too badly. So far there hasn't been much in the way of leads on that front. He's gonna go talk to the guy who was a bartender here forever and a day. Meanwhile, we're still on for tomorrow— we'll go through all of Lonnie's stuff and see what we can find."

Jonah stopped behind Rachel, peering over her shoulder at what she was making. "Danishes?" His hand curled around her hip.

Feeling the heat of his palm soak into her skin, Rachel took a firmer grip on the rolling pin to keep from turning into him. "Mmm. Cream cheese and peach. I want to make little roses out of peach slices for each one."

"Sounds delicious." Jonah crossed to the prep sink and began scrubbing up.

Rachel took an unsteady breath, grateful she hadn't been holding a knife when he'd touched her.

"Okay, man, you've held down the fort all week while I played hooky and nursemaid. Go on home and spend some time with your family."

"You don't have to tell me twice." Holt slid his apron over his head and hung it on a hook by the door. "Those muffins have another fifteen minutes."

"On it. And thanks, brother."

"Any time."

The two of them exchanged some kind of complicated fist bump that had Rachel smiling. Their friendship reminded her so much of John and Hudson and the third member of their trio, Steve. They'd been the Three Musketeers growing up. Thick as thieves and closer than brothers. They'd stayed that way all their lives, going into the fire academy together and coming out to work for the same unit in Syracuse. Now Hudson was the only one left.

"You okay?"

Blinking at the sound of Jonah's voice, she realized Holt was gone, and she'd been standing there, lost in thought, the rolling pin in one hand. "Yeah, I'm fine. I was just thinking. We should do a savory scone for the late breakfast crowd. What kind of cheese do we have on hand?"

She fought not to squirm under his long, assessing look.

"Don't know. I'll see what's in the cooler."

He came back a minute later with a wedge of Asiago in hand. "We could pair it with ham."

"I think we can do better. Something a little more complex in flavor. Caramelized onion and bacon?"

His eyes lit. "You know I never turn down bacon."

"Neither does anyone else. Start pulling ingredients while I finish these danishes."

Time slipped by, with Jonah moving in and out of the kitchen to handle customers between prepping components. When they hit a bit of a lull, they assembled the scones together, working side-by-side as they had countless times before when she'd taught him to bake. But it felt different now. The tension humming between them was overt instead of implied. They'd acknowledged their attraction, made a plan to act on it. The crackle of awareness skated along her skin with each brush of his body against hers. The occasional catch of his breath was the only thing that told her she wasn't alone.

They cut the scones into wedges, spacing them on the baking sheet with far more deliberation than the task called for. Then he slid them into the waiting oven and set a timer.

Rachel tipped back a bottle of water and closed her eyes.

"Getting tired?"

She met his gaze. "No." Every inch felt electrified, alive again for the first time in too long. Her hands itched to reach for him, so she set her bottle aside and curled her fingers around the edges of the table she leaned against.

Jonah edged into her space. "You've got a little something just—" He lifted a hand, brushing at her cheek.

Eyes on his, she turned into the touch, wanting so much more than this simple caress.

"You're dangerous when you look at me like that." His voice was full of gravel.

Rachel swallowed. "Like what?"

"Like you want to devour me."

Yes, please.

"Well, I did promise you honesty." She couldn't actually remember if she had, but she certainly intended it. Her fingers curled into the front of his shirt. "And you promised to take care of me."

"So I did." He closed the scant distance between them, pressing his lips to hers.

On a hum of pleasure, she opened for him, welcoming the fresh blast of lust as he took her mouth in a slow, devouring kiss. He trapped her between the hard planes of his body and the worktable behind her. His hand slid into her hair, his fingers massaging the base of her skull. His free hand snuck beneath the hem of the T-shirt she wore, skimming just high enough to claim the skin along her spine. She shuddered, needing to feel those calloused hands everywhere. Rising to her toes, she pressed into him, chasing more of the delicious heat he stirred.

"Oh, shit. Sorry, dude."

Jonah's head snapped up on a growl. "What the hell are you doing here?"

Griff backed toward the swinging kitchen door, hands raised in surrender. "Sam and I just came to say goodbye and pick up some snacks for the road. Didn't mean to... uh... interrupt."

"Honey, what's going on?" Sam came through the door, the baby in a sling across her middle. Her eyes widened at the sight of the two of them. "Oh. *Ohhhh.*" She drew the word out, an unmistakable realization.

Cheeks flaming, Rachel released the fistful of Jonah's T-shirt she held. A blotch of flour remained, along with another clear handprint on his shoulder. Nope. No hiding that. Awesome. So much for keeping things low key.

An oven timer went off. Needing to do *something*, she ducked out of Jonah's hold and retrieved the next batch of danishes, setting them in a rack to cool. Schooling her features into something she hoped approached normal, she turned to face Jonah's sister and brother-in-law. "So, you guys are headed back to Chattanooga?"

"That is the plan," Griff confirmed. His own mouth was set in a carefully blank mask, but Rachel didn't miss the glint of amusement in his blue eyes.

"That's for the best," Jonah agreed.

Okay, so they were both taking the party line of pretending nobody saw a thing. Good to know.

"And you'll keep us updated on how things are going here?" Sam pressed.

"Yeah." Jonah's agreement came easily, and Rachel wondered if he realized she was asking about more than just the case.

He moved toward the door, obviously trying to herd the two

of them out of the kitchen. "C'mon. I'll box up some stuff for you to take back with you."

Sam flashed a grin back at Rachel. "It was great meeting you, Rachel. Hope to see you again soon."

They all disappeared through the door before she could do more than throw up a quick, awkward wave. Then she was alone, wondering how complicated this friends-with-benefits thing had just become.

7

"Um... Are you sure this place is safe?" Rachel sounded skeptical as she looked up at what remained of the house.

Jonah bumped her shoulder with his. "Can you get tetanus if you step on a nail in there? Probably. Is it going to fall down on your head while we're inside? No."

The arch of her brow said she didn't quite believe him.

He couldn't blame her. Paint had peeled from most of the wooden siding. The roofline of the front porch sagged like a swaybacked horse, and Virginia creeper and vines of poison everything had swallowed one end. Multiple floorboards had rotted beneath, leaving gaps big enough to break a leg. He knew from his prior trips out that much of the interior was only a little better.

His mom's expression was regretful as she looked up at the place. "It was my grandmama's house. She passed nearly twenty years ago and left it to me. It wasn't practical for us to live this far out, and we didn't have the money to fix it up at the time. Kept putting it off. Then it got damaged in a storm, and it reached a point where it wasn't worth trying to fix it up."

A faded blue tarp still covered the roof on the side of the house a huge tree limb had fallen on. They'd removed the tree and replaced the tarp a few times over the years, boarding up things as best they could, but the mountain was doing its level best to take back the spot. Jonah wondered if he'd finally find the time and motivation to do something about it now that he was home for good.

"The land is valuable, so we haven't sold it off, but we can't actually *do* anything with it without knocking the house down, which also costs money." Rebecca spread her hands. "So here we are."

"It made for a convenient place to toss Lonnie's crap until we could go through it." Jonah moved toward the front stairs. "Mind your step. I haven't checked to see what condition they're in, and I haven't been out here in more than six months."

Carefully picking his way over the rotted wood, he unlocked the door before returning to hold out a hand, first for Rachel and then his mother, to see them up the rickety stairs. Holt brought up the rear, hauling a couple of camp chairs. There were more in his truck, along with garbage bags, a cooler full of drinks and snacks, and a Bluetooth speaker to make this feel a little less like the chore that it was.

Their footsteps echoed through the house as he led them to the living room. Unlike much of the rest of the house, there were few leaks here, and it was the most structurally secure space available, so this was where he'd piled all his father's worldly possessions.

"Holy shit." Holt paused at the edge of the space, taking in the stacks and stacks of boxes. "This is... more than I was expecting."

"I don't have the first clue what's in here. I just threw every damn thing into boxes for us to deal with later."

"Is there furniture?" Rachel asked.

"Only a few pieces I kept in case they could be salvaged. A

desk. A cool old trunk. Chest of drawers. They're under all this shit... somewhere. I just had Goodwill pick the rest of it up, and whatever they didn't want went to the county dump. If the flash drive was hidden in that somewhere, we're SOL."

"Maybe there will be a backup or paper copies of some kind," Holt suggested.

"Or some other evidence entirely." If this didn't pan out and give them some kind of legitimate lead, or proof of his father's involvement in whatever this was, Jonah didn't know what their next steps would be.

Rachel's hand settled on his shoulder. "One thing at a time. This is going to take a while."

He laid his hand over hers and squeezed, refusing to analyze how much comfort he took at her touch. "True enough. I'll go get the rest of the chairs and the speaker. Holt, you wanna help me with the cooler?"

"Sure."

They went back out to his truck, hauling the ice chest he'd filled with drinks and picnic fare out of the back.

"I appreciate you helping with this, man."

"Of course. I've got your back. And it's in my best interest to get to the bottom of this shit, too." He shouldered one of the remaining camp chairs. "Rachel seems to be recovering well."

The bruise had mostly faded, and the gash on her temple had started to heal. But Jonah hadn't been able to stop watching her like a hawk, monitoring the dilation of her eyes, keeping watch on her gait, looking for signs of dizziness or nausea or anything else that would indicate longer-term problems from the head injury.

"I wish she'd take some more downtime, but I'd have to handcuff her to a chair to make her. She doesn't sit well."

Holt smirked. "Sounds like someone else I know."

"Yeah, yeah."

Holt had certainly been around in the early months when

Jonah had kept pushing, kept demanding his body do more than it was capable of. He'd seen the rage when Jonah's body had given him the middle finger and refused. There'd been a lot of setbacks because he didn't listen to his doctors or his brain. He didn't want that for Rachel.

"I like you two together."

Jonah glanced at Holt over the cooler. "We're not together." It felt wrong to say it, but the friends-with-benefits thing was temporary. Neither of them was looking for more. No reason to get their friends excited about something that wasn't going to be a real thing.

Holt arched a brow. "You sure about that? You've been spending an awful lot of time together."

"She's staying at my house. And I've been on nurse and bodyguard duty. Of course, we're spending a lot of time together."

"You spent a lot of time together before that. You kept up with her when the rest of us didn't."

Jonah fought the urge to grind his teeth. "We're friends."

"Cayla and I were friends."

That had been Holt's excuse for stepping in to act like her husband when her ex had unexpectedly been released from prison. Then he'd married her for real, to keep his lie from coming back to bite her in the ass. But the rest of them had known the truth from the beginning: Holt was crazy about her. He'd just needed to get out of his own way.

"It's not the same. She's going back to New York when all this is finished."

His buddy held up a hand. "All right. I was just making an observation."

Jonah wished he'd keep those thoughts to himself. He hadn't talked with his friends about his reasons for not pursuing a long-term relationship. It wasn't just about Rachel. He didn't intend to cross that bridge with anyone. But with both of them wrapped in marital bliss, he supposed it wasn't surprising that they figured he'd be the next to fall. His friends meant well by it. They were simply wrong.

By the time they came back inside, someone had found the breaker box and restored power, turning on the window unit air conditioner. Jonah couldn't believe the thing still ran. It chugged along like an asthmatic train, spewing out an anemic stream of cooler air. With the ceiling fan going, it was just enough to combat the oppressive late summer heat. The women had set up sorting stations: Keep, Toss, Donate, Investigate. Each one was designated by a sign taped to a different wall of the room. He and Holt set down the cooler. Camp chairs were unfolded.

Jonah set up the speaker with a bluesy playlist as their unpacking backdrop. "Well, everybody pick a box, I guess, and dig in."

There didn't seem to be any rhyme or reason to what was in each box. Lonnie couldn't have been called a hoarder, but there was a whole lot of crap Jonah didn't know why he'd kept. Old issues of *Motor Trend*. A bunch of empty mason jars. A box of assorted cables belonging to out-of-date electronics. A bag of bottle caps. Some beat up baseball cards that definitely weren't collectibles. None of it had anywhere to hide a flash drive, and there were no signs of paperwork that amounted to anything incriminating. The mounds of stuff on the Toss wall continued to grow.

"Is this you?"

At Rachel's question, Jonah rose and crossed to where she was sorting through yet another box. She had a vinyl photo album in hand, open to a picture of him in T-ball uniform, hat too big for his head, broad, gap-toothed grin on display for the camera. His dad had been so excited he'd played. He'd come to every game. That was before everything had gone to shit.

Jonah swallowed. "Yeah. I think I was about six."

"You were adorable." She flipped through, and there were more photos of him and of Sam. Birthdays. Christmases. Images of the family that had been a lie.

He grunted, his gaze dropping to the rest of the contents of the box. He spotted the T-ball trophy from that year, and the peewee baseball mitt he'd outgrown. Beneath it, one of the plastic dinosaurs he'd prized peeked out. They were pieces of a childhood so long distant, he barely remembered it. Why had his father kept this stuff when he hadn't wanted to keep his family?

Rachel's hand curled around his. "Hey. I'm sorry. This is hard on you."

"I'm fine." The protest was automatic. Something he'd said for decades, whether it was true or not. But he knew she saw through him, so he relented and squeezed back. "Okay, it's weird. But I will be fine."

Having her support while traversing what was turning out to be a field of emotional landmines meant more than he wanted it to. Because he needed time to think, he stepped back and raised his voice.

"Who's ready for some lunch?"

JONAH HURLED another bag of trash onto the pile in the back of his truck. "Okay, I'm calling it."

Rachel handed him the one she carried, so he could heft it over the side. "You sure?"

He rolled his shoulders and jerked his chin toward where the sun had sunk behind the mountain, painting the sky in a vibrant wash of oranges and pinks. "It's getting late. We've gotta be up early for work tomorrow, and we're not getting through the rest of this crap tonight. Plus, I don't think we can cram any more bags or boxes of garbage in here."

Holt had headed out a couple hours before, so he'd be home for the bedtime routine with Maddie. They hadn't found anything overtly useful, and there was still plenty of stuff to sort through. The job was bigger than any of them had anticipated, made more complicated by the fact that they were combing through things so carefully, hoping to find anything that might amount to evidence. One thing Rachel knew for sure—she wasn't cut out to be a cop. She didn't have the patience.

"Fair enough. Are we going to run by the bakery to toss all this in the dumpster?"

"Yeah, we'll hit that on the way home."

Her heart did a quick tap dance against her ribs at hearing him include her in home. He didn't mean it like it sounded. They were going to *his* home. But she couldn't deny that, after their intensive forced proximity during her recovery, it was starting to feel like hers, too. Maybe that was just because nowhere had really felt like home since John died. Home for her had never been a place. It had been him. She didn't want to think too hard about what it said that Jonah was starting to slide into that position. They'd agreed to short term. Casual. She wasn't the new woman in his life. She was his right-now. That was all.

Rebecca made her careful way down the rickety steps, a box in her arms. "I'll drop the donations off tomorrow. I've got time between appointments."

Jonah plucked the box out of her hands. "I've got it." He shoved it in the backseat of the truck and wrapped an arm around his mom's shoulders. "You've helped enough."

"I don't mind, baby. You've got so much on your plate already."

"And I'll feel better if you get on home before it's full dark." To move her along, he opened the driver's side of her car and gestured to the seat.

It was a polite dismissal, but a dismissal nonetheless.

Rebecca's brows drew together, her lips pursing in disapproval. "Stubborn boy."

"I come by it honest." He brushed a kiss over her brow. "Please head on home, so I don't worry about you."

"Fine. But I'll be back out here to help again, whether you like it or not."

"Thanks. Love you, Mom."

"Love you, too." She waved in Rachel's direction. "Bye, Rachel. Don't let this one railroad you too badly."

She chuckled. "No, ma'am."

Then Rebecca was gone, rolling down the rutted, overgrown driveway to the county road beyond the treeline. Jonah's shoulders seemed to relax as she disappeared.

"You okay?"

He seemed surprised by the question. "Yeah. Why?"

"You don't actually have to do everything by yourself, you know."

"I know. But it just doesn't seem right, her having to do anything related to Lonnie's crap after how he treated her. It's not her responsibility."

"Fair point."

Rachel knew little about Jonah's dad, other than he hadn't been in the picture much. Just the mention of his name had a disgusted coldness sparking in Jonah's eyes. He hadn't done right by his family, and that was a cardinal sin for Jonah, who put everyone ahead of himself. But it was clear from his reactions over the course of the day that things with Lonnie hadn't been so cut and dried as Jonah had believed.

She waited until he'd locked up the house, and they were on their way back to town, before trying to dig a little deeper. "How are you feeling?"

"Fine."

"Jonah, I know today was harder on you than you were expecting. I'm just checking in on you."

She watched him swallow his instinctive response. Probably something akin to, "Well, don't."

He blew out a breath, his fingers tightening on the steering wheel. "It's just weird that my dad had anything related to our family."

"Why? You were his kids."

"Because he completely walked away. Totally hands off from the time I was eight years old."

The idea of it hurt her heart. "That had to be so hard on all of you."

"It wasn't great. He didn't carry his weight, so I stepped up to be the man of the house. To take care of my mom and Sam."

And that right there was the origin of that overgrown sense of responsibility. He'd been carrying that load for a long, long time. No wonder he didn't know how to set it down.

"Why did he leave?"

"I don't know for sure. One day, he just up and left. I don't remember them fighting. He was just gone. Not far. Still in town. But not a part of our lives anymore."

Rachel couldn't imagine the blow that must've been to all of them. "Was there another woman?"

"If there was, I never heard anything about it. Mom never mentioned it and over the years, he was never tied to any one person in particular. He just chose to remove himself from our lives entirely. That wasn't Mom's call. After about a year, once the divorce was finalized, she changed our names because he wanted nothing to do with us."

"He didn't fight that?"

"Didn't lift a finger." Though his gaze didn't stray from the road, a muscle jumped in his jaw.

Rachel couldn't wrap her head around any of this. He and his family were awesome. The credit for that clearly went to his mom, who'd had to be strong as hell to get through something like that. And Jonah himself for stepping up when he'd been only a child himself.

Needing to comfort, she reached across the center console to lay a hand on his thigh. After a long moment, he dropped one hand from the wheel to curl his fingers with hers. He said nothing else for several miles, but he held on, and that link was enough for now.

Unloading the bags and boxes from the truck to the bakery's dumpster took longer than they'd planned. More than one split, and they had to scoop up and toss the detritus in by the armful. By the time they'd finished and made back to the house, it was full dark.

As they climbed out of the truck, Jonah came around to take her hand again, his fingers dancing along her palm. "How do you feel about going home, showering off the sweat of the day, nuking some leftovers, and cuddling up to watch another episode of *Great British Bake Off* before hitting the hay?" If he still felt any discomfort over their prior conversation, his voice didn't betray it.

Sleeping wasn't specifically what Rachel had in mind. Neither was a solo shower, but now didn't seem the moment to push him on that front. "That sounds like exactly the kind of chillaxed evening to round out the day."

He opened the door, and they stepped inside.

Two paces into the kitchen, she ran into his back when he went stock still.

"What is it?"

His body had gone taut as a bowstring. "Someone's been here. Stay put."

Releasing her hand, he pulled a gun from a holster hidden in the back of his jeans. Seeing him armed, knowing he must have been carrying it all day, gave her a bit of a jolt. He was never truly off duty, and that was something very, very different from John.

As he moved away from her to search the house, she saw what had stopped him in his tracks. The kitchen had been tossed. Drawers and cabinet doors hung open, the contents of some spilling out. The old radio that had sat on the counter had been smashed to bits. She could just see into the living room, where more signs of a hurried search showed in the cushions on the floor and the overturned basket of books and movies.

Jonah returned a minute later. "They're gone. I'm gonna call the police. Check your stuff and see if you can tell if anything's missing, but don't touch anything."

Rachel hurried to do as he asked. Her room had received a similar treatment to everywhere else. The contents of her dresser and suitcase had been strewn about. Her toiletries were scattered across the bathroom cabinet and all the drawers and doors were ajar. Everything in her itched to clean up and put things back to rights, but the police would need to dust for prints and check for other evidence.

Sheriff Kincaid was in the kitchen when she came back out. His expression was grim. "I don't like this. It's another escalation. One outside the bakery itself. This feels personal to you."

"To my dad, just like we thought." Jonah pointed to the remains of the radio. "That radio was in the bar. He kept it up there for years. It was one of the few things I kept when he died."

"You think something was hidden in it?"

"There wasn't. I already took it apart to check, but obviously somebody thought it might be a hiding place. Why else smash it?"

Xander blew out a breath. "Is anything missing that you can tell?"

"We won't know for sure until we do a full clean up, but offhand, it looks like no." Jonah turned to face her. "What about your stuff?"

"Like you said, it doesn't look like it. Everything was just pawed through." She crossed her arms over her middle to ward off the chill that swept down her arms. This was supposed to be her safe space. Now someone had violated it.

"Was there anything on the alarm system?" Xander asked.

Jonah looked disgusted with himself. "I forgot to set the damned thing, so no."

"All right. I'll be getting my people in here to see what other evidence they can find. In the meantime, y'all might want to find somewhere else to stay for the night."

"I've got it covered."

Rachel looked at Jonah. "Where are going? The inn? To your mom's?"

"No. I've already talked to my buddy Porter, who owns this place, to let him know what happened. He's got another cabin further out that has a hell of a security system. We're going there."

"Ty's old place?" Xander asked. "That place is wired up about like Fort Knox. It's a good option."

Someone knocked on the door.

"That'll be Clyde. We'll get started on your bedrooms so you can start packing things up to take with you." Xander strode to answer the door.

Rachel stared around the kitchen at the chaos. "Do you think he found what he was looking for?"

"No. The mess is worst in the back, probably because he *didn't* find what he was looking for." Jonah closed the distance between them and wrapped his arms around her.

Rachel held on, letting the warmth of him soak in to combat the chill. He sucked in a breath, but before he could speak, she beat him to the punch. "Don't ask me to go home, Jonah."

He huffed a noise that, under other circumstances, might have been a laugh. "Am I that predictable?"

She tipped her head back. "In this, yes. But my reasons for refusing remain the same."

With a gentle finger, he tucked a strand of hair behind her ear. "Okay. I get it. You're in it now. You want to see it through. I respect that, even if I don't agree with it. As soon as we're cleared, we pack our bags and move out."

"Move out entirely?"

"For now. This location's compromised. The cabin will be more secure. It'll make a better safe house."

Compromised. Secure. Safe house.

Toto, I am definitely not in Kansas anymore.

8

A motion-activated security light snapped on as Jonah pulled his truck up to the cabin. The building was nestled in the trees, as if it were a part of the mountain itself. He knew from Porter that the nearest neighbor was half a mile away, and the only vehicle access was this driveway that was barely even visible from the road above. That could be a blessing and a curse, but he didn't intend to leave Rachel here on her own at any point, so the remote location suited his purposes for the time being.

She'd been quiet since they'd left the house, but he couldn't decide how much was upset and how much was just tired. It had been a long-ass day, even before the break in, and Jonah hadn't missed the worry in her eyes. No matter that she hadn't been the target, her space had been invaded. She had to be rattled.

Wanting to put her at ease, he shoved open the driver's side door. "C'mon. Let's get inside and get settled."

She slid out of the truck when he did. "I bet it's cute in the winter, when there's snow on the ground."

Cute.

If he hadn't already had plenty of evidence of exactly how far apart his world was from hers, that was it. He didn't think he'd ever look at a space without evaluating it from a tactical perspective immediately.

Rachel glanced up at him. "Do you even get snow this far south?"

"Yeah. Not the kind of snow that would live up to your Yankee standards, but we get some." Using the keys Porter had brought over, he opened the door and punched in the security code.

She stepped in behind him and fumbled along the wall for a light switch. When it came on, they both blinked at the glare. The place was tiny. Porter had warned him, but Jonah hadn't quite grasped how much he'd meant it. A single room, with a kitchen tucked into one corner and a sofa and armchair set in front of a wood stove. A loft above them held the lone bed, accessed by a steep, narrow set of stairs that might as well have been a ladder. The single bathroom was tucked beneath the overhang of the loft. Only the vaulted ceiling saved it from feeling claustrophobic.

Jonah moved to the wall and slid back a hidden panel where the brain of the upgraded security system lived. It only took a few minutes to follow Porter's instructions for pairing the system with his phone.

Rachel peered over his shoulder at the panel. "Why is this place so heavily secured?"

"Ty Brooks—He's one of Xander's deputies. Former Army Ranger—When he lived here, a stalker came after his then-girl-friend/now-wife, Paisley. I don't know all the details exactly, except that she was kidnapped, and after he got her back, he vowed never again. They lived here until they got their house built. Porter didn't see any reason to take the extra security out. It comes in handy from time to time."

She folded one arm across her middle, betraying the

discomfort she hadn't voiced. "Do you think we really need all of this?"

Skimming his hands from her shoulders down her arms, Jonah tugged her closer. "I don't know. But if it makes you feel safer, it's worth it."

She wrapped around him with that easy physical affection he was coming to crave and lifted those blue eyes to his. "You make me feel safe."

Her words seemed to carry the weight of something other than their current predicament. He wasn't sure he deserved that trust, but he'd do everything in his power to earn it.

Because he couldn't stop himself, he brushed a soft kiss to her lips. The unhesitating way she melted into him had his resolve wavering. "Let's haul in our stuff. It's late."

It only took a couple of trips. As neither of them was keen on taking a header over a stray bag if they got up in the middle of the night, they elected to go ahead and unpack, stowing their clothes in the dresser and half closet beneath the slope of the roof and their toiletries in the small bathroom. They'd still need to stock groceries. He hadn't grabbed more than the bare minimum to get them out of the house, figuring they'd get breakfast and coffee at the bakery when they went into work. That was a problem for tomorrow. For tonight, they both needed sleep.

The moment Rachel stepped out of the bathroom, sleep was the last thing on Jonah's mind. There was nothing overtly sexy about the oversized T-shirt, except that it hung down so low, it looked like that was the only thing she was wearing. Logically, he knew she probably had on the sleep shorts she'd been lounging in for much of the week, but all his brain could focus on was the long, lean expanse of her legs. Legs he wanted wrapped around his waist while he buried himself inside her.

"I'll sleep on the sofa." The words came out in a croak as he struggled to get a grip on his libido.

Those lips that were becoming his obsession tipped into a frown. "Don't be ridiculous. You aren't going to fit on that sofa. We're grown adults. And that aside, given our arrangement, it doesn't seem like there should be any issue with us sharing a bed."

Their arrangement. The benefits portion of their friendship. The part he'd been doing his damnedest not to think about because he couldn't quite get past seeing her injured, his brain continuing to superimpose that image over her face. The dissonance was killing him.

At his continued silence, she crossed one arm over her middle again, her expression shuttering. "Unless you've changed your mind."

Jonah cursed himself for his incessant need to recheck himself, re-ask the question, to make absolutely certain that whatever he did was the best for her. He stepped toward her, wanting to smooth hurt feelings and find some way to reassure her.

"It's not that. I definitely haven't changed my mind." He stroked her hair back, running his fingers softly over her temple. There was no flinch, no sign of residual tenderness. "I just need you to be okay." Beyond her injuries, he needed her to come out of the other side of this change in their relationship unscathed. And that was something he didn't know how to guarantee.

"I am." She closed the distance between them, fitting her body flush to his, her hands on his chest. "I need you to see me, Jonah. Not my injuries. Not what happened to me. That was why I was drawn to you. Why I chose you. Because when everyone else saw my circumstances, you saw me." Rising to her toes, she pressed the softest part of her against the hardest part of him, angling her mouth a mere breath away from his. "Come to bed. I need you."

Jonah shuddered, the remnants of his resolve crumbling

under that simple statement. Nothing and no one was more important to him in that moment than her, and he was willing to do anything and everything she asked.

Banding his arms around her, he bent his head until they shared a breath. "Be sure."

Her fingers slid into his hair. "I am."

RACHEL HELD, trembling, at the threshold of everything she'd wanted for months. On a basic biological level, Jonah wanted her. That was obvious enough. But he'd held back and hesitated often enough that she wasn't certain where he stood. She needed him to make the next move, to close that infinitesimal distance. To prove he was actually in this, not just humoring her because he didn't want to hurt her feelings.

He didn't disappoint.

On a sigh, he took her mouth, threading his fingers in her hair until he cradled her head, angling it exactly how he wanted it. She opened for him as he sipped and savored, drugging her with his patient exploration. There was more than gentleness in his touch. There was reverence. Rachel's heart stumbled. She'd known he wasn't the man for a fast, hard tumble. He took too much care with everyone and everything. But she hadn't expected this.

Nerves sprang to life inside her. It was one thing to think about doing this. To dream about it, even. But it was very, very different to face the reality. She and John been each other's first everything, and they'd been happy and satisfied together. But for all that, she lacked experience. What if she disappointed Jonah? What if her body betrayed her, and this was all a supremely terrible idea? What if sex ruined their friendship?

But Jonah just kept kissing her and kissing her, his fingers still in her hair, until the nerves gave way to sensation, and her arms felt heavy and languid around his shoulders. Only then did he pull back far enough to lightly nip her bottom lip. "Let's go upstairs."

She took extra care climbing up, not entirely trusting her dexterity after he'd kissed half her brain cells away. The queen-sized bed seemed huge, as if it had grown two sizes in the space since she'd put her clothes away. It was the only thing she could see.

Jonah's hands settled on her shoulders, his lips pressing against the side of her neck from behind. "Do you want me to stop?"

Dropping her head to give him better access, she whispered, "No."

She felt the shape of his smile against her skin as he kissed her neck again, his big hands curving around her hips, drawing her back against the erection straining his jeans. Those lips cruised across her collarbone, his beard brushing the sensitive skin of her throat, and her knees threatened to buckle.

"God, you make me weak."

"Only with pleasure." With a quick spin, he tumbled them onto the bed.

His weight pressed her into the mattress, lighting up nerve endings that had long been dormant. All those lovely, languid sensations sharpened to need. She wanted more. Wanted skin against skin, slick and heated. Wanted, too, to feel the rasp of his beard against her sensitive flesh. It was a new sensation for her, completely Jonah.

Restless now, she dragged at his shirt until he tugged it off and tossed it to the side. It was her turn for reverence as she ran her hands over the planes of his chest. He was beautifully made, battle-hardened, even this far out from his military service. Dark hair dusted his pecs, narrowing down to a trail that disappeared into the waistband of his jeans. She could just make out the V-grooves at his hips. She definitely wanted to spend some time admiring those. With her tongue.

He went back to kissing her, his hands sliding beneath the hem of her sleep shirt to coast up her torso, lighting little fires along the way as they passed so close to where she wanted him to touch and taste. With one arm, he lifted her up, pulling off the shirt and sending it to the floor with his. Those green eyes went dark as pitch as he stared at her bare breasts. Her nipples pearled under his gaze, begging for attention.

"So damned beautiful." The rasp of his voice had moisture pooling between her thighs.

When he took one nipple into his mouth, curling his tongue around the stiff peak, she almost exploded off the bed. After two years of feeling next to nothing, this was almost too much. He palmed her other breast, rolling the nipple lightly between his callused fingers, and Rachel pressed her head back into the pillow, searching for some kind of purchase. She could almost come from this alone.

"Jonah." His name was all she could manage in the moment, but he seemed to understand the inherent plea.

One hand slid down her belly, into her sleep shorts, to cup the heat between her legs. That intimate, possessive touch had her bowing with a whiplash of an orgasm that left her blind and gasping.

By the time she saw anything but the stars behind her eyes, he was laying more of those languorous kisses along her throat and jaw. "You okay?"

The absurdity of the statement had an impossible giggle bubbling up in her chest. "It's been a really long time, but I'm having a hard time finding a reason to complain about having a hair-trigger orgasm at the moment."

"Been a long time for me, too." His lazy smile turned smug. "But I can absolutely work with a hair-trigger orgasm."

She speared her fingers into his hair and dragged his mouth back to hers for a fierce, decadent kiss. "Then get to it."

"Yes, ma'am." On a grin, he scooted away, down the bed, his fingers snagging the waistband of her shorts to drag them off as he went, leaving her entirely bare. He hummed in satisfaction, his eyes full of so much hunger as he stared at the apex of her thighs. A flush worked its way up her body, the muscles low in her belly pulling tight with fresh need.

Jonah's gaze lifted to hers. "Can I taste you?"

"God, yes."

Hooking his hands behind her knees, he dragged her to the edge of the bed, keeping his tone conversational as he knelt, pressing her legs apart to fit his shoulders. "I've been thinking about this almost from the moment we met, wondering if you're as sweet here as you are everywhere else."

He'd wanted her from the start. It did something to her deep inside to know that. To know he'd seen her as a woman first. Then his mouth was on her, driving her on a fast, reckless ride up the peak again. He backed off at the crest, bringing her down just a little, only to drive her higher. Over and over, he repeated the pattern, until her breath sobbed out and she was half-mad with wanting, her hands fisting in his hair. At her ragged, "Please," he relented and sent her flying again.

When the pieces of her knit themselves back together under the ministrations of more of those drugging kisses, she took in his justifiably self-satisfied smirk. She wanted to break that smirk. Wanted to wreck him physically, as thoroughly as he'd wrecked her. Curling a hand around his nape, she kissed him back, tasting herself on his lips.

"I need you inside me."

He pulled away, shucking his clothes in short order and donning a condom before rejoining her on the bed. Then he was over her, the blunt head of him nudging her entrance.

"Are you sure? There's no going back after this."

She framed his face between her palms. "Yes."

He pressed forward, sliding into her wet heat, and she kept her eyes on his, needing him to know that she was with *him*, not imagining someone else. Despite the double orgasms, she was still incredibly tight. But like everything else, he took his time, giving her body a chance to adjust to his girth, inch by slow inch, until he was seated fully inside her. They sighed as one, and he dropped his brow to hers.

"You feel incredible."

"Jonah." His name was all she could manage past the knot of emotion that lodged itself behind her breastbone. Gratitude that this amazing, generous man had consented to become her lover. That he was hers, if only for now.

She didn't realize she was crying until he brushed the tears from her cheeks, his face twisted in concern.

"Did I hurt you?"

"No." She brushed her lips against his. "No. This is perfect. Beautiful. Thank you." Levering up, she kissed him again, drawing him down, wrapping her legs around his waist and rolling her hips in a silent plea for him to move.

After a moment's hesitation he did, beginning a slow thrust and retreat that seemed to fill her deeper with every stroke, lighting up all the dark places she hadn't been willing to acknowledge. And as he dragged them over the edge together, she knew this could never be the simple friends-with-benefits affair she'd asked for.

9

J onah linked his fingers with Rachel's, enjoying how they so neatly laced with his. "You know my favorite part of being a baker?"

"Mmm?" She hummed the question from her position draped over his chest.

"That we close at two, and I get the whole rest of the afternoon to do whatever I want." He traced a finger down her bare back, enjoying her little purr of pleasure.

She lifted her head and blinked sleepy eyes at him, her mouth curved in a satisfied, feline smile. "I definitely can't complain that an afternoon delight heads up that list of activities."

And if she kept looking at him like that, he'd be up for another round in short order.

For the past four days, they'd headed back to the cabin right at closing time, barely making it inside before they dove at each other. Though they hadn't discussed it, they were both acutely aware that their time together was half through, and neither of them wanted to waste a minute of it. So they made love and slept and talked, then did it all over again. And if Jonah had used this escalation in their relationship to keep her away from all things related to his father—well, he told himself he was letting Xander do his job.

Their connection was electric. Jonah had no idea whether it was because of the unshakable foundation of friendship they'd built first, or if it was simply her. He only knew he'd never experienced anything like it. Beyond the incredible sex, he simply liked having her around, in his space. They'd fallen into a weirdly comfortable and domestic partnership that should have alarmed him. Instead, it just made him want more. If there was a part of him that had begun to whisper, *"What if?"* he ignored it. Their expiration date made sense. She didn't actually live here. New York was twelve hours away. Above and beyond all that, he could never put her through what a lifetime with him would mean. Not after all the trauma she'd already experienced.

But he could give her a taste of a real relationship. Show her how she should be treated. The things she should expect from whoever came after him. The idea of someone coming after him soured his gut. But Rachel deserved to find that second chance at forever with someone who was better equipped to give it to her. Somebody who didn't have a ticking time clock of good years before the long-term consequences of his injuries detonated.

Not wanting to think about an end to them that was far too close, Jonah dragged his mind back to the present. He was with her now. That was what mattered. He was going to make every second count, and that meant going all in for however long they had. They hadn't been actively trying to hide the change in their relationship. It was too hard to stop themselves from all those little touches and gestures that betrayed a deeper level of intimacy. But they hadn't been parading it either. He was proud to be with Rachel, proud she'd chosen him. And abruptly, he wanted to take her out, show her off.

"Get dressed." He punctuated the order with a light smack to her butt.

"If this is about your aversion to cooking naked, I swear I've never burned myself."

"It's not an aversion. It's self-protection to make sure we actually get fed, which wouldn't happen if you paraded around the kitchen in your very fine birthday suit. But no, we're going out tonight. On a date."

"A date?" The confusion in her tone had him wishing he'd thought to do this before.

"Yep. A night out on the town. Such as it is."

"Isn't that kind of outside the parameters of the whole friends-with-benefits thing?"

"Yeah." But they'd already gone beyond that in his mind. Fighting back a wave of disappointment, Jonah slid away from her, sitting up. Maybe she didn't want to go all in on this. On him. "If you don't want to call it a date, just call it dinner. I'm starving. You still haven't had the grilled mac and cheese sandwich from the diner, and I can't let you leave Eden's Ridge without it."

Maybe they both needed the reminder that she *was* leaving.

Rachel's arms came around him before he could stand. "Jonah." She pressed a kiss to his shoulder. "Look at me."

Fixing his face into a neutral mask, he twisted to face her. "What?"

Her smile was a little shy. "I would love to go on a date with you."

The knot in his chest untangled. Not wanting her to see the profound relief on his face, he kissed her again, fast and hard. "Dress comfy, and wear shoes you can walk in."

"Aye, aye, sir!"

Forty minutes later, they strode into Crystal's Diner, just before the Wednesday night dinner rush. Spying an empty booth along one wall, Jonah made a beeline, dragging Rachel with him. He nudged her onto the bench seat and slid in after her, where he could see most of the restaurant. Which meant he noticed all the other patrons noticing them.

Yeah, I'm here with her. Eat your hearts out.

He stretched a deliberate arm along the back of the booth, making his claim.

Rachel plucked a laminated menu from behind the napkin dispenser. "I don't think I've sat on the same side as my date since college. Not like this anyway."

"The easier for you to steal my fries."

She gasped in mock outrage. "I am not a fry thief."

"You are when you order onion rings when you really want both. But don't worry. I can share."

Her eyes sparkled as she batted those long lashes at him. "Your nobility knows no bounds."

"Jonah Ferguson, where *have* you been hiding?"

He flashed a smile at the comfortably rounded, fifty-something Crystal, where she hovered by their table. "Hey, Crystal. Been working my tail off. How are things here at the diner?"

"Good, good. Can't complain." Her lively eyes skated over to Rachel. "And who's your lovely companion?"

"This is Rachel McCleary. Rachel, Crystal Blue, creator of the grilled mac and cheese sandwich that's going to ruin you for life."

"Nice to meet you. Jonah's been telling me tales of this sandwich for a very long time."

"Oh?" Crystal's glance ping-ponged between them.

"Rachel was my teacher in Syracuse. She's the one who taught us all to bake," Jonah explained.

Crystal brightened. "Well, Lord have mercy, we owe you a debt, young lady. The addition of that bakery to town has been so wonderful. And of course, we're thrilled to have our boy home again."

"Eden's Ridge is a really great little town," Rachel said.

"Will you be staying long?"

Jonah had known this would be a fishing expedition. Part of him welcomed getting the word out this way. But he felt Rachel stiffen beside him. Curling his hand around her shoulder, he gave a little squeeze.

"She's in town helping out while Brax is on his honeymoon."

"That's so nice of you! Home to New York after that?"

Rachel hesitated, and he was about to step in to redirect the conversation when she straightened her shoulders. "I'm not sure. Things are a little up in the air with my plans just now."

What did that mean?

"Well, I hope you enjoy your time in Eden's Ridge, however long you stay. What can I get y'all?"

After Crystal sashayed toward the window to put in their order, Jonah turned a little in his seat to better see her. "You're not going back to Audrey's program?"

"I had her find a replacement for me. He's willing to make that permanent if I choose not to come back. And right now, I don't think I want to."

"Why not?"

"For a lot of reasons. But mostly, I think I need to get out of Syracuse entirely. Start over somewhere new. I'm thrilled to be down here right now, because my anniversary is next Tuesday, and if I were home, everybody would make a big sad production of it. I want to remember. But I want to remember the good, not the end. So, part of what I hoped to achieve while I was here is figuring out whether I like small town life, because that will impact where I think about relocating."

Here.

Jonah had to bite back the word that came instantly to his tongue. There were reasons why that was a terrible idea. The biggest one being he didn't think he could stand being around when their time as lovers came to an end and she moved on with someone else.

"Well, trying it out for a while seems sensible before picking up stakes and making a change that big. And it seems like that means I need to show you the best small town life has to offer."

She aimed that heart-stopping smile in his direction. "I was hoping you would."

"THE BRIDE'S ex one-thousand percent pulled a 'Friends in Low Places' at the reception."

Rachel's mouth fell open. "He did not!"

From where she leaned against one of the prep tables in the bakery kitchen, Cayla lifted her palm. "Hand to God. He straight up started quoting the lyrics. I thought the groom was going to blow a gasket, but thankfully the best man and one of the other groomsmen managed to haul him out before he got to the third verse."

God, Rachel was so enjoying this pipeline of small-town gossip.

At another table across the kitchen, Jonah kneaded and stretched his latest batch of sourdough. "Video or it didn't happen."

Cayla scowled. "Now what kind of professional would I be if I took video that was YouTube worthy at one of my clients' weddings instead of working to smooth things over with the bride and her parents?"

Holt snagged her around the waist and pressed a kiss to her cheek. "One smart enough to know somebody else was totally gonna do that, and find it online later."

Her smile was very cat that ate the canary. "You are not wrong."

Rachel efficiently wrapped the pastry she'd just made in cling wrap and popped it into the walk-in cooler to chill. "This I've gotta see."

They all crowded around Cayla to peer at her phone as she brought up the video. Jonah pressed against Rachel's back, his hand sliding possessively around her waist. She leaned against him, enjoying the feeling of being claimed in all these tiny ways. She'd spent so long being part of a pair. Not that she couldn't be alone. In the years since John had died, she'd learned how. But it meant she didn't take it for granted now.

She and Jonah had crossed some line. Past being friends-with-benefits and into something more that she didn't dare analyze. She'd told him about her intention to relocate, and he hadn't immediately suggested she move to Tennessee so they could keep pursing this relationship. But he'd been true to his word, making an effort to show her everything Eden's Ridge had to offer. Surely, that meant *something*? She didn't know how to ask him without risk of damaging this fledgling thing building between them.

The bell over the front door jangled as another customer entered. Patting Jonah's hand, Rachel stepped away. "My turn."

Since the bruising had faded from her face, she'd been taking shifts out front, filling orders and ringing people up. Jonah had involved her in the development of their business from its beginning, taking advantage of her experience building and growing a bakery from the ground up. She wanted to get a feel for how theirs ran from all sides, so she could make suggestions for how best to strengthen it.

A familiar brunette with a toddler on her hip stood at the counter. The child caught sight of her and reached out chubby arms. "Ray-Ray!"

Grinning, Rachel skirted the counter to give the girl a little belly tickle. "Hey there, Bailey. How are you?"

Bailey giggled and stretched those little arms out in the

universal sign for *up!* When Rachel held out her hands in return, her mother, Pru Reynolds Bohannon, one of the quartet of sisters behind The Misfit Inn and Spa, relinquished her. "I'd heard you were back in town and staying with Jonah."

Rachel settled Bailey on her hip, soaking in the comforting weight of a cuddly child. "For a couple of weeks now. I came back for Brax and Mia's vow renewal and stuck around to help while they were on their honeymoon."

"Xander mentioned the trouble y'all had. How are you feeling?"

Rachel blinked in surprise. *Small towns,* she reminded herself. And the sheriff was Pru's brother-in-law. "I'm okay. All recovered now."

Pru's brown eyes were worried as they scanned the fading scar at Rachel's temple. "Aren't you a little anxious? I know they haven't caught the guy."

She couldn't hold back the wry smile. "Hard to be anxious with a former SEAL as a bodyguard."

"Fair point. Even before the Navy, Jonah had a protective streak a mile wide."

It was weird for Rachel to think about how many people here had known Jonah longer and perhaps better than she did. "You've known him a long time?"

"All my life. He was just a year behind me in school and friends with several of my brothers. Everybody's glad to see him home."

It was another reminder of the roots he had here. This was his place. She wondered if it could really become hers, too. Shaking off the thought, she shifted Bailey to her other hip. "What can I get for you today?"

"The tiny terror there can be bribed with C-A-K-E. We've got a houseful at the inn this weekend, so it seemed prudent to be prepared."

"I feel like we can help you out with that. What are you looking for?"

"Cake!" Bailey trilled, leaning over to press her little kid hands to the glass display case, where the day's offering of cupcakes sat like frosting-covered jewels.

"Oh! Bailey, don't touch!" Pru's voice held that edge of motherly exasperation that said she was in dire need of a break.

Rachel shifted her out of reach of the case and bounced a little. "It's fine. Nothing that won't clean right up." She made faces at the girl, wringing out more giggles. "If you have a few minutes, we could all sit down for a little snack and a visit."

"That sounds amazing," Pru breathed.

"Go, sit. I've got this."

Juggling Bailey on her hip, Rachel gathered up a couple of the fresh lemon blueberry scones and snagged bottled waters from the mini-fridge behind the counter, before joining Pru at one of the four-top tables.

"So, how's everything at the inn?" Rachel had loved every minute of her past stays at The Misfit Inn. Their spa was top-notch, and the inn itself was delightful and cozy.

"Crazy. We're at peak season and growing by leaps and bounds. Which is a fantastic problem to have, so I shouldn't complain."

"Wishing you had some breathing room doesn't qualify as a complaint."

"You're sweet for saying so. We're gonna have to look at expanding staff again soon. My sister Athena's been handling the lion's share of the breakfast stuff, but her *Misfit Kitchen* web series is taking off since her cookbook came out, so she really doesn't want to deal with that anymore, you know? She's a chef, not a baker. It's not her passion."

Rachel's brain began to spin. "Are you looking to hire someone in-house, or would you consider contracting with the boys?"

Pru blinked. "I don't know yet. I guess it would depend on how the numbers broke down."

"I think I might could help you out either way." At her questioning look, Rachel continued. "I'm thinking of leaving Syracuse."

It took all her control not to look toward the kitchen and Jonah. But it didn't stop Pru.

"And moving here?" *To be with Jonah?* was what she was really asking.

Rachel took advantage of handing Bailey her sippy cup to avoid Pru's gaze. "I don't know. It's too early to say at this point. But gainful employment is certainly a factor."

"You don't want to open another bakery?"

"I haven't decided." She'd done it once. She could do it again. But she wasn't sure she wanted to. "I think I might like a different kind of challenge."

Eden's Ridge couldn't support another bakery, and she was reasonably sure Bad Boy Bakers couldn't support a fourth person. Certainly not at the level they operated at now. To seriously consider coming here, she had to have a viable option for employment. If the Misfit Inn was seriously looking to expand its staff, it might be the ideal solution.

"How long are you in town?"

"At least until Brax and Mia get home. After that, I don't have firm plans." She hoped Jonah would ask her to stay, but she couldn't count on that.

"Let me talk to my sisters. I think they'll go with me on this, but if you'd be willing to stick around for another week or so, we could maybe do a trial run to see what we all think about having an in-house baker. You could give us a better idea of the numbers involved, and that would help us figure out whether that's a viable option for all of us."

"I'd love that."

By the time they'd finished their snacks, and she'd sent Pru and Bailey on their way with two boxes of treats to get them through the weekend, Jonah was ensconced in the little office off the kitchen.

Rachel slid into the narrow room behind him and glanced at the spreadsheets on the screen. "Inventory?"

"Unfortunately. It's my least favorite part of the business."

"Necessary evil."

"Have a good visit with Pru?"

"I did. I got to know her a bit during my previous stays at the inn. I really like her and her sisters."

"They're good people," he agreed.

"Our conversation gave me some ideas about Bad Boy Bakers."

"Oh?" Jonah tipped his head back against her ribs, and she automatically began kneading at the muscles in his neck and shoulders.

"Have you been keeping track of what sells the best, broken down to cost per unit?"

"Um, no? Not to that deep an extent. We're keeping up with what sells best, sure. And we've got a better handle on how much to make to avoid waste. But we haven't looked at what it costs to make each thing."

"I can help you put together a spreadsheet that will do that by linking to your existing inventory spreadsheet."

Jonah tipped his head back to stare at her. "Why, Miss McCleary, are you secretly a math nerd?"

She squeezed his shoulders. "I'm a data geek and proud of it. It meant I knew down to the penny how much it cost me to run my business. That was especially important in the lean beginning years. How are your sales running?"

Holt came to lean in the doorway. "Sales are holding steady. They're not quite as high as they were at the very beginning when things were brand new and everybody was excited to come check us out, but we've settled into something that's probably going to be our normal. I'm getting more cake orders, largely courtesy of Cayla, and we've definitely got our share of regulars."

All of that was good and more or less what Rachel had expected. "Have you considered how you want to grow?"

"Grow?" Jonah protested. "We're barely started."

"Yeah, but it's never too early to think about how you might expand. What other product lines you might carry. The ways you can really shore up your business. Because there are three of you, and this is a small town. There are only so many ways you can expand your market base in terms of the people who live here."

Holt folded his arms. "What did you have in mind?"

"Well, for one thing, you should absolutely look into partnering with some of the local restaurants to see about providing baked goods and desserts on their menu. If they don't already have someone in-house doing that, chances are, they're purchasing something pre-made. You can offer better quality, fresher options, which serves to elevate their menus and also functions as free advertising for the bakery, provided they disclose the source to patrons—which you should absolutely ask for. Then there's also the possibility of mail orders."

Jonah scoffed. "Mail orders? For baked goods? Have you actually seen the state of packages that go through the postal service in our country?"

"Yeah, smart ass. That's actually something I was looking into for my bakery before I decided to close. There's a real market for that kind of thing. Obviously, not every kind of baked good is suited to survive being mailed, but there are certain products that absolutely can. I know of several bakeries that have created a demand well outside of their catchment area."

"I'd think that's a pretty involved process," Holt observed.

"Something that might need more people? More equipment and space."

"It can. But it depends on the degree. There are ways to do it in phases, so you're not overwhelmed straight out of the gate." Rachel could see they'd already hit the point of overwhelm. Probably this wasn't the best thing to bring up while the issue of who was targeting the bakery was still up in the air. "It was just an idea. And certainly something y'all should discuss among yourselves once Brax gets back."

Jonah grabbed one of her hands and pressed a kiss to it. "It's a good idea. Maybe a bit too ambitious for where we are just now. But the talking to local restaurants we can absolutely do. I know Logan Maxwell's farm supplies a hell of a lot of the produce and meats for them, so it seems like there's a good chance they'd be open to that kind of partnership."

"You're the local," Holt pointed out. "Seems like you're the logical person to talk to them."

"I'll add it to the list."

10

On Sunday, Jonah glowered at the remaining piles of his dad's stuff. He didn't want to be here. He didn't want to waste his dwindling time with Rachel digging through this crap, searching for something that had probably been tossed or stolen or lost. If they hadn't found a flash drive or financial records or anything remotely useful on the previous trip when they'd had all hands on deck, why should they expect to find something now?

Beyond all that, he could acknowledge, in the privacy of his own head, that he was anxious about what else he might find. The childhood memorabilia they'd uncovered that first day had unsettled him more than he wanted to admit. It didn't fit with the picture of the man he'd carried in his head all these years. Were there more pieces that didn't fit? More evidence that would make him ask questions Lonnie was no longer here to answer?

Rachel's hand settled on his shoulder. "I don't think glaring is going to improve your X-ray vision."

"Maybe I'm trying to incinerate it all with my eyes."

"How's that working for you?"

He grunted.

She only laughed. "C'mon. There's not that much stuff left. If we push hard, I think we can get through the last of it today, and then it's done."

Except, if they didn't find anything, would it be done? Did that mean there was nothing *to* find? If Xander had uncovered more leads to follow, he hadn't shared, probably for fear that Jonah would interfere in his investigation. But if all the possible trails petered out, they'd be up shit creek. And who knew whether the person or people behind the vandalism and break-ins and Rachel's attack would ever just cut their losses and give up?

Jonah didn't want to live with that uncertainty, so he sucked it up and opened another box. Rachel did the same, and for a while, they worked in companionable silence. That was something he'd always liked about her. She was easy to be with, never pressing for needless conversation because she couldn't handle quiet. Yet, she could just as easily talk with him for hours about anything and everything. It was a gift to be easy with both.

He checked the water reservoir of an ancient Mr. Coffee before adding the coffee maker to the donate pile and moving to the next box in the pile. On top was a manilla envelope full of photos. He slid them out, braced for... something. The sight of his mom's smiling face was a bit of a sucker punch.

She was so young in this shot, no more than seventeen, with her arms around two guys of similar age. One was Lonnie, who'd had none of the hardness Jonah remembered of his father. He could see his high school self in the lanky frame he'd had before football and the Navy had bulked him up. The other guy was a stranger. With blue eyes and shaggy brown hair long enough to be pulled into a stubby tail, he looked like a young pirate, or maybe one of the Lost Boys from *Peter Pan*. Where Rebecca and Lonnie looked at the camera, this guy was looking at Rebecca, a half-smile on his lips.

Mixed in with several other group shots from some social function or other, there were more pictures of the three of them. Some of just Lonnie and the other guy. Some of Lonnie and his mom. The pictures chronicled what seemed to be a friendship between the three of them that spanned several years. The more he studied the other guy, the more Jonah felt a niggle that something about him seemed familiar, but he couldn't place why. Maybe he knew the guy's kid or something growing up. There were more pictures of just Rebecca that dated into their early marriage. In one she aimed that dazzling smile at the camera, her hand laid on a very pregnant belly. That would've been him in there, he realized.

How long after this photo had things started to devolve between his parents?

Knowing his mom might want to keep these, he set them in the keep pile and moved on to the next folder in the box. It was full of newspaper clippings. His instinct was to put it immediately in the toss pile, but he'd already discovered that Lonnie's filing system was more like sweeping all papers from a flat surface into a single container. Or maybe that was just a result of his own hurried and apathetic packing. So he took the time to page through the contents of the folder.

He froze as he saw his sister's face peering out from the article. It was a story from the local paper about some academic achievement or other when she was in middle school. Why had Lonnie cut it out and kept it? There were more articles. Stories chronicling Jonah's high school football career. Graduation announcements for them both. Even some slightly blurry snapshots from each of their high school graduations, which, as far as Jonah knew, his father hadn't attended.

"This makes no sense."

Rachel abandoned her box and came to peer over his

shoulder. As he continued to page through, her hand settled on his shoulder again, a quiet support.

"Why the hell would he keep all this shit? All this suggests that he gave a damn, at least on some level. But he walked away and made no effort to maintain a relationship with us. It doesn't add up. Doesn't fit with the man I remember."

"What do you remember?"

Jonah tossed the folder aside and scrubbed both hands over his head as his temples began to throb. "He basically dropped out of our lives. Didn't even fight for visitation or partial custody when Mom divorced him. Child support was spotty, and Mom didn't think it was worth fighting about. She just wanted to be done, and I don't blame her. He didn't go so far as to run the other way when he saw us in town, but he simply wasn't a part of our lives. Everything I saw him do was selfishly motivated. That's part of why I went into the SEALs. I felt this need to do something to karmically balance him out. I wanted to do something honorable with my life."

He dropped his hands. "Of course, that got blown all to hell. Literally."

Rachel knelt in front of him, reaching up to massage his temples. "You're still doing something honorable with your life, Jonah. You are an everyday hero. You take care of everybody and everything in your orbit. You gave Brax and Holt a purpose, a community they could become a part of. You turned an eyesore into something that's a great addition to this town. You regularly help your family and your friends, putting everyone ahead of yourself. I know this isn't what you expected out of your life. My life didn't turn out the way I expected, either. But that doesn't mean either of us is on a lesser path."

Under her gentle ministrations, the pulsing in his head began to ease. "That's better. Thanks."

She brushed a kiss to his temple and moved back to her box.

Jonah watched her for a moment, debating whether to voice the question she'd opened the door to. "What did you expect out of your life?"

Methodically, she began to page through another folder of paperwork. "The things most people expect, I guess. Family. Children with the man I loved. That was really hard for me to let go of when he died."

Jonah thought back to seeing her with Pru's little girl the other day. She'd looked utterly natural and comfortable with a toddler on her hip, and it had been more than obvious she took joy in the child. It was easy to picture her with her own. Smiling and laughing as she instructed little hands in baking and decorating cookies or making salt dough ornaments for the Christmas tree. A live one. One of the firs that grew out on the mountain. They'd make strings of popcorn and construction paper chains, and he could lift the kid up to put the star on the top...

The sound of the screen door slapping cut through the fantasy that had taken root in his brain.

"Yoo-hoo! Y'all back here?"

What the actual hell is wrong with you, Ferguson?

Swallowing hard, he turned to face his mother. "What are you doing out here? I told you we had it handled."

"Oh, psshh. I promised I'd still help, and what else did I have to do this afternoon? Looks like y'all have made another big dent."

"We're getting there. I found some pictures you may want." Jonah jerked his head toward the tiny keep pile. "That envelope there."

Dropping her purse, Rebecca picked up the envelope and slid out the contents. Her face immediately softened with nostalgia.

"Oh, wow. This was a long time ago." She began to flip

through the photos, her gaze lingering. Remembering when things were still good?

"Who's that other guy in all those pictures with you and Dad?"

"That's our friend Grey. He and your dad and I were like the Three Musketeers back in high school."

"How come I've never heard anything about him?"

"Well, he left Eden's Ridge not too long before Lonnie and I got married, and we all lost touch. I don't know what happened to him."

"Didn't you ever try to stalk him on social media to see what he was up to?" Rachel asked.

Rebecca hesitated, regret clouding her gaze. "No. No, I didn't. We had a big fight right before he left. I don't think he'd have wanted to hear from me." She twitched her shoulders. "It was a lifetime ago. We were all kids."

How might her life have changed if she'd waited for someone better than his father? Jonah looked down at the folder of stuff he'd tossed to the floor, unable to hold back a question that had haunted him for years. "Mom, what did you see in Dad?" He lifted his gaze. "You're awesome. He wasn't. How the hell did you end up with someone like him?"

He cursed himself as pain flickered over her face.

"He wasn't always like you remember. When we were young, he was fun and funny, and I thought we wanted the same things. We got married really young. Sometimes that works out. Sometimes it doesn't. But I got you and Sam out of the deal, so I consider everything else absolutely worth it."

Jonah felt like a slug for bringing it up.

"Oh, don't look at me like that. It was my choice. I don't regret it. Now, have y'all found any evidence of his bookkeeping for the bar?"

"Not yet, but this might be something." Rachel held out a stack of papers.

They both crossed to join her.

"They're deposit slips for a bank in Johnson City. See? Here's the account number." She pointed to the bottom corner.

Jonah frowned, trying to think through the echos of the headache. "I don't remember there being any mention of a bank account in Johnson City in any of his stuff that went through probate. The bar's account was here in town. So were his personal accounts. He died unexpectedly, so his records weren't what you could call organized. I guess it's possible an account slipped through the cracks on that front. Or maybe they're from an old account that he closed."

"Or maybe he hid it deliberately," Rebecca added. "If he was doing something shady involving blackmail or otherwise illegally obtained funds, I wouldn't think he'd want to run that through his primary accounts."

"That's a completely fair point. Either way, we'll have to go through the attorney who was executor to find out."

"While you're at it, maybe you could get copies of the old bank statements," Rachel suggested. "Maybe we can reverse engineer his financials from that. It wouldn't be perfect, but isn't that what they're all the time saying on cop shows on TV? Follow the money?"

"It's better direction than we've had up to now. I'll call him tomorrow. Meanwhile, let's try to get through the rest of this crap. I want to be finished."

"And here's your change. Thanks for choosing Bad Boy Bakers." Rachel handed over the bakery bag to the latest customer, automatically glancing at the pass-through when she heard the kitchen door open.

Jonah strode inside.

She tagged off with Holt and went to greet him. "Well? What did he say?"

"He'll look into it. This one wasn't on the list of accounts he dealt with as executor, so he's going to find out whether there is an account, and get copies of the transactions for the year prior to Lonnie's death if there is. It all means more waiting." Everything in his posture was restless.

"I know you hate the waiting, but it's a positive step." Knowing he needed to do something productive, with visible results, she nodded to the rack of proofing baskets. "Meanwhile, the sourdough is about done with its latest proof and ready to go in."

He jerked his head in a nod. "On it."

They fell into a familiar rhythm, juggling customers and recipes and conversation. As the scent of baking bread filled the air, Jonah's shoulders seemed to relax. He needed answers. Needed this situation to be resolved. But once it was, would it change things between them? If he was thinking about what came after this week, Rachel didn't know and was terrified to ask, even if she was working on an option for how she could realistically stay.

Pru's sisters had been extremely enthusiastic about the idea of potentially bringing her on, so Rachel had been pulling together a business proposal to give them some numbers. She needed more information from them, in terms of volume of their clientele, but the creative side of her brain was running wild, thinking of the presentation she wanted to give around the food. Showing everything she could do. Above and beyond the breakfast offerings, she was thinking about the sort of food she could put together for events. They didn't do a lot of events, and she didn't know why. The space was fantastic. Maybe it was a capacity thing? A staffing thing? She intended to ask during her trial run next week.

Hungry again, Rachel nabbed one of the fresh boules of

sourdough and sliced off a heel. The warm, yeasty taste of it melted on her tongue, and she sighed with pleasure. "This would make a fantastic grilled cheese."

Jonah perked up. "Mmm, that does sound good. You wanna whip some up for a mid-morning snack while I get the next round of loaves in the oven?"

"Sure. Holt, you want one?"

"Absolutely."

While the boys shifted gears to replenish stock after the biggest of the breakfast rush, Rachel browsed the walk-in for cheeses. Opting for a mix of mild and sharp cheddar, she brought the lot of it back to her station and began to slice. The scent of grilling butter on bread began to fill the kitchen, making her mouth water. Their breakfast was hours ago.

The guys barely waited for the sandwiches to hit a plate before they were snatching them up and biting in.

"You'll burn yourselves."

There was a lot of hissing of breath to cool off the bites already in their mouths.

"Damn, this is tasty," Jonah moaned. "Great call."

Holt took another bite and hummed an agreement. "It's a big step up from the white bread and American cheese ones I grew up on. Though I still have a fondness for those. So does Maddie."

"Everybody loves a grilled cheese." Rachel sampled her own sandwich, appreciating the way the sharp saltiness of the cheddar balanced with the sweet of the sourdough bread. As the flavors melded on her tongue, her brain began to spin. "I think we should try an experiment."

"Thinking about a new recipe?" Jonah asked. "I volunteer as tribute for taste testing."

She laughed. "No, I think we should test out a flash lunch special. A single sandwich option. Or maybe something with small variations like... one of these just like this, one with some apple or pear slices, and maybe one with bacon. We could post it on social media and see how many people show up."

"Do we want to get into offering lunches?" Holt sounded skeptical.

"As a full-service restaurant, no. But having an extremely limited menu lunch special would be a way to get people in the door who might not otherwise show up. Folks who aren't inclined or can't show up for breakfast. There aren't that many dining options in town. So I think people would be excited about something different. They'd come in, try the sandwich, and maybe pick up a cupcake or tart for dessert or a baguette to take home for dinner. It gets bodies through the door, which is the name of the game."

Thinking through the whole thing, she nabbed a pencil and notepad, beginning to make notations and calculations about how many loaves of sourdough they had and how much cheese was on hand. She'd finished her own sandwich by the time she came up with a per-sandwich cost to produce. "This is how much you'd have in raw ingredients. You currently make this much profit selling the loaves on their own. Each loaf would get you four, maybe five, sandwiches, and you could toast the heels to make croutons, which would be another potential side item. There's a higher profit margin in the actual sandwiches, depending on what you charge for them. And it means you're less likely to have stock left over at the end of the day."

In response to Holt's questioning eyebrow, Jonah shrugged. "I mean, the worst that can happen is we sell three sandwiches and call it a failed experiment."

"Let's do it."

While they settled on a price, Rachel made another grilled cheese to take photos of. Holt posted it to the bakery's social media pages, along with an announcement about the lunch special of the day before the three of them devoured the sample.

"The word is out, so I guess we'll see."

What they saw a couple hours later was their first ever lunch rush. Holt was manning the range while Rachel and Jonah juggled orders and comments from customers.

"Oh my God, this is delicious."

"Please do this again!"

"This is awesome!"

"Is this going to become a regular thing?"

Rachel grinned at Jonah's flummoxed expression. "That's still up for consideration. But please, tell everybody. The more people who show up, the more likely we are to do it again. Be sure to follow us on all our social media to see the announcements!"

Holt slid the next couple of sandwiches onto the ledge of the pass-through. "I'd say we have ourselves a successful experiment."

"Yeah, you do!" Pleased with herself, Rachel swung toward the jingling bell of the front door. "Welcome to Bad Boy Bakers. What can we get you?"

An auburn-haired woman with a crown of daisies on her head peered around a massive bouquet, her nose twitching as she sniffed the air. "I'm actually here to do a delivery, but can I get one of whatever smells so good?"

"That'll be today's lunch special. A grilled cheese on sourdough," Holt answered from the kitchen.

"Sign me up. Meanwhile, you must be Rachel."

She blinked. "I am."

The woman extended the bouquet with a smile. "These are for you."

"Oh. I—Thank you." She took the vase, noting the gladiolus and forget-me-nots, among bold lilies and assorted greenery. Her throat went thick even before she pulled out the card and read the inscription.

To remembering all the good stuff. Happy anniversary. -Jonah

She'd known the date as soon as she woke up this morning. Her eleventh wedding anniversary. And it had felt incredibly weird to know that and be waking up beside someone else. To be happy with someone else. So she'd tried to put it out of her mind, not wanting to dwell on John when her time with Jonah might be drawing to an end. They hadn't talked about what came after this week, once Mia and Brax were back. She hadn't told him about her audition for a job at the inn next week. She'd been too afraid to rock the boat.

But he'd remembered what she'd said about wanting to remember with joy instead of sorrow, and he'd bought her flowers to do exactly that. He was a man who could help her celebrate her anniversary with another man and not be threatened that she'd had a full life and all those memories with him. How could he not be the right guy for her? How could this not be exactly where she was supposed to be?

Swamped with love and gratitude, she turned to find Jonah. His face was uncharacteristically blank, but she recognized his anxiety in the twitch of his hands. Needing to reassure him, wanting to thank him for making this so much easier on her, she closed the distance between them, sliding her arms around his neck and pressing her lips to his in a kiss that had their lunch patrons cheering.

She dropped back to her feet in the circle of his arms. "Thank you."

"Not too much?"

"It was perfect."

And she was pretty sure he was, too.

11

J onah drummed his fingers on the steering wheel of his truck as he hit the outskirts of Johnson City. He didn't want to be here. Didn't want to be away from Rachel, not when he had no idea how much longer he had with her. It had been on the tip of his tongue to ask a hundred times over the past couple of weeks, but he hadn't been able to bring himself to say the words. Because that would bring up a discussion of what legitimately came next, and he was afraid she'd want more than they'd originally agreed to. And that was on him, because he'd changed the rules and pushed them beyond the basic friends-with-benefits she'd asked for. He'd wanted as much as he could have with her, even if it was only for the short term. But Brax and Mia got back tomorrow, and that meant their short term was up and his grace period for avoiding the subject had run out.

Instead of figuring out how he was going to end things in a way that wouldn't destroy their friendship, he was going to meet with the attorney who'd been executor of his father's estate. That the guy hadn't just emailed him digital copies of the bank records he'd requested told Jonah there was more to talk about than just an old account. He hoped it meant a legitimate break in the case, so he'd made time for the appointment and left Rachel back in the Ridge with Holt, in hopes the alone time would give him some genius clue how to handle her.

A police car was leaving the parking lot as Jonah arrived. It might've been nothing. The guy could've had business with the attorney and stopped by while on duty. But something told Jonah that wasn't it. He was on alert before he stepped through the doors and into what had been a comfortably plush waiting room on his last visit. Now there were papers everywhere, as if a tornado had gone through the office. Elias Craggs was frowning as his frazzled secretary gathered papers from the floor.

"Looks like y'all have had some trouble."

Elias looked up and ran a hand over his balding head. "Yeah. Somebody broke in last night. Doesn't look like they actually took anything, as far as we can tell, but they definitely went through our files. We're trying to figure out what information might have been compromised and who all needs to be contacted. It's a damned mess."

Coincidence? Jonah didn't tend to see those anymore. But Johnson City was a fair piece away from Eden's Ridge, and Craggs had lots of clients. There was no reason to automatically assume this had anything to do with Lonnie.

And yet.

"Was my dad's stuff among the files that were gone through?"

"As far as we can tell, nearly everything was gone through." He gestured to the mess. "Whoever it was tossed things willy-nilly, obviously, to cover up whatever it was they were looking for. We won't know for sure until we get mess sorted."

"And that's going to take a while," the secretary groaned.

"Do I need to come back later?"

"No. I've still got everything I needed to give you." Elias waved a hand for Jonah to follow. "Let's go into the conference room. It's less of a mess."

They took a seat at the end of the conference table that wasn't covered in files. "Well, you gave me a little mystery. I'm not entirely clear on how your dad managed to slip this one through the cracks, but he did, in fact, have a bank account with Trust Financial here in Johnson City. As of today, that account has a balance of $264,396.72."

Jonah stared. "I'm sorry, what?"

Elias flashed a wry smile. "I had much the same response."

"But... how?"

"That's a good question. I got copies of bank statements from this account and from the others that you requested, going back for a year prior to his death. If we need more than that, I'll have to make another request. They just came in this morning, so I haven't had a chance to look through them all, with everything going on, but at a glance, it looks like he mostly used it for savings. When he pulled money out, it was always in cash. I saw some corresponding values in the bar's business account, so this was apparently what he used to keep the business afloat."

"Afloat seems generous. I mean, you saw the bar. His house. You saw his other accounts. If he was sitting on that kind of money, why was he living the way he was?"

"I don't know, given the state of things you and Samantha inherited. I have no idea why he wouldn't have poured extra funds into the business. But you know people do all kinds of strange things. And he was more ill than anyone knew, apparently. Could be he wasn't quite all there mentally by the end."

As far as Jonah knew, Lonnie had done nothing to treat the aggressive cancer that had killed him, choosing to continue to live as he always had. On his own.

"This account wasn't a part of probate. Will we need to do something on that front?"

"Probate is over and settled. All claims were made on the estate and debts were settled, so the money officially belongs to you and your sister as his sole heirs. Do you know what you'll want to do with it?"

He didn't have the first clue what they'd do with that kind of money or whether his sister would want any of it at all. "I'll have to talk to Sam about that. I appreciate you looking into all this."

"Of course. And if I find that your father's files are impacted by this unpleasant business, I'll let you know."

Jonah rose, accepting the thick packet of bank statements. "Thanks."

Craggs escorted him out. At least the meeting had been short and sweet.

Jonah tossed the envelope onto his front seat. What was the likelihood that this break-in could have anything to do with his father? Probably not high. Why would somebody be breaking in now, instead of while the estate was in probate? Still, he decided to mention it to Xander, so he could get in touch with whoever was in charge of that investigation in Johnson City, just in case. For now, he wanted to get on back to the Ridge and comb through the records to find out exactly where Lonnie was getting his money.

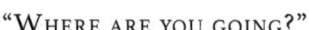

"Where are you going?"

Purse in hand, Rachel went brows up at Holt's sharp question. "To the grocery store?"

"Jonah's not back from Johnson City yet."

She gave an exaggerated look around the bakery kitchen. "I

am aware. Last time I checked, I'm not under official house arrest."

"Of course not. It's just, I'm supposed to look out for you while he's away, and I'm stuck here finishing up this cake for tomorrow."

"Are you seriously going to tell me I have to stay here under full bodyguard protection in the middle of the afternoon on a Friday, because you can't escort me to Garden of Eden to pick up the ingredients for dinner?"

The fierceness of Holt's scowl was undermined by the ballerina pink fondant in his hands. "Yeah, I know how that sounds, but if anything happens to you on my watch, Jonah will kick my ass."

"It's the *grocery store*. Right downtown. In public. In the daytime. Nothing has happened since the break-in. Nobody's even looked at me sideways. I promise I'll come right back and text you when I get in and out of my car. The car he let me drive to work on my own this morning, I might add."

Holt scrubbed a hand over his face, then swore when he ended up with fondant in his beard.

Rachel's lips twitched. "Pink is a great color for you."

"Smart ass." He grabbed a towel and began to wipe at his beard. "I know it's ridiculous, but Jonah didn't play around with Cayla or Mia's safety, so I'm sure as hell not going to be careless with yours."

Softening, she laid a hand on his arm. "Thank you. I do appreciate it. Straight there and back. Promise. There's homemade manicotti in it for you."

His blue eyes turned wistful. "Manicotti?"

She could make two batches if it got her out of this kitchen. "With from-scratch sauce. Assuming I can get there before all the fresh tomatoes are gone."

"Fine. Be careful. No playing on your phone while you walk to and from the store. Pay attention to your surroundings."

"Cross my heart. Back in a flash." Rachel scooted out the door before he could change his mind.

She slid into the car she'd barely used since coming to Eden's Ridge. This was the first time she'd actually been alone since her injury. It was odd being without Jonah after being practically attached at the hip these past few weeks. Brax and Mia got back tomorrow night, and the subject of what she was doing next was one she couldn't avoid any longer. So she'd opted to make one of Jonah's favorites for dinner in hopes of getting the conversation off on the right foot. Whatever foot that might be.

Familiar faces greeted her as she grabbed a shopping cart at Garden of Eden. More than one person called her by name as she began to traverse the aisles, picking up the necessary ingredients. This was part of that small-town dream. Being known and recognized. She didn't know all their names, but it was enough to know their faces from the bakery. These were tendrils of that connection she wanted to build, and she was surprised by exactly how much she wanted to foster them.

"Rachel! Hi, sugar."

She blinked and found Rebecca standing on the other side of the tomato display. "Hey. How are you?"

"I'm good. Finished with my clients early today and figured I'd get the grocery shopping done. I'm guessing you had the same idea."

"Yeah, I wanted to get started on some manicotti while Jonah's in Johnson City meeting with the attorney."

"Any word yet on what he found?"

"No. But it must have been something since he asked Jonah to come in to meet with him about it."

Worry flashed over his mother's features. "I hope all this stuff gets sorted soon."

"You and me both."

Rebecca hesitated. "Listen, would you like to go get a cup of coffee?"

She ought to get straight back. She'd promised Holt. But saying no felt rude, somehow, and she had the sense Rebecca wanted to talk about something. What that something might be gave Rachel more than a little anxiety, but she genuinely liked Jonah's mom. "Sure. I can't stay too long or Holt will send out a search party, since he's on babysitting duty, but I'd love a cup of coffee."

As there was nowhere else to get one, they ended up at the diner, settling into one of the booths in the back. An early twenty-something waitress, with a perky ponytail and more than a passing resemblance to Crystal herself, took their orders. She flipped over the white ceramic mugs on the table and filled them from a nearby pot without spilling a drop.

"Y'all want any pie with that?"

Rachel smiled. "Just coffee for me, thanks."

"This will be fine. Thanks, Nicky." Rebecca wrapped her hands around the mug. "So, how have you enjoyed your time in Eden's Ridge?"

Okay, so they were beginning with small talk. She could do that. "I like it. It's really different from Syracuse. A lot smaller. Slower. But that works for me."

"So, what comes next?"

Playing dumb, Rachel began to doctor her coffee. "What do you mean?"

"Well, Brax and Mia get back tomorrow. That was the whole reason you were coming down to help. Are you headed back to New York? Are you sticking around here?"

Rachel looked down at her mug, as if the answer were swimming in its caramel-colored depths. The woman had been nothing but kind to her, so she decided to be transparent and as honest as she could be. "You really want to know what's next with me and Jonah."

On a huff of laughter, Rebecca lifted her mug. "Well, there is that."

"I don't know. None of this was the plan. We sort of fell into whatever this is we're doing, and we haven't talked about what comes next. We haven't even talked about what's happening next week. He's been so consumed with trying to keep me safe. With trying to find the answers to whatever's going on. With keeping the business going. I think we're both a little afraid to bring up what happens next, because neither of us knows exactly where the other stands." She tapped her fingers against the mug. "This was supposed to be temporary."

Rebecca nodded. "And then it became more."

What the hell was she supposed to say to that? It was true, but this was *his mother*. It was one thing to allude to being something more, but she didn't want to spell it out.

Rebecca just smiled that former-pageant-queen smile. "I have eyes. I see how you two look at each other, and I think it would be a real shame if y'all let that slip away."

Rachel's throat went thick because this felt like a blessing for whatever they decided. "I don't want to let it slip away. I didn't expect to find anyone else after my husband died. We were high school sweethearts. Each other's first everything. We were together for seventeen years. And they were really great years. Starting over with somebody else is intimidating and overwhelming. And beyond all that, I just didn't think I could be that lucky twice. But Jonah's... Jonah." She laughed a little. "We recognized something in each other back in New York. We were both a little broken. Drowning in grief. That's what led us to being friends in the first place, and it's a contributing factor to what's made us more. But I don't know what he wants. I don't know how he feels."

"Have you asked him?"

"No. I've been trying to figure out logistics and options.

Because, you may have noticed, your son likes to know all of those things before he does anything."

Rebecca's rich, rolling laugh filled the diner. "Oh, honey, yes. You do know him. You talk about logistics. Would you consider leaving New York?"

"I was already thinking of leaving Syracuse even before I came down here. And then this happened, and I don't know. I would never ask him to leave what he's built here. This is his place. I know that, and I'm trying to figure out if it could be my place, too." She sipped her coffee. "I have a job interview here next week. I... haven't told Jonah."

"Do you think he'll be upset?"

"I don't know. For all we've been friends for a long time, being... more is still very new. I don't want him to think I'm being presumptive, or like I'm trying to force him into some kind of commitment. And, I guess, there's a part of me that wants him to ask me to stay first."

Rebecca covered her hand. "There's nothing wrong with that. Everyone wants to be chosen." There was something in her tone, some look in her eyes that said she knew that desire, knew what it felt like not to be.

"True enough."

"Well, none of it's really my business, but for whatever it's worth, I really like you two together. You make him happy, and he hasn't been happy in a really long time. There's a softness in him with you I've never seen before. I like seeing that in my boy. Too much of his life made him feel like he had to be hard."

"He takes on so much. He wants the best for all the people he cares about, but I think, a lot of the time, he believes he doesn't count. Like as long as he does all the things right and his people are safe and happy, then his own wants don't matter."

Rebecca studied her for a long moment. "You really see him."

"He sees me right back."

"Then I hope he's smart enough to see that you're the best thing that could've happened to him."

That knot was back in her throat. "Thank you. That means a lot to me. And what is it you guys say down here? From your mouth to God's ear?"

Rebecca lifted her mug for a toast. "Here's to exactly that."

12

"Welcome back, man." Jonah pulled Brax into a back-thumping hug.

"Good to be back. Everything go okay while we were gone?"

Holt scratched behind his ear. "More or less."

Brax sobered, his gaze bouncing between the two of them. "What happened?"

Cayla waded into the fray. "It'll keep for a bit. Let's get the dogs outside and get the food going." With her special brand of mom-wrangling, she managed to herd her six-year-old, their mutt, Banana Bread, and Mia and Brax's pit bull, Leno, out the back door.

Mia closed her eyes. "Just tell me whether I have more stuff to repair."

Jonah swung an arm around her shoulders and squeezed. "Nope. The bakery is fine."

"Okay, then somebody get me some alcohol. I have a feeling I'm gonna need some for this discussion."

"Way ahead of you, girl. I made margaritas." Rachel dragged her into Cayla and Holt's kitchen.

"C'mon." Holt jerked his head toward the back door. "I've got the grill fired up and the kebabs ready to go on."

They collectively migrated out to the back patio. Jonah lit the tiki torches lining the perimeter to ward off mosquitos. Maddie's shrieks of laugher echoed off the fence as she raced around with the dogs. He couldn't tell who was chasing who, but they seemed to be having a hell of a good time. As the women spilled out of the house, Holt began laying skewers of meat and vegetables across the grill.

Brax snagged beers from the cooler. Passing one to each of them, he twisted off the top and sipped. "On a scale of mildly problematic to completely FUBAR, what are we looking at here?"

"I'd say we're sitting at a SNAFU," Holt decided.

Jonah scowled. "A concussion isn't normal."

"Who got a concussion?" Brax demanded.

"I did." Rachel crossed the patio to slip an arm around Jonah's waist. "Stop growling. I'm fine."

Brax went brows-up. "I thought you said everything at the bakery was okay?"

"It is. I apparently interrupted the latest attempt at a break-in."

"Oh my God! Are you okay?" Mia took two steps forward, as if she needed to check Rachel over herself.

"I'm really okay. Jonah took good care of me. No lingering effects from the concussion."

"Why the—" Brax shot a glance out at Maddie in the yard and lowered his voice. "—H-E double hockey sticks—didn't you let me know?"

Holt opened his own beer. "Dude, you were on a very delayed honeymoon. We weren't going to do anything to interrupt that. The business was fine, and we've been handling everything else."

Mia took a hefty swallow of her margarita. "Okay, maybe you could start at the beginning?"

Jonah took a breath. "Okay, the short version is that we're a whole lot more sure that Holt's theory from back in the spring that none of this had anything to do with Mia is almost certainly correct. And I'm pretty sure that it was because of something my father was involved in that's spilled over onto all of us, because I'm the one who inherited all of his property and the bar."

Brax slid an arm around his wife. "How do we know this?"

Jonah laid the whole thing out for them.

At the end, Brax pinched his nose. "So, where are we now?"

Holt interrupted. "Five minutes on food."

"Well, my dad apparently had a secret bank account in Johnson City. I'm not actually sure if it was legitimately secret or if his record keeping was just that bad, but it's got over two hundred grand sitting in it."

"Two hundred grand?" Brax whistled. "If your dad was sitting on that kind of cash, why was the bar in such lousy shape?"

"There's a question. One of many. I've done some digging, got copies of all his bank statements for the year before his death. Rachel and I spent last night going through them and trying to reverse engineer the books for the business to see if we can determine what was actually going on." And yet again, they hadn't talked about what came next with them.

Rachel picked up the thread. "Most of it is exactly as you'd expect. Vendors related to running a bar. Regular bills. Some medical expenses. That kind of thing. The weird part is that all the deposits in this account came from Percipience Unlimited."

"What's that?" Cayla asked.

Jonah crossed his arms. "We don't know. I used my GoogleFu to try to dig something up online, but I didn't find jack, which seemed odd. There's no reason I can find that my dad should've been receiving regular payments—no pay stubs or invoices or anything in his stuff."

"Were the deposits always the same amount?" Holt asked.

"They varied," Rachel said. "And they didn't keep to any particular schedule either, so far as we could tell."

Holt pulled the kebabs off the grill and onto a waiting tray. "So, let's call Cash and see what he can dig up."

"Who's Cash?" Rachel wanted to know.

"Good friend of mine. Former Army intelligence. He's into cybersecurity now, and he's one hell of a hacker." Tenting some foil over the kebabs, he pulled out his phone and dialed, putting the call on speaker.

It rang three times before someone picked up. "Yeah?"

"Hello to you, too."

"Hey man. Hang on a second." There were clear sounds of a hand being placed over the receiver, followed by a low murmur, then evidence of Cash changing locations. "Okay, sorry about that."

"Everything okay?"

"Yeah, I'm just in the middle of something. What can I do for you?"

"We need you to dig up whatever you can find on Percipience Unlimited. Jonah's dad was getting payments from them, and we're trying to figure out who they are and what they're about. Jonah wasn't able to find anything about them online."

"You thinking shell company?" Cash asked.

Jonah stepped closer to the phone. "Maybe. Seems like a convenient way to hide things. We'd appreciate it if you could work your magic."

"Sure, I can do that. It might be a couple of days. I've got some other things going I can't walk away from at the moment."

"Of course. Appreciate it, man," Holt told him. "And hey, you need to find time to come out for a visit. I want you to meet Cayla and Maddie."

"Love to. I'll be in touch."

As Holt ended the call, Jonah felt a vague sense of relief. Like maybe they were actually starting to set things in motion. "Guess now we wait."

"Now, we eat," Cayla announced.

Hands were washed, the outdoor table was set. Soon they were seated and passing the bowls of fresh-cut watermelon and the tomato corn salad to go with the kebabs. Conversation turned to Brax and Mia's trip across Europe, and Jonah relaxed a little further. All his people were home and safe, exactly as he wanted them.

"So, now that Mia's home, I demand a girls' night. Rachel, you are required to be in attendance," Cayla declared.

Jonah stiffened. Would she even be here for a girls' night?

"Of course, I'd be happy to."

She would?

As if sensing his question, Rachel looked up at him. "I wasn't planning to go back to Syracuse immediately. I'm here for at least another week. If that's okay with you."

"Yeah, of course. Stay as long as you like." *Stay forever.*

Except that wasn't an option. And he had to find a way to get okay with that.

RACHEL SET down her bag of groceries on one of the makeshift plywood and sawhorse counters in what would eventually be the kitchen of Mia's new house. She'd gutted the original monstrosity, taking it down to the studs.

"Okay, I know we were all technically here for your reception, but I didn't actually get to see the house. Will you give a quick tour?"

Mia brightened. "Love to."

Cayla lifted a bottle. "But let's open the wine first." She

pulled the cork and poured them each half a Solo cup of pinot noir.

Rachel lifted the cup to sip. "I'm having flashbacks to college. Although this is a much better vintage than anything I had back then."

"It is a mark of adulthood that we've graduated from crappy wine coolers." Cayla lifted her cup for a toast.

Leaving the provisions for their girls' night in the makeshift kitchen, they followed Mia through the house.

"The bedrooms are done. They were pretty straightforward. Mostly new paint and crown molding. We replaced the fixtures in all the bathrooms and put in new tile. And I found this fantastic old clawfoot tub that I had refinished for the master."

They ooed and ahed over the tub, and even more over the view out the picture window above it. Rachel trailed the two women, soaking in the house. It was a good space. Like the bakery, she hadn't seen the starting point, but she'd heard stories. As they moved through from room to room, Mia explained what she'd started with and all the changes she'd made.

Returning down to the first floor, they entered the living room.

"This is my current pride and joy." Mia paused in front of a massive river rock fireplace that stretched from the floor to the top of the vaulted ceiling. "I found this gorgeous slab of live edge cherry for the mantle. It was a tricky as hell installation, but the end result is exactly what I wanted." She ran a hand over the mantle in much the same way Rachel had seen her touch Brax. With love.

"And these. These make the space." Mia crossed over to unlatch several doors. With a few strategic shoves and pulls, she opened the newly installed accordion doors to the expanse of deck outside where their reception had been held.

"It made for a hell of a party." Rachel strode out to the deck, wandering over to the corner where she'd kissed Jonah what felt like months ago.

Cayla wandered out to join her. "Do you think y'all will be in by Christmas?"

"We're basically down to the kitchen, so unless something goes horribly wrong or we have supplies on back order, then yeah." Mia knocked on the nearest piece of wood, the deck railing.

"There's so much room here." Rachel turned to take in the sprawl of the house that seemed to have grown out of the mountain. "What are you two going to do with all the space?"

"Well, that's a thing." Mia took a hefty swig of wine. "Brax and I are working on getting approved as foster parents. We want to adopt."

"Honey! That's amazing!" Cayla set her cup aside and pulled Mia into a fast, hard hug. "You two will make wonderful parents."

Rachel's heart gave a squeeze. Brax had come so far since she'd known him. But nothing had done more for him than reconnecting with his wife. Getting the chance to see him pursue the dream of family he hadn't even been willing to admit he wanted was just the icing on the cake.

"I'd say that deserves a toast." She lifted her cup. "To the family you make."

The three of them clinked cups and drank.

"So, Rachel, how long have you been in love with Jonah?"

The sip of pinot noir she'd taken promptly slid down the wrong pipe. She bent double, coughing.

Mia shot a bland stare at Cayla. "Way to be subtle. Aren't you the one who says the point is to, like, lead up to stuff?"

"Girl, we already did that. We talked about your house, and I waited a whole twenty minutes. I want the tea. What is going on with you two?"

For the past three weeks, she'd been almost exclusively

hanging out with men. Either Jonah himself or Holt, as they'd traded off guard duty, so she wasn't left on her own. She loved the guys. She really did. But the prospect of discussing the situation with other women, especially women she wanted to get closer to, was incredibly appealing. If she came here, these would be her friends. Maybe they'd have some insight.

"That's... complicated. We need more wine and snacks for this discussion."

They retreated inside and began divvying up the appetizers they'd brought onto plates. Rachel took more time than necessary to pile pieces from their makeshift charcuterie board onto a paper plate. Meats, cheeses, olives, and crackers were built into tidy little stacks.

Cayla topped off their wine. "Okay, girl. Spill."

"We've been nothing but friends since we met two years ago. Good friends. But neither of us was in a place where more would have been an option. We weren't looking for anything. Then I kind of kissed him at Mia's wedding."

The bride's dark eyes peeled wide. "Holy shit. Really?"

Rachel winced. "There was a lot of champagne involved."

"Wait, when was this?" Cayla asked.

"Like... seconds before Sam went into labor."

"So you laid one on him and then he up and went to the hospital with his sister?"

"That about sums it up, yes. Since he was there for something like thirty-six hours, I had time to sober up and realize I'd made a terrible mistake. Which was why I went to the bakery so ridiculously early on my own, and how I managed to surprise our resident bad guy. Jonah's the one who found me."

Mia's face twisted in sympathy. "I bet he was losing his mind."

Don't you dare die on me. Don't you fucking dare. I can't lose you.

Had it been Jonah she'd heard? Or her own mind taking her back to the trauma of being in the hospital with John?

"I was unconscious, so I missed most of it. But it wasn't good."

"He basically would barely let her even walk on her own after," Cayla confirmed.

"He blamed himself. Probably still does, to some extent."

Mia popped a slice of salami in her mouth. "So how did you get from him being your live-in nurse and bodyguard to, you know, playing doctor?"

She'd literally been around the two of them *once* since she'd gotten back from her honeymoon.

"Is it that obvious?"

Mia smirked. "I mean... we were assuming. But thanks for that confirmation."

Rachel's cheeks heated. "I basically proposed a friends-with-benefits situation for while I was down here, and he agreed."

Cayla's brows drew together. "Y'all look like a lot more than friends-with-benefits."

"I think we both got more than we bargained for."

Nodding sagely, Cayla reached for more cheese. "Been there, done that. But it worked out beautifully for me."

"You and Holt are perfect together. Jonah and I are... I don't know exactly what we are. We keep sort of avoiding talking about it. I think we're both terrified of what the answer is going to be. We went into this with certain expectations in mind, and we've gone so far beyond those expectations. He's very... methodical about things. He likes to know the answer to everything, so I'm trying to come up with all those answers before we actually discuss it. I'm looking at the possibility of moving here."

Mia whooped. "I mean, I'm new at this whole girlfriend thing, but I'm absolutely down to have another one."

Cayla beamed. "Awesome! Would you work with the guys at the bakery?"

"I can't ask that of them. Bad Boy Bakers is theirs. I can and will certainly help with that, but I'm not going to horn on that or expect them to take me on as some kind of fourth partner if I do come down. I've actually got a job interview tomorrow. Well, more of an audition, all this week, as the potential in-house baker for The Misfit Inn."

"Oh, that's a fantastic idea! I planned all of their weddings. They're great people."

"I like the notion of working for the inn with a lot of other women. I like the different format. I wouldn't need to make the same thing every day, and I think it would be a fun new creative challenge for me."

"What did Jonah say?" Mia asked.

Rachel winced. "I still haven't told him yet."

"Why not?"

"See also the whole part about him wanting all the answers. If they offer me the job, then I have a real means of supporting myself if I come down here. I don't want him to think I'm trying to push him into something. We're both in over our heads, and I don't think either of us was prepared for that. I certainly wasn't prepared for this. I didn't think I had it in me to feel this way again after John died. And the fact that I can is both wonderful and horrible, because what if he doesn't feel the same way?"

Cayla scoffed. "I've been watching y'all for months. Every time you came down here, and then over the past few weeks. There's no way he doesn't feel the same way. I'm pretty sure Holt and Brax have been taking bets on when he was gonna make a move."

"I can confirm they have indeed placed bets on that." Mia's expression turned speculative. "Not sure who wins if you were the one who initiated."

"Well, even if he does feel more for me, that doesn't mean he wants to do anything about it."

"Girl, you have to talk to him. You have to clarify everything," Cayla insisted.

"I know. I know decisions have to be made. I just want to get through the interview first and be able to tell him that there's an option if he wants it."

"He's going to want it." Cayla refilled their wine. "Now, what are you going to bake for the interview?"

13

How the hell had Jonah's life changed so much in the past three weeks? Rachel was off with the girls, and he'd been left to his own devices for the evening. She'd consumed so much of his focus, he had no idea what to do with himself. Somehow, in the past weeks of intensive one-on-one companionship, he'd forgotten how to be on his own.

Considering his impending return to being single, that was... not a good thing.

Not that he'd broached the topic with Rachel yet. Again. Because he was some kind of chicken shit procrastinator who didn't want to ruin their last days together. However many they had. He didn't know what would be worse—if she was upset that their friends-with-benefits arrangement was over. Or if she wasn't. She was the one who'd asked for this to be a temporary thing. It had been him who'd pushed for more, in typical Jonah Ferguson fashion. Over-delivering. He knew he couldn't give her a forever, but he wanted this time together to have meant as much to her as it had to him.

She'd said at dinner last night that she was here at least for another week. That made it sound like her plans were open-ended. Why hadn't she discussed them with him? Why the hell hadn't he asked her?

It all boiled down to a truth he didn't want to admit to himself: He'd been in love with her from the start, and he'd gone and fucked everything up by changing things between them when he'd known they couldn't have a future. He'd been lying to himself that feelings wouldn't get involved. Or thinking he'd be able to shove them back in that box he'd kept in his mental attic as long as he'd known her. Turned out self-delusion was a personal talent of his. He was afraid that the end of this arrangement would be the end of them as anything at all. Going back to a life without her in it felt every bit as bleak as a life without the SEALs.

But he'd survived that loss. He'd survive this, too. He just had to convince her she was better off without him.

Scowling at the idea of it, he yanked open the fridge in search of a beer.

The phone in his pocket began to ring.

Cash.

"Tell me you have something."

"Hello to you, too."

Jonah took a breath. "Sorry. I'm in a shit mood. Shouldn't take it out on you."

"No worries. And yeah, I found something. We were correct that Percipience Unlimited is a shell corporation. I had to dig through several layers, but ultimately I traced it back to a Howard Danforth. Does that name mean anything to you?"

Jonah kicked back against the counter and tried to think about what he knew of the guy. "He's the rich guy in town. Made his money in real estate, if I remember correctly. I don't know him personally, but everybody in town knows who he is. I went to high school with his son, who was a real prick. Why would a guy like that have been doing business with my dad?"

"Well, you did speculate it was probably something on the

illegal end of the spectrum. Blackmail? Some kind of money laundering? There's a pretty long list of possibilities. You want me to keep digging into the guy?"

Much as he wanted to say yes, Cash had done a hell of a lot of pro bono hacking on their behalf the past six months. Jonah didn't want to abuse the connection.

"You've got your own business to run. Let me take this to the sheriff, see if he knows something I don't. If we come up with a more specific thing for you to find out, I'll let you know. Thanks, Cash."

"No problem."

Abandoning the quest for a beer, Jonah put in a call to Xander.

"Is this a social or professional call? Because I just sat down with a beer on my back deck."

"Technically professional. I have some information to pass on."

"Do I need to go into the station?"

"Probably not."

"Then why don't you come on over and have a beer with me? Kennedy took Caroline over to the inn, and I'm on my own."

"Be there in twenty."

The sun was sinking behind the mountain by the time he dropped into an Adirondack chair beside his buddy, appreciating the fact that he'd left the seat open, placing Jonah's good ear where he could hear. Xander pulled a long neck bottle from a tub of ice between the chairs and handed it over. Twisting off the top, Jonah took a long pull, savoring the yeasty flavor on his tongue as he took in the view. God, he'd missed this place when he'd been in the Navy. More than he'd let himself think about.

"I'm guessing you found something," Xander prompted.

"Maybe. It looks like Lonnie was receiving payments from Howard Danforth."

Xander went brows up. "Payments?"

Jonah explained the bank account and what he and Rachel had pieced together. "Cash traced the company name back to Danforth. I can't think of a single legitimate reason why they'd have had any regular interactions."

"Danforth definitely wasn't the type to set foot in a place like The Right Attitude. You think the payments were some form of blackmail?"

"Maybe. But if it was blackmail, why were they inconsistent? Each one was a different amount, and the timing wasn't regular. Did Lonnie just get a wild hair and periodically threaten to release whatever he had on Howard? That doesn't seem to quite fit what was going on."

"Could be he was doing something for Howard," Xander speculated.

"Like what?"

"Being some kind of go between, maybe. The Danforths are the kind of people who got rich off the backs of others. On the surface, they're squeaky clean. The people who show up to church on Sunday to look good in the eyes of the congregation, but don't actually practice what's preached, if you know what I mean. And then, of course, Bradley got arrested for statutory rape and sent to prison a few years back."

Jonah stared at him. "Shit. How'd I miss that?"

"You were overseas. And when you got back, you had a lot of recovery to do."

"I mean, I knew in high school Brad was an entitled asshole, but I didn't imagine that."

"Yeah, he didn't improve with age. Anyway, that kind of entitlement comes from somewhere. On the surface Howard has managed to come off as squeaky clean, but I wouldn't be surprised if the apple didn't fall far from the tree. Porter certainly has no love lost for him."

"What's Porter got to do with Danforth?"

Xander tipped back his beer. "Oh. Yeah, I guess you missed that, too. Danforth is Porter's biological father."

Stunned, Jonah took another long pull on the bottle. "Well, I guess that's a clear case for nurture over nature." He couldn't imagine someone further from the spoiled asshole Bradley had been.

"True story. Anyway, the fact that Howard was paying your dad isn't actually evidence of any wrongdoing. It's not an actionable item or the kind of thing that would get us a warrant to really dig into Howard. Can you get records going further back?"

"I'll have to request them, but I'll see that we get a copy going back to the start of the account, if I can. Not sure how long that'll take or what it'll prove."

"It might be a timeline for... whatever is going on. That's another piece to the puzzle. And knowing there was a connection between them somehow gives us some other directions to probe."

Jonah tipped back the last of his beer. "Probe how?"

"Don't know yet. Gotta be real careful how we approach this. Howard's a guy with money and power, which means he's potentially got a lot to lose. If he's somehow behind all this, if your dad had something on Howard he didn't want getting out, and he thinks you've got it, that could paint even more of a target on your back."

Better on him than anyone else he cared about. But Jonah kept the thought to himself.

"Fair enough. I'm gonna go talk to Mom. See if there's some history between Howard and Lonnie that I don't know about."

"I'll check our records and talk to my dad. It might be he has some insight from all his years as sheriff."

"You think we're actually going to solve this thing?"

"I think we're closer than we were before. Let me know what your mom says."

"Will do." Jonah rose and bumped his fist. "Thanks for the beer, brother."

The drive into town to the little three-bedroom ranch he'd grown up in only took about five minutes. He parked in front of the house, automatically going to the kitchen door in the garage and letting himself in as he'd done all his life.

"Mom?"

"In here!"

He followed her voice to the living room, where she was curled up on the sofa with a glass of wine and a book. "Hey. Why wasn't the door locked?"

"I haven't gotten ready for bed yet."

Jonah frowned. "You're here by yourself. With everything going on, you should be locking your doors."

"Have you eaten?"

"What?"

She closed her book and set it on the end table. "Have you eaten? You're grumpy. That usually means you need to eat something. I've got meatloaf in the fridge. Want some?"

"I will never turn down your meatloaf. But that doesn't change the point."

"I'll fix you a plate, and I promise to lock the door after you leave."

Jonah had a feeling she was only humoring him, so he'd make sure to lock it himself. Trailing her into the kitchen, he leaned his elbows on the counter while she began pulling things out of the fridge. "I came to pick your brain."

"What about?"

"Were you aware of any connection between Howard Danforth and Lonnie?"

His mother paused in the process of slicing the meatloaf. "Well, that's out of left field. Why?"

"Because it looks like Lonnie was getting money from him for at least the last year of his life, and probably beforehand."

He repeated the story, explaining what they'd uncovered as she loaded his plate with mashed potatoes and green beans and popped the whole thing in the microwave.

"I don't have anything earth-shattering to tell you. We all knew each other back in high school. Your dad never liked him, but they really had nothing to do with each other. He didn't have any kind of active hate on for him, he just never really cared for him. Howard was every bit as much of a prick as his son grew up to be. Arrogant. Entitled. We all tended to steer clear."

"Did you ever know of them having interactions after high school?"

"Not that I'm aware of. I mean, we ran into each other as you do in town this size. But nothing sticks out in my memory as significant." She slid the plate in front of him.

Jonah forked up a bite of meatloaf and dipped it in his mashed potatoes. "Have you heard any whispers of anything about Howard at the shop?"

"Not apart from rumors about who he's sleeping with. I don't know how his poor wife keeps her head held high with all his philandering. I guess, for her, money is enough to make up for it. I wish I could be of more help."

He shrugged. "It was a long shot. And worth it for mooched meatloaf."

She grinned and ruffled his hair. "And why is it you're available tonight to mooch meatloaf? I'd have thought you'd be with Rachel."

A warning began to sound in his brain. "She's at girls' night with Cayla and Mia."

"I'm sure she'll enjoy that. She's a sweet girl. I really like her."

Jonah fixed her with a stare. "Don't go there, Mom."

"If you're about to feed me some line about the two of you

only being friends, please remember I did not fall off the turnip truck yesterday."

"I am aware. But she'll be going back to New York soon. This is all just temporary." And damn it, that word kept sticking in his throat.

"Does it have to be?"

"Yes." And if he kept repeating it, maybe he'd start to believe it again so he could do the right thing and walk away.

IT FELT odd to show up at The Misfit Inn with bags of groceries on Monday morning. But Rachel had determined that as much as she could talk numbers and projections, nothing would speak as well for her as her food, so she'd come prepared.

Pru's sister Kennedy answered the door, her green eyes going wide. "Oh, wow. You've got a load. Can I help with any of that?"

"I've got it. If you could just direct me to the kitchen?" She technically knew where it was from her prior visits as a guest, but it felt rude to just go on back.

"Sure. Everybody's already in there. You want coffee?"

"I wouldn't say no."

The other three Reynolds sisters sat around the long farmhouse table. They looked up as she came in.

"Rachel! Good morning. What's all this?" Pru asked.

"Well, if you guys are okay with it, I thought while we talked through whatever interview questions you had for me, I'd make you some of the food that I'm proposing for the menu, if you were to put me in charge of this."

"Breakfast I don't have to cook myself?" Athena Reynolds Maxwell, the award-winning chef of the family, lifted her mug in a toast. "Sign me up."

Rachel flashed her a smile. "So you don't mind if I take over your kitchen for the next little while?"

"Knock yourself out."

"Thank you, Chef."

Athena pointed. "She's got kitchen manners. I like her."

Rachel set her bags down on the counter and pulled out some folders, passing them out to each woman. "I put together a selection of menus. Obviously, these would change to take advantage of whatever produce is in season. I'm assuming you would like to highlight products from Maxwell Organics for the guests."

"Always a bonus," Athena conceded. "Logan does love to show off his food."

Switching the oven on to preheat, she began pulling out bowls and utensils, appreciating the clear and obvious organization of the kitchen, probably because of Athena herself. "I know from my prior stays that you guys regularly offer cookies and snacks in the afternoons. There is also a sampling of menu options for that as well. I'd need to see some more specific numbers in terms of guests, but I have general breakdowns of each dish and the average cost per head. I would expect a setup like this to have some consistent offerings, plus a limited menu of rotating options that guests could choose from to order on the spot. A breakfast or brunch buffet could also be an option, but that would depend more on the size of your guest list as to whether that would be a profitable option."

From the opposite side of the table, Maggie lifted her hand. "Hang on, I need a minute."

Rachel flushed a little. "Sorry. Am I going too fast?"

"No, I'm just glorying in the fact that you speak spreadsheet. Please continue."

Kennedy set a mug of coffee at Rachel's elbow as she scooped flour for a batch of biscuits and another of scones. As she worked, she continued to talk, going over the benefits of the different menu options.

"There's also the issue of events. You have a fantastic space here, but I know you don't do a lot of them. Why is that?"

"That's on me," Athena admitted. "Because I hate catering. I'll do it for people I really, really like, but my plate is full with *The Misfit Kitchen* and my boys. Events weren't something I wanted to take on."

"That's fair. Is that the only major limitation you have?"

"I mean, there's staffing," Kennedy pointed out. "But we could hire some temps for that."

"Well, if this were to work out, and I were to get the job, I certainly have the capacity to cater for events. Weddings for sure, and other parties. At the end of the day, I'm a master baker. If you'll page through to the back of the packet, you'll see a listing of the sorts of dishes I regularly prepared when I was running my own bakery."

"Why aren't you running your own bakery now?" Maggie asked.

It was odd being around people who didn't know her history. Her hands shook a little as she poured an egg mixture into prepared mini-quiche cups, sloshing over the sides. She took a moment to wipe the spill off before answering.

"My husband was a firefighter. He died because of a traumatic brain injury sustained in a fire a few years ago. After I lost him, I needed to do something different. It's how I ended up teaching as part of Audrey's program and working with Jonah and the guys."

The four of them exchanged a look, and it was obvious Pru had mentioned her involvement with Jonah.

"And now you're looking to relocate here?" Kennedy asked.

"I need a change. Eden's Ridge would be my first choice because I have friends here."

"And because of Jonah," Athena prompted.

"We can't ask that," Maggie warned.

"Oh, bullshit to that. This isn't a corporation. If she's moving here to be with him, we need to know she's not going to bail if it doesn't work out. This is a tiny town. Would that be something you could tolerate? Because we don't want to hire somebody, open up the doors to all these potential changes, and then have it all falling apart because a relationship tanked."

Maggie closed her eyes and sighed. "I apologize for my sister. You don't have to answer that."

Rachel huffed a laugh as she slid a plateful of steaming biscuits and fresh apple cinnamon scones onto the table. "Maybe not, but it's a valid question. Is Jonah a consideration in my decision? Yes. Do I know what will happen with us long term? No. I know better than many that life gives no guarantees. But if I were to be offered the job and accepted, I wouldn't leave anybody high and dry. I'd be more than willing to sign a contract locking me in for some period of time if that would make you more comfortable. And if things didn't work out at the end of that time period, then we could all part ways, no harm, no foul. If I were, for whatever reason, the one to move on, I'd see that a replacement was found and installed so that there wouldn't be an interruption in service. I assure you, I'm up for this challenge. And I'm willing to put my skills where my mouth is and try it for the rest of the week, if you're willing."

Athena bit into a biscuit and made a humming noise. "Oh, I'm more than willing. I swear to God, if I hadn't already married Logan, I'd ask you to marry me right now. These are fantastic."

"These scones are good enough proof for me," Kennedy declared.

"Well, I was the one who brought it up, so I'm in," Pru added.

Maggie nibbled her way through half a biscuit. "What would you think about a six-month trial period? Guaranteed employment for that term, during which we'd provisionally try some of these other options, test out the events, see how it goes, with the option to renew on a more permanent basis at the end or part ways, if that's what everyone decides?"

It was more than Rachel had hoped for.

She extended her hand. "I'd say we have a deal."

Athena reached for another biscuit. "Can you start tomorrow?"

14

Holt slid a tray of cookie bars into the oven. "It feels kinda weird being here without Rachel. I got used to being back in a kitchen with her the past couple of weeks."

Jonah only grunted and continued to knead butter into the brioche dough. He could've used the stand mixer and let a dough hook do all the work, but he needed the physicality of kneading to distract himself from the fact that she wasn't here.

Brax worked his way down a row of puff pastries, folding and rolling each one before returning the lot of them to the cooler to chill. "What's she up to today, anyway?"

"No idea." And Jonah hated that.

Holt went brows up. "Really? You've kept her in your pocket since she got hurt. I'm surprised you didn't make her give you a detailed itinerary."

"She's free to come and go as she chooses. My pressing her about it would've come across as an interrogation. She won't be foolish or go anywhere alone." He'd exacted that much of a promise from her last night when she'd told him she wasn't coming into the bakery with him this morning. Somehow they'd gone from being able to talk about anything to walking on eggshells, trying to avoid the elephant in the room.

"You say that like you're chewing glass, man," Brax observed. "Did you two have a fight?"

"No." He just didn't know where they stood, and didn't know how to ask her because his heart wanted one answer and his brain knew he had to settle for another. It was what was best for them both. Anything else was pure selfishness on his part.

"Right. So that brioche personally attacked you and insulted your mom?" Holt asked. "Because it's gonna be like rubber if you keep that up."

Jonah growled and braced his hands on the worktable. This would've been so much simpler if she'd just gone home as she'd originally planned. Their arrangement would've come to its natural end, and it would've sucked, but it wouldn't have required a hard conversation. They could've slid back into their familiar roles as friends, and he'd eventually figure out how to sleep without being curled around her.

Brax came back from putting the pastry in the cooler. "You could ask her to stay."

"Why would I do that? Her life isn't here." And he had to keep ignoring the fact that she'd made it clear it wasn't in Syracuse anymore, either.

"Oh, I don't know, maybe because you're in love with each other," Holt drawled.

His words slid like a knife between Jonah's ribs. It was one thing for him to love Rachel. He'd gone into this whole thing knowing it would hurt when it was over. But he didn't want to hurt her. He didn't want to break her heart. She'd had enough of that in her lifetime. In his quest to give her as much of himself as he could in the time they had, had he inadvertently helped her skate across that line?

"She's already extended her trip," Brax pointed out. "She

doesn't want to walk away from you. She's just waiting for some sign from you that you don't want her to go."

Jonah scowled. "You haven't even been here."

"Didn't have to be. None of this is a shock to me. We've been waiting on you two to get out of your own way for two years."

Blowing out a breath, he admitted the truth. "I can't do forever. Not with her. Not with anybody."

"Why the hell not?" Holt demanded.

"I've got my reasons."

Brax rolled his eyes. "Well, are you sure they're worth a damn? Because you seem pretty upset at the prospect of things with her being over."

"It's the right thing for her."

The look they exchanged made it perfectly clear they thought he was full of shit. But they didn't know. They didn't understand. They hadn't been the one she'd told about her anguish sitting by John's hospital bed, day after day, losing him by degrees. They hadn't seen her cry and watched her break apart as she finally let loose of the grief she'd been carting around since his death. He had. And he'd do anything to keep her from hurting like that ever again. But none of that was his story to tell, so he ignored them both and began slicing baguettes for the jambon beurre lunch special of the day.

Evidently correctly interpreting his mood as vile, they let him be, falling into the usual routine of rotating who went out front to deal with customers. The last person Jonah expected to see on the other side of the counter was Howard Danforth. He was in line behind two other people who'd showed up for lunch. Nothing about the guy specifically said villain, but there was no hiding the layer of entitlement that clung to him and his khakis and polished loafers like a stain. Entitled money spent just as well as the hard-earned kind, so Jonah resisted the urge to kick him out. Instead, he decided to do just a little poking.

"What can I get you today?"

"I'll have the lunch special and a sweet tea to go."

"Sure thing." He punched in the order, calling it back to Brax, who was currently on sandwich assembly. "Can I ask you something?"

Howard went brows up. "I suppose so."

"Did you go to high school with my parents?"

After a beat of hesitation, Danforth nodded. "Yes, I did. Long time ago. Why?"

"No reason. I was just looking through some of my dad's stuff, going through old pictures and things. Saw some faces I recognized in some photos from back in the day, from what I was guessing was high school, and I wondered if that was actually you. It's weird to think of my parents being that young." And that was the God's honest truth. Seeing them at half his own age, knowing his mom had been married and pregnant only a few years later, was straight up mind-boggling.

"You're still going through your dad's things? Didn't he pass quite some time ago?"

Jonah jerked a shoulder as he rang up the order. "Yeah, he did. But I had a lot of stuff going on at the time, and my sister wasn't interested in wading through it, so we just kind of tossed it all into storage until we had time to mess with it."

Howard handed over his credit card to pay. "I was sorry to hear about your father's passing."

It was the sort of remark that was polite to make, and might not have made Jonah blink if his dad hadn't been who he'd been and this man hadn't been from a whole other world.

"We weren't close. But thank you."

Brax brought out the sandwich and tea. "Order up."

Danforth took the bag with a nod and left.

"Was that wise?" Brax murmured.

"Don't know. But I gave him a piece of information he didn't have before. Let's see what he does with it."

~

RACHEL HUMMED to herself as she unloaded groceries in the tiny cabin kitchen. She'd gone on a spree at Garden of Eden, wanting to cook something awesome and celebratory as a backdrop for finally telling Jonah about her job offer and admitting she didn't want them to be over.

He'd been acting odd the last couple of days, and she figured that was entirely because he didn't know what was happening. She was grateful to finally have an answer. Or at least one of the answers. There were still a million and one details to work out, but this somehow felt like one of the biggest.

If she hurried, she could get started on the puff pastry before Jonah got home. The thought made her pause, glancing around the cabin. It was odd to think of this place as home. To realize that some part of her already considered it hers. But it wasn't about the space. It was about Jonah himself. He'd opened his life to her, and she wouldn't take the gift of that for granted. Wouldn't take him for granted. She was ready to fully open herself to love again. And wasn't that a miracle after everything she'd been through?

Ingredients and bowls were scattered across the counter by the time the door opened and Jonah stepped inside.

He went brows up. "What's all this?"

"The fixings for dinner. I thought I'd make beef Wellington."

"Fancy." He dropped his keys in a bowl by the door. "What's the occasion?"

Nothing in his tone was anything but pleasant, but something in the carefully neutral expression he wore stopped her from saying, "We're celebrating." Instead, she wrapped the pastry in plastic wrap and put it into the fridge to chill. "It sounded good. And I really wanted to talk to you about something."

His shoulders loosened a little, and only then did she realize how stiffly he'd been carrying himself. "I really wanted to talk to you, too. But you go first."

As it was far too early to start the rest of dinner, and it would be some time before the pastry was ready to roll out and fold again, she had nothing to do with her hands. She'd wanted to broach this subject over a good meal, with a glass of wine.

The best laid plans.

Considering and rejecting different approaches as she washed her hands, she ultimately decided the Band-aid method would be best at this point. "I'm not going back to Syracuse. At least not to live."

Jonah went still, all traces of emotion vanishing. God, she hoped this was his surprised and processing face.

"I already told you I needed a change. That I was thinking about relocating before I even got down here, and this was my chance to try out the small-town life." She shrugged with a casualness she didn't feel. "Turns out, I really like it. And, on top of that, I have to factor you in."

Not wanting the little butcher block island between them, she circled around it, stepping closer to him. "When we started all this, it was supposed to be simple. Friends-with-benefits. But I think both of us can admit it's become more than that. Neither of us is wired for casual to begin with, and circumstances maybe nudged us along some."

He watched her come closer like some big jungle cat, those green eyes unreadable.

"We're more than we intended to be. More than I ever expected to find again, and I don't want to let that go." When he said nothing, she swallowed and pushed on. "I know you like to have all the information and all the data and answers before you make a decision, so I've been working on a way I could realistically stay. I had a job interview this morning to be the new in-house baker at The Misfit Inn. It went really well. They want me to start tomorrow."

"You found a job here?"

She couldn't tell if that toneless reply was shock or disbelief.

"Yeah. The bakery is yours. I'd never presume to try to horn in on what you and the guys have built. I know this comes as a surprise, and I don't want you to think this is supposed to be some kind of pressure. I'm not being presumptive or asking for some kind of commitment beyond where we already are right now, because I know a lot of things are up in the air. But we both put off talking about this way longer than we should have, and I just needed you to know where I stand. I'm in this with you. I want to see where it goes."

As the seconds ticked by, Rachel realized that her hope he'd grab her in his arms and hold on, admitting he didn't want to let her go either, wasn't going to be realized. He'd barely moved since she'd begun talking. And, in fact, his face twisted, as if he was in pain. A sick feeling began to churn in her gut as he squared his shoulders.

"That's not what we agreed to."

Really? That's what he was focusing in on? "I know that. But Jonah, you were the one who pushed for more. We became more. I don't want to walk away from that. Do you?"

He broke his paralysis and began to pace, scrubbing a hand over his head, his fingers automatically seeking his scar, as they often did. "No. No, I don't want to. But I have to."

Whatever she'd expected, it wasn't this. "What are you talking about?"

The eyes he fixed on hers were grim. Resigned. "I agreed to get involved with you on this level because it was temporary. Because you weren't asking for a full-on relationship. And yeah, we definitely crossed a bridge and are more than we intended to be, but that doesn't change the end result. I still can't give you the kind of forever relationship you deserve. If I'd known it was going to be like this, I never would have said yes in the first place."

If he'd taken out a combat knife and driven it into her heart, she'd have been less surprised.

"Why?" It was the only thing she could choke out around the pain blooming in her chest.

"Because it's not what's best for you."

A thread of temper began to lick through the pain. "It's not what's best for me? And what exactly is best for me?"

"You deserve someone who will be there for you through thick and thin. Someone who will take care of you and respect you. Someone you can build the family you want with. Who you can grow old with."

How could he not see himself in every one of those traits when she so clearly could?

"And that's not you?"

"No. It's not me. It's never gonna be me."

The finality in his tone had tears burning the back of her throat. "I don't understand. Where the hell is this coming from? Why would you have pushed for more with me if you always had some kind of end in mind?"

"I wanted to give you as much of myself as I could for as long as I could. I thought it was the right thing, but in the end it was really selfish of me." Looking miserable and full of regret, he dropped his hands. "I never wanted to hurt you."

Oh, but he had. She'd begun this with her expectations managed, held in check. He'd been the one to give her so much more than she'd asked for. To show her what they could have together if only she risked the heart that had only just begun to beat again. And now he was taking it all away. The depth of that betrayal made her shake.

None of this was an explanation, but it was clear he'd made

up his mind, made a decision for them both without even talking to her. Swallowing against the pain of that, and struggling to hold back the wave of tears that so desperately wanted to fall, she reached for the scraps of her pride. She'd given him everything else. She wouldn't give him her devastation. "Fine. I'm not going to beg. I'm not going to force you into something you don't want."

He finally took a step closer, reaching out. "I'm not saying it's over right now."

"It sure as hell seems like you are."

"We had an expiration date on this for a reason. I'm just saying we should stick to that."

She stepped out of his reach. If he touched her, she'd break. "Well, it seems like we both miscalculated. I'm leaving."

When he opened his mouth, no doubt to say something cautionary about her protection and safety, she just held up a hand. "I'm going to see Cayla. I'll be back to get my things later so I can move to the inn."

"Rachel—"

"Don't. Just don't."

Skirting out of his reach, she snagged her purse and walked away from the man who'd just destroyed her heart.

15

Jonah was the worst kind of selfish bastard. Because he hadn't been able to resist reaching for more, he'd given her unrealistic expectations, and now he'd gone and done the one thing he'd never wanted to do. He could still see the pain in Rachel's eyes, still feel the edge of that knife sliding into his own gut. He should never have gotten involved with her at all, because he didn't know how they could go back to being friends after this. Why should she trust him with any part of herself? And how could he ever be satisfied with less?

The sound of her car pulling out of drive propelled him into motion. She'd been upset, on the verge of tears. He'd tail her into town, just to make sure she got there okay. It was probably as close as she'd let him get from here on out. Resisting the urge to drive a fist through the wall, he jogged out to his truck.

It didn't take long to catch up with her. Once her car came into view, he slowed down and dropped back. No reason to make her feel crowded or like he was some kind of deranged lunatic who wouldn't let her walk away. She did exactly as she'd said, going straight to Cayla's office across the street from the bakery. Rather than pull in behind her—what the hell could he say that she'd be willing to hear?—he kept going, leaving her to go unload on his buddy's wife exactly how horrible a person he was.

He drove aimlessly through town, crossing side streets, circling back until he found himself driving past his mom's salon. Through the window, he spotted her on a stool doing God knew what. Before he thought better of it, he whipped into a parking space and stalked back to the shop. She looked over at the jangle of the bell announcing his entrance.

"Hey, baby."

"Why don't you let me take care of this?" He took the box of lightbulbs from her hands, gesturing her off the stool beneath the fluorescent lights.

"My three o'clock rescheduled, so I thought I'd finally tackle changing out the bulbs this stupid light fixture." She climbed down, gaze zeroing in on his face. Without another word, she crossed the space and locked the door.

Jonah arched a brow. "What are you doing?"

Her eyes narrowed. "What are *you* doing? What happened?"

For ten seconds, Jonah considered lying and saying "nothing." But his mother always seemed to see too much, and his capacity for prevarication wasn't exactly up to mission standards just now. So he shrugged and climbed onto the stool himself. "The inevitable."

"Which was?"

He slid the cover off the light and set it aside. "Rachel and I basically broke up. I don't know if you can call it breaking up when we weren't exactly together in the first place." They'd never defined a thing past that initial friends-with-benefits status. It hadn't seemed necessary.

Rebecca fisted both hands on her hips. "Oh, bullshit."

The vehemence in her tone had him glancing down.

"I've seen how you two are with each other. You *were*

together, whether you put a label on it or not. And that girl is the best thing that ever happened to you, so what did you do?"

Stopping by to see his mother in his current state of mind probably wasn't his best decision. He obviously wasn't going to find comfort here. Reaching over his head, he began twisting the blown bulbs free. "I simply stuck to the original terms of our agreement and let her go so she can find someone who can be what she actually needs."

Rebecca stared at him, shaking her head as she accepted the bad bulbs. "You know, you're my son. I love you. But I did not know that I raised an idiot."

Surprise had him dropping his hands. "What?"

"I refuse to believe that there is anybody out there who is better for her than you."

She was his mom. She had to say that. "Yeah, well, you're biased." He lifted the first replacement bulb, fitting it into the slot.

"Right now I'm not. I feel confident you're being an idiot. I know Rachel isn't the one who did this, so why did you? Why is it you don't think that you can have a real relationship with her?"

"That's not my story to tell." He reached for another bulb.

"Do you love her?"

"Doesn't matter."

"The hell it doesn't," she snapped. "Do you love her?"

He snapped the bulb in place with more force than necessary and leapt down from the stool. "Yes. And that's exactly why I'm doing this. It's for her own good. She'll thank me later."

"Well, you're just spewing forth all kinds of bullshit, my boy. No woman is ever going to thank someone for breaking her heart. Not like this."

He stalked over to the switch and turned the light back on, watching the bulbs flicker to life. "It's not her. I can't have a long-term relationship with anybody."

"Why not?"

"Because I can't guarantee I'll be around forever. I can't guarantee that I'll be myself forever." He'd been warned by his doctors, and he couldn't afford to ignore those cautions anymore. There was too much at stake.

His mother's face softened. "Baby, I know you've been through a lot. But nobody has that guarantee, with or without a traumatic brain injury. Did you tell her any of this?"

"It wouldn't change anything." He stepped back on the stool and replaced the light cover.

"If this is truly how you feel, that's your right and your decision. It's a dumb decision—and you've made some doozies in your lifetime—but it is your decision. But at the very least, Rachel deserves to know why. I think you're selling her short by not actually talking to her about this. You just took the information and made the decision like you always do, thinking you know best for everybody."

"I do know best."

She blew out a frustrated breath. "That may be the most arrogant, entitled thing to ever come out of your mouth. I thought I raised you better." For a moment she closed her eyes, and Jonah knew from experience she was trying to hang on to her not inconsiderable temper. "I'm sure you're well intentioned. You think you're doing the right thing. The noble thing, because that's how you've always tried to live your life. But baby, you don't have the right to make this decision for both of you without giving her the full story. Believe me, that's never the right choice."

There was something in her tone, some thread of deep regret that had him wondering. But before he could ask about it, she kept going. "I guarantee she's not going to react like you think she will."

"I know exactly how she'll react. That's why I'm making this decision. Because I don't want her to ever regret wasting time on me." He didn't think he could bear ever seeing that look in her eyes.

"Love is never a waste of time, and if you think it is, then I have failed in teaching you some of the most important lessons in life." The self-recrimination in her tone had him stepping forward.

"Mom, no."

She just shook her head. "I can't look at you right now. I am so disappointed in you."

The words landed like a physical blow. He'd lived his entire life trying to be the good son, to earn his mother's approval, to do the right thing for everybody and everything because, if he didn't, who would?

Closing the distance between them, she reached up, framing his face in her hands. "You are not your dad. It has never been on you to make up for him in this world. And it's long past time for you to stop acting like it is."

Releasing him, she stepped back. "Go on. Get out of here. I have a client shortly, and I need to work off my mad before she gets here."

With no comeback at hand, he did as she ordered and strode out, feeling more lost than he ever had in his life.

He'd followed her. An unwilling hope warred with the hurt on Rachel's whole drive into town. Maybe seeing her walk out had been a wake-up call. Maybe he'd realized he'd made a terrible mistake.

But when Jonah drove on past Cayla's office, she realized that was wishful thinking on her part. He was just making sure she got there, because no matter what they were or weren't to each other, he still felt like her safety was his responsibility, and that wasn't something he'd ever shirk. Why the hell didn't that responsibility extend to her heart?

No other car was in the tiny lot. She was relieved because she hadn't bothered to call or text first, and Cayla could've just as easily been with a client. That would've seriously put a crimp in Rachel's need to fall apart with a friend, and she didn't think she could hold it together much longer.

Stepping inside the little house, she dimly registered the cozy feel of the place, with its fun vintage accents and refinished furniture. They were all details she'd appreciate under other circumstances. But not today. "Cayla?"

Footsteps sounded from around a corner, and the woman herself appeared, her smile spreading wide. "How did the interview go this morning?"

The interview that she'd nailed. For the job she was no longer even sure she could do. God, how had everything gone so wrong, so fast?

She tried to find a smile and felt it wobble around the edges. "I got the job."

"That's awesome!"

In the face of Cayla's enthusiasm, the dam broke, and the flood of tears she'd been holding back spilled down her cheeks.

"Oh, honey!" Cayla pulled her into a tight hug. "Why isn't this good news?"

"Jonah d... doesn't want me." Saying it out loud added a new layer of finality to the situation that only had Rachel crying harder.

Cayla pulled back. "Crazy man say what?"

"I... I..."

"You know what? Wait just a bit. I'm going to make you some tea. Here, have a seat and catch your breath, okay? You can tell me when you're ready."

She nudged Rachel into one of the chairs around the table by the window and moved to the little kitchenette, adding water to an electric kettle and pulling cheerful mugs off a shelf. By the time she doused the tea bags with boiling water, Rachel had found a little composure again.

She wiped at her face with a fist full of tissues from the box Cayla had set on the table. "The interview went great, and they want me to start tomorrow. So I got all the stuff to make a nice dinner. I wanted to set the stage for the surprise, you know?"

"Of course."

"He was... off somehow, when he got home from work. I thought it was because he was twitchy, not knowing what was going on. The last couple of days have been a little weird. So I told him about the job and that I plan to stay. He said that wasn't what we'd agreed to."

The timer went off. As Cayla finished prepping the tea, Rachel explained what had happened, what he'd said, feeling every word like a fresh blow as she recounted the story.

"His mind is made up. He's done." The devastation sank into her very marrow as she admitted it. "I don't know if I can stay in Eden's Ridge knowing he's here. Knowing I'll run into him at the grocery or the diner. I don't know if I can build a life here without him in it. I don't think I can face those reminders that he didn't want me."

Cayla pressed a mug of tea into her hands. "I don't think this is about him not wanting you. A blind man could see that he does. Something else is going on. Why would he think breaking things off was for your own good? That it's the best thing for you?"

Rachel clutched the mug, wishing the warmth would soak through her palms and into her bones where the chill had settled. "Hell if I know. He wouldn't tell me."

On a huff, Cayla rolled her eyes. "Well, that's a typical presumptive male. God forbid they explain themselves on the front end. Putting his idiocy aside for a minute, he doesn't think he's good for you. And he seems very hung up on the permanency of a relationship."

"And I don't get that. I'm not *asking* for that. I mean, was I hoping that we were headed in that direction? Yes. But I, of all people, know there are no guarantees in life. I just wanted a chance to see what we could be, and he's killing it off before we have an opportunity to follow through on it." If he hadn't pushed for more, if they'd kept things the casual friends-with-benefits connection she'd asked for, would this hurt so damned much? Would she have been able to walk away with exactly what she'd asked for and been satisfied, ready, and able to move on with her life?

"He's obviously scared of something," Cayla concluded. "You said he went off on a tangent about what you need and deserve. Why wouldn't he think he could give you those things?"

"I don't know. Because he's been doing all of that already. He *is* that guy, so what is he so afraid of?"

"I have no idea. If he's got some kind of relationship trauma fueling all this, I'm not aware of it." She sipped her tea. "Do you love him? I mean, I know I teased you about being in love with him last night, but are you really?"

"Yeah. Yeah, I am. Every maddening, stubborn, noble piece of him." And oh, how she wished she could turn that off like a light. She'd welcomed it when he'd made her feel again, but she hadn't been prepared for the pain.

"Then regardless of how badly he's just hurt you, I think you owe both of you, and the possibility of what you could be together, more of a fight. Talk to him. Make the stubborn cuss tell you what the hell this is all about. Maybe it still won't work out. But then at least you'll have some kind of answers. And maybe after he's had a little bit of time to think about it, and you drag out whatever the truth is, he'll pull his head out of his ass and realize he's being ridiculous."

Rachel wasn't sure she could cope with that conversation, and she definitely didn't know if she could pry the truth out of him when he was so set on this path. But she knew she'd regret it for the rest of her life if she didn't try.

"Thank you for the tea and the pep talk."

"Any time." Cayla wrapped her in another hug. "And if the talk doesn't go well, and he needs his ass kicked, I can promise Holt will volunteer. He's on your side."

One corner of her mouth twitched up. "Hopefully it won't come to that."

"Hopefully."

Bidding her friend farewell, Rachel got back into her car to go confront the most boneheaded man she knew.

16

Courtesy of his mom, Jonah felt even more like shit by the time he headed back for the cabin. But maybe she was right. Not about his decision, but about giving Rachel a full explanation. Because he knew in the absence of one, she'd fill in the gaps herself, and he didn't want her to think it was her fault. This was all on him, and she needed to know that. Maybe she'd hate him for it, but if it eased her mind somehow, it would be worth it.

Her car was parked in front of the cabin when he finally got back. Relief flooded through him that he hadn't missed her. Needing to see her, to assess how she was, he rushed up the steps and let himself in. A bag dropped from the loft to the floor. Even from the brief glimpse he had of Rachel's face before she moved to the ladder, he could see she'd been crying. Damn it.

Guilt and regret twisted in his chest. "Rachel."

"I'll be out of your way in a little while. I just need to finish getting my toiletries together."

Obviously, she was serious about moving to the inn. He shouldn't have expected anything different. "Wait."

She glanced at him, her expression full of pain and expectation and not a little bit of impatience.

"I owe you an explanation."

Some of the impatience faded, her shoulders relaxing a bit. "That would be appreciated."

"Sit. Please."

With clear reluctance, she moved to the seating area. That she chose one end of the sofa instead of the chair was a small victory. He sat at the other end, close but not touching her.

"Do you remember the night I found you in the school kitchen?" He didn't have to clarify which night, because it was clear she knew exactly what he was talking about. Was every detail of that encounter as indelibly etched in her mind as it was in his?

Unable to settle, he'd come back hours after class, needing to do something. She'd already taught them the soothing power of taking a recipe from ingredients to completion, of being able to lean into that predictability and control when it seemed everything else was out of their hands. He'd found her there, sobbing and broken. They hadn't really known each other at that point. Not beyond teacher and student. But no matter how much he despised tears, he couldn't walk away from her pain. Without a word, he'd wrapped her up and held her until she'd cried herself out.

He could still remember how she'd felt in his arms. What seemed like days later, she'd begun talking, her voice hoarse and broken from weeping. Jonah had known these were confidences she hadn't shared with the other students.

"I lost my husband." Her voice had been small in that kitchen, but the story she'd told had imprinted itself upon his damaged soul. "He was a firefighter. A damned good one. But sometimes good isn't good enough. He managed to save his best friend, but the roof collapsed on him. By the time his company got him out, he was unconscious, with severe head injuries, smoke inhalation, and a whole host of other problems."

Her head had rested against Jonah's chest, her whole body lax with exhaustion as she'd continued.

"He was in a coma for three months, and I was there, every single day, wishing, hoping, praying that he'd wake up. Even though I knew that every day, every hour that passed, the lower the chances that he was going to recover. There was a part of me that knew, long before he actually died, that he wasn't coming back to me. And I thought I'd made peace with it. Put it away. But I haven't made peace with it. I just shoved it down, and for whatever reason, right now, it's all bubbling up. And I don't know how to come back from the pain of that."

Jonah hadn't had any major wisdom to impart. He hadn't known how to help her. But he'd wanted to lessen the burden she carried.

"I don't think there's anything quite like the pain of losing the most important thing in your life, whether that's a person or a mission. You build everything around it, and then suddenly you're unmoored. Adrift at sea, trying to figure out how to reshape your life when the biggest piece of it is missing. Dr. Graham would say that we have to remember that we're still here. That we still have a purpose. We just have to figure out what it is."

And in that kitchen, for the first time since he'd left the SEALs, he'd felt as if he'd finally found one. To give this woman a safe harbor and a chance to purge her grief. That was what he'd done, and it had healed something in both of them.

He couldn't break open those wounds again. He just had to make her understand that.

"Our friendship began out of shared pain. I know what it did to you to lose John, and that's why I can't give you more than what we already have. Because of this." He tapped the scar on the back of his head.

A furrow appeared beneath her blonde brows. "But you're fine. You recovered."

"For now. But I had profound post-concussion syndrome, and the doctors made it clear that there is a significantly increased chance of depression, aggression, suicidal thoughts. I could have difficulty walking, muscle weakness and tremors. Memory loss. Dementia." It would be a living death to lose himself, to lose his mind. "I care way the hell too much about you to put you through that. I'm not going to be selfish enough to rob you of the chance for the life you want with someone else."

He expected understanding. Acceptance. Maybe even a little relief.

"That's bullshit."

Jonah sat back, surprised at both the words and the matter-of-fact delivery. He was doing this for her. Didn't she see that?

Those usually soft eyes flashed with temper. "First of all, there's no guarantee you're going to get any of that."

"But I very well could. You've endured enough pain for a lifetime, and I can't do that to you."

Rachel pinched the bridge of her nose. "You don't get to make that decision for me. You don't get to decide how much pain is too much for me. You don't get to decide how much I am willing to endure." Eyes blazing, she slapped at her chest. "I'm the one who gets to decide what I'm willing to risk. Do you think I regret being with John for so little time because of how things ended? No. He was a good man, and I'm grateful for every day I had with him. I wouldn't go back to change that, even if I knew our time was limited. I loved him. I will always love him. I feel the same about you, you stubborn jackass. I love you, and I'm willing to take however much time I get, whether that's a week, or a year, or fifty. Because love is worth it, however long it lasts. I know that better than anybody, and I never expected to find it again. So no, I'm not going to sit back and be grateful that you're trying to take my choice away from me. Fuck that. You don't have to accept my love, but you don't get to make that decision for me."

She loved him. On some level, he'd known. He'd seen. But it hadn't been real to him, and because of that, he'd been able to convince himself that she'd get over it. Over him. But having her say it outright like this hit him like a thunderbolt of truth. And with that realization came the first glimmers of doubt about his position.

"That's not... I wasn't trying to take your choice away. I'm trying to stop you from hurting."

"Life is pain, Jonah. It's how you know you're still living. It's why the joys are so much sweeter. Because you know both sides of the coin." She shoved up from the sofa, all but incandescent in her rage. Panic that she might be leaving crawled up his throat, but before he could reach for her, she spun back to face him.

Her expression was softer, a mix of hope and grief and yearning that reached out and squeezed his heart, even as she spoke. "Let me ask you one question."

"What?"

"Do you love me?" The words were softly spoken, with a tremor that betrayed her fear of the answer.

She'd laid herself bare to him, and he couldn't hold this back from her. Not now. "Yes." The word felt as if it was being ripped from somewhere deep. An admission he'd never come back from.

Her hand cupped his cheek, tipping his face up so he had to look her in the eyes. "Then let that be enough. Know that it's enough for however long we get. And trust that I can handle whatever happens."

He'd told her his greatest fear, shared his greatest weakness, and she was accepting all of it. All of him. She not only loved him, she loved him enough to risk the hurt of losing him by degrees, exactly as she'd lost before. That unwavering bravery made him realize just how deep her feelings ran. The idea of it humbled him and absolutely wrecked his world.

He didn't deserve her. Didn't deserve this chance at everything. But neither could he hold himself back from it any longer.

Jonah breathed her name, pulling her down and into his lap. She fell against him, her mouth finding his in a fevered demand. The taste of her lit a fire in his blood, a need to imprint the flavor and feel of her on every part of him. Even as he thought it, she reached for the hem of his shirt. Then clothes were flying and frantic hands were grasping, until they were naked, and he plunged into her, driving them both desperately up, until the wave of release took them both. Eyes locked, the enormity of the moment struck like a tsunami. This was bigger, more potent than ever before, because there was love here. A love they'd nearly lost.

He'd hold on to it, hold on to her, for as long as she'd let him. Because nothing and no one would ever be more precious to him than this, and he'd spend the rest of his life showing her how much.

RACHEL TREMBLED in the aftermath of her release, her arms locked tight around Jonah. He'd left her wrecked and raw and emotional, and she couldn't let him go. Not yet. Maybe not ever. Because she wasn't absolutely certain he'd come back. He'd said he loved her. But the admission had been grudging, and she knew better than to believe that was enough to overcome his misplaced sense of responsibility. It was only a step in the right direction.

"Don't let me go. Please don't let me go." She murmured the

words against his throat, a plea she wasn't even certain he was conscious to hear.

He shifted, levering himself up from where he'd collapsed on her, proving he was, in fact, awake. The motion had him flexing inside her, setting off flutters of aftershocks. With a gentle finger, he stroked the hair back from her face, his eyes searching for... something. He opened his mouth to speak, but his phone began to ring.

With a frown, he glanced toward the floor. "It can wait."

"It might be important."

"So is this." But he groped around for his pants. It had stopped ringing by the time he unearthed it to check the display. "Mom. I'll call her back."

The screen lit up in his hand as it began to ring again. Back-to-back calls were never a sign of anything good.

"Hello?"

Because they were still fused together, Rachel clearly heard his mother's reply. "Nanna's house is on fire."

"What?" Jonah bolted upright. "Where are you? Have you called 911?"

"I'm outside. The fire department is already on the way."

He reached for clothes. "Stay far back from the house. Better yet, get in your car and stay there. I'm on my way."

Rachel grabbed up her own clothes and stood to dress, feeling wetness on the inside of her thighs.

What the...?

The breath clogged in her lungs. Oh, God. They'd forgotten to use a condom.

Jonah was dragging on pants, still snapping orders at his mother. "Do not, under any circumstances, go into that house."

Okay, one emergency at a time. Now was not the moment to mention the oversight. Rushing to the bathroom, Rachel hastily cleaned up and pulled on her clothes. She came out just as

Jonah snagged his keys. They raced out of the cabin, jumping into his truck. Gravel spit as he reversed to get on the road.

"I don't know what the hell she's even doing out there on her own," he grumbled. "The place is dangerous. There was probably a short in one of the electrical lines or something. That window unit has been on borrowed time. It probably finally blew up."

Knowing nothing she could say would calm him, Rachel simply laid a hand on his thigh, keeping a connection between them as he sped toward the house, breaking all kinds of speed limits. Given the location of the cabin, they were actually closer than the fire department. In only a couple of minutes, they spotted the plume of smoke billowing up from the distant trees.

Jonah swore, his knuckles going white as he gripped the wheel.

"We're nearly there. Just keep your eyes on the road."

In less than five minutes, they were skidding to a stop beside Rebecca's car. Jonah hurled himself out of the driver's seat. Beyond where they'd parked, the house was already well on its way to destruction. Flames licked behind windows and at the roofline, eating through the wood siding.

The noxious scent of smoke struck Rachel as she got out of the truck, and an anxious sweat broke out along her spine.

"She's not in the car. Mom? Mom!" Jonah's shout seemed to echo, but there was no reply.

They circled the house, checking the perimeter, finding no trace of Rebecca.

"Where the hell is she?"

Rachel stared at the house, spotting movement in one of the windows. "Jonah! Look! She's inside."

He whipped around, his face paling as he spotted his mother, arm raised against the blaze that had spread to the living room, where all of Lonnie's things had been stored.

Without hesitation, Jonah charged toward the house, kicking in the front door. Flames spewed out from the darkened doorway.

"Jonah!" Terror clawed through Rachel as she watched him race directly into the fire without a single piece of safety equipment to protect him.

Time seemed to slow to a crawl, each second stretching into minutes. The flames spread, licking up the rickety porch and eating through what remained of the supports, until it collapsed in a shriek of breaking wood, blocking his exit route. The wail of sirens sounded in the distance as she sprinted around to the back of the house, hoping to spot Jonah coming out the other door. But he didn't emerge. She didn't see any sign of him at all as the fire truck rolled up the drive.

Incoherent prayers fell from her lips as she raced to meet them. Though this was a volunteer unit, the firefighters spilled out in tightly organized fashion, already leaping to attach the hoses and get water on the blaze. The house was fully involved now.

"There are two people inside." She struggled to speak past the panic that gripped her chest. "Jonah went in after his mother at least five minutes ago and hasn't come back out." She directed them to the part of the house she'd seen Rebecca in.

The lead firefighter gave a nod and began shouting orders as she turned back to face the house. Where the hell was Jonah? Fear was a living thing, eating through her as surely as the flames were consuming the house. What if he didn't make it out? What if she'd just found him and she lost him in the same horrific way she lost John? She didn't think she could survive it again.

Glass shattered as the windows exploded outward from the heat. Rachel dropped to her knees on a sob as the firefighters made their way into the mouth of the beast. She hardly dared breathe as she waited, counting the seconds and praying.

Two interminable minutes later, one of them emerged

with a small figure draped over his shoulder. Rebecca. He hustled her away from the blaze. The sound of her coughing was only the smallest relief. She was alive. Awake. Jonah was still lost.

Another minute later, the second firefighter emerged, struggling under the weight of Jonah's bigger body. Rachel's heart seized. Was he even still alive?

She rushed forward, but two of the other volunteers beat her to him as the man who'd carried him out lowered him to the ground. Jonah wasn't moving, and his eyes weren't open. She could see angry red blisters along one arm.

"Is... is he—" Rachel couldn't finish the question. Could give voice to that deepest of fears.

"We've got a pulse, and he's breathing."

It wasn't a guarantee. She knew that better than anyone. But it was a start.

As they scrambled into action, covering his face with an oxygen mask, she slid to the ground in sheer relief while the house burned down behind them.

"Don't you dare die on me. Don't you fucking dare. I can't lose you."

The fierceness in the voice cut through the black. Something in Jonah turned toward it, recognizing an order when he heard one.

"The Universe did not put you in my path to take you away this soon, so wake the hell up, Jonah. I mean it. You don't get to pull this shit. I won't stand for it. Wake up. Wake up! Oh God, please wake up." The last of her words trailed off into a terrified whisper.

It was the fear that had him swimming up toward the increasing pain. He knew how to battle through pain. How to get to the other side. Never mind that he felt like absolute shit. Rachel was afraid, and he couldn't let that stand.

Why did everything smell like smoke? And what the hell was that beeping?

His eyelids weighed a thousand pounds apiece, but he pried them open anyway, wincing at the burn of the light. Everything was a blur. He tried to speak, but the words came out in a meaningless croak. Christ, his throat was on fire.

"Jonah!" The vise-grip on his hand tightened, and then his vision was full of Rachel, her face absolutely ravaged from tears.

Guilt punched him in the gut. This was exactly what he'd wanted to prevent. He never wanted to see this look of fear on her face over him. Not ever. He tried to sit up, to reach for her, but she pushed him back down.

"No, lie back. Stay still."

There was something on his face. He batted at it, his hands feeling like paws instead of limbs with opposable thumbs he could actually control.

"Oxygen mask. Here." She reached off to the side and came back with a cup. Nudging the mask down, she angled the straw into his mouth. "Sip. Just a little."

He sucked, and the cool water felt like glory in his throat. Far too soon, she took the water away and settled the mask back in place.

Her hand lingered on his cheek, fresh tears streaking down her own. "I'm really damned happy to see you."

"Don't... cry."

She hiccupped a laugh and wiped her face against her shoulder. "I'll stop in a minute. Promise. I'm just so relieved."

He glanced around the room, and holy shit, the movement hurt his head. But it was clear enough he was in the hospital. Same kind of emergency bay where he'd brought her all those weeks ago. Shit, that couldn't be good.

"What..." He licked his lips. "What happened?"

Somewhere in the haze of his mind, the pieces began to swim. The fire. His mother. Then he remembered and terror had him jack-knifing up. "Mom!"

"She's okay. She's down the hall. Brax and Holt are with her. The firefighters got her out." Rachel pressed her lips together, but he didn't miss the trembling. "They got you out."

He'd run into a burning building to save his mother, and he hadn't come out under his own steam. Jesus, what had that done to Rachel?

Dragging the oxygen mask down again so he could speak clearly, he squeezed her hand. "I'm so sorry."

Her fingers tightened on his. "Don't. Don't you start apologizing or blaming yourself. Don't you dare think I'm going to walk away from you because of this. Maybe you scared ten years off my life, but nothing is more terrifying than a life without you. Nothing. Do you hear me?"

He didn't have time to respond because the doctor and a nurse strode in.

"Mr. Ferguson, it's good to see you awake. I'm Dr. Johnson." The lean man dropped onto the rolling stool and scooted across to the bed, one hand shoving his glasses up his nose. Everything about the guy was neat and tidy, from the trim goatee to the close-cropped black hair. Jonah wondered if he'd been military at some point.

Over the next little while, he got examined, poked, and prodded. He answered questions. Had the burns along his left arm checked out. Shit, that hurt. This time Rachel was the one who took all the instructions and details of aftercare.

She was sticking. Even after all this.

His aching head circled back to what she'd asked him back at the cabin. To trust that she could handle whatever happened. Hell, it seemed like maybe she could handle things better than he could. That said so much about her strength. His mom had been right. He was selling Rachel short, and it seemed the only thing he'd been protecting them from was a chance at real happiness. Maybe there'd been a part of himself that hadn't believed he deserved that. Like he hadn't earned it yet. Maybe he wouldn't ever feel like he'd done that, but God, he wanted to spend the rest of his life trying, because these past weeks with her had been the best he'd ever had, despite all the peripheral stress.

"Jonah?"

He blinked and realized the doctor and nurse had left.

Rachel moved in again, taking his hand. "They're working on the discharge paperwork for you and your mom."

That was good. His whole body hurt, and he just wanted to get the hell out of this place. With luck, he wouldn't see it again for a good long while. But that wasn't his first priority just now.

He laced his fingers with hers and held tight. "I'm not letting go."

"What?"

"I should've said it before everything went to hell. I love you, and I'm not letting go. I'm sorry I was an over-presumptuous jackass."

Her eyes went glassy with unshed tears, but the corners of her mouth twitched. "Did you hit your head while you were in that fire?"

"Not that I remember. I just didn't want you to worry anymore."

"This isn't the first time, and I'm sure it won't be the last. But you're absolutely worth it." Rachel bent, brushing her lips against his in a tender kiss.

"I'll try to make sure you don't regret it."

"I'll never regret you."

He just hoped like hell she was right.

17

"**S**it." Rachel punctuated the snapped order by pointing at the sofa in Rebecca's living room.

Jonah's expression turned mutinous, but before he could spout whatever nonsense he thought would justify staying on his feet any longer, she stepped into him and poked him in his massive chest.

"Don't even think about arguing with me. I might not be able to haul you around bodily, but I had to endure your mother-henning, so you will damned well endure mine."

After the exertion of changing into the fresh clothes Brax had brought, his face was too pale, and his arm was covered in bandages. She knew the burns hurt, and he needed to be still. To rest and recover. And she needed a quiet shower later to finish falling apart now that the worst was over.

"But—"

"Jonah." She softened her tone and let some of her own exhaustion show. "Please, sit down. I need to fuss. It will make me feel better."

He lowered himself to the sofa.

"Thank you."

Brax arched a brow. "You sure you wanna take on Grumpy here? Because he's a totally shit patient."

"I'm aware. But his bark is worse than his bite, and he's not the first stubborn man I've ever dealt with." She moved past him into the kitchen to pour fresh glasses of water for Jonah and his mother. The doctor had said they needed to drink as much as possible to flush the smoke from their systems.

The garage door opened, and Holt strode in with grocery bags in hand. "I've got ice cream and popsicles galore. Everything a sore throat could want. Along with all those supplements the doc suggested. And Cayla's on her way with dinner for everybody."

As he set down his load, Rachel moved in to give him a squeeze. "Thank you for being here." She shared a look with Brax. "Both of you."

Holt hugged her in return. "We've got your back."

"Even if it means tying down your charge," Brax added.

That pulled a laugh out of her. "I don't think that'll be necessary, but I'll keep it in mind."

The door opened again, and Cayla came in, two large bags from the diner in hand. "Dinner specials all around, and loaded potato soup for the invalids."

Rachel winced. "Don't call Jonah that. He'll riot."

"I heard that!"

"Behave!" she called back.

Cayla handed the bags off to her husband and pulled Rachel in. "You okay?" she murmured.

"Getting there." It was going to take a year or twenty to forget the sight of Jonah running into that burning house without even a turnout coat. But it looked like she'd get the chance to replace that memory with others.

Cayla pulled back, searching her face. "Did you two get to talk before all this?"

Rachel nodded. That whole conversation felt like half a lifetime ago.

Before Cayla could ask anything else, Mia strode in.

"Man, I'm sorry I'm late. I only just managed to shake loose from the job." She headed straight for the living room. "Way to give us all a heart attack, you two."

Because she needed to keep busy, Rachel began divvying up the food among all the guests. Wanting to keep close, but too restless to fully sit herself, she perched on the arm of the sofa beside Jonah, balancing a plate in one hand as conversation inevitably shifted to the events of the day.

"Does anybody have actual news about the fire or the house?" Brax asked.

"The house is a complete loss," Rachel announced. "I could see that before we even left for the hospital." If there'd been anything left of Lonnie's that might have been useful, it was ash now.

"Can we maybe talk about what actually happened?" Holt suggested.

"Yeah, let's. What in the hell possessed you to go into that house? I ordered you to stay put." Jonah's tone was harsh, but beneath the snap of it, Rachel could hear the worry.

Rebecca flinched, her shoulders bowing with shame. "It didn't look that bad. I thought I could get in and out."

"There was *nothing* in that house worth your life. You could have *died*."

They all heard what he didn't say. That he could have died, too, coming after her.

Tears spilled down his mother's cheeks. "I'm sorry. I'm so sorry I took the risk. I'm sorry I put you at risk. But I remembered something about that desk of your dad's. The whole reason he was in love with it was because it had a hidden compartment in the drawer. I thought there might be something inside."

"If there was, it wasn't worth the risk."

"But what if it was? Where's my stuff from the hospital?"

Hearing the urgency in her tone, Rachel retrieved the bag, including her purse.

Rebecca pawed through the soot-stained jeans she'd been wearing, checking the pockets. She held something up in triumph.

"What's that?" Jonah asked.

Rachel was closer and had a better view. "A key." She reached out to take it, turning it over in her hands. "A safe deposit box key. John and I had one very much like this. We kept all our important documents and things at the bank, so if anything ever happened, they'd be safe."

They all stared at each other.

Was this literally the key to the answer they'd been looking for all this time?

The doorbell rang, startling them out of the shocked silence. Brax went to answer it and came back with Xander. He was in his sheriff's uniform, with a casserole dish in hand.

"Evenin', y'all. I came to check on everybody. Kennedy sent a broccoli and rice casserole."

Cayla rose to take it, heading to the kitchen to put it away.

"Why do I get the feeling that's not the only reason you're here?" Jonah asked.

"Well, I hate to be the bearer of additional bad news, but that fire was no accident. Even our volunteer guys could see clear signs of arson."

"Like somebody set the fire and walked away, or rigged with some kind of remote detonator situation?" Holt asked.

"We'll know more once the fire marshal has a chance to actually inspect it. He won't be able to make it out until tomorrow. But I'm leaning toward the former."

A muscle ticked in Jonah's jaw, and his uninjured hand curled into a fist. His eyes met Brax's and then Holt's.

Rachel reached for him, laying a hand on his leg. "What is it?"

"This might be my fault."

"How's that?" Xander asked.

"I kind of baited Howard Danforth."

Xander swore and paced a circuit around the living room. "Why the hell would you do that, you dumbass? Beg your pardon, Mama Ferguson."

"It seems appropriate, under the circumstances."

"I didn't tell him where we were keeping anything. I just mentioned how I'd seen him in some pictures when I was going through my dad's stuff. Which I had. I just wanted to see what his reaction was."

Xander propped his hands on his hips and glared at Jonah. "Yeah, well, if this was it, it's not something we can prove. Not unless there's something left that the fire didn't destroy. We won't know that until the fire marshal has time to go through everything."

"What if something survived the fire?" Rachel held up the key.

"Does that go to a deposit box?" Xander asked.

"We're not sure. But maybe," she conceded. "If it does, we'll still have to figure out which bank it goes to, and we'll probably have to go through the estate attorney again, because none of you guys were on the signature card anywhere, were you?"

"Either way, it's after business hours, so you won't be able to do anything tonight," Mia pointed out.

"It'll give me something to do tomorrow, since I won't be able to work. Again." Jonah sighed.

"Seems like if it went to the bank here, somebody would've said something when he died," Holt said. "Logic suggests the most likely location is that bank in Johnson City where that other account was."

After securing Jonah's promise to let him know the results

of the search, Xander took his leave. Everyone else began to clear dishes and pick up the remains of dinner. Then they took themselves home, leaving Rachel alone with her two charges.

With no more necessary actions, she felt the exhaustion hit her like a freight train.

Jonah reached out and snagged her hand, pulling her down beside him on the sofa. "Your turn to sit. You look like you're about to fall down."

"I mean, it's a very attractive option at the moment."

From her perch in the overstuffed chair, Rebecca eyed her son. "Did you pull your head out of your ass?"

Rachel sat up. "Uh?"

Jonah just put his good arm around her shoulders and tugged her against his side, pressing a kiss to her brow. "Yeah."

"Good." On a satisfied nod, Rebecca rose. "I'm going to bed."

"Do you need any help changing into your pajamas or need help checking your bandages?" Rebecca asked.

"I'll let you know if I do. Thank you, sweetheart." She disappeared down the hall.

"What was that about?"

"My mom kind of read me the riot act for being a dumbass earlier. So I was already primed by the time I got back to the cabin to talk to you."

"Oh." Rachel tucked her head against his shoulder, feeling a smile tug at her lips. "I really like your mom."

He laughed. "She really likes you, too."

THE BANK MANAGER set the long, narrow box on a table in the middle of the room and stepped back. "I'll be right outside. Let me know when you're finished."

"Thanks." Jonah didn't move, even after she'd left the room.

As Holt had surmised, Lonnie had used the same bank in Johnson City where he'd kept the secret account. Elias Craggs had done whatever was necessary to get Jonah access as the heir to the estate. Now, faced with what might be the end of this long quest, he just stared at the box with a surreal mix of excitement, anticipation, and dread. What were they going to find inside?

Rachel laid a hand on his back. "There could be answers in there."

"There could also be more questions. I've been trying to prepare myself for that. With the idea that some of my questions may never have answers." And he didn't know what he was going to do if that was the case. He didn't give a damn if he never understood who his father really was. But if he didn't find some kind of evidence to tie Howard Danforth to the multitude of threats that had faced his friends, family, and business, he wasn't sure if he'd ever rest easy.

With a bracing breath, he stepped forward and lifted the lid of the box.

The only thing inside was a single, slim envelope with *Jonah and Samantha* scrawled across the front. Frowning, he picked it up, looking underneath for anything else. But there was no flash drive hiding in a corner. He patted the envelope, looking for a telltale bulge. Nothing.

"This doesn't make sense. Why would there be a letter to me and Sam if he didn't even leave indication that this box existed?"

"Well, you said he died rather suddenly. Maybe he didn't have time to finish putting his plans in place."

"Maybe."

"Do you want to open it here?"

This probably wasn't the answer that he wanted. The

evidence to take down Howard Danforth wouldn't be found in a few thin sheets of paper. Not unless Lonnie had been on the nose about the whole thing and drawn a map with X marks the spot.

"No. Let's get out of here." Tucking the envelope in his back pocket, he took Rachel's hand and stepped out of the room, waving to get the attention of the bank manager.

"Was everything as you expected, sir?"

Jonah resisted the urge to flash a bitter smile, as the bank had been perfectly accommodating. "Well, I didn't have any expectations. But we've emptied the contents, so the account or whatever can be closed."

"Understood. I'll just need you to sign some paperwork. And we've got the rest of those records you requested."

Jonah did as asked, and five minutes later, they were back in his truck in the parking lot. He passed Rachel the thick manilla envelope of bank statements and ran his fingers around the edges of the smaller one bearing his name. How could something so small feel so heavy?

"You okay?"

"I don't know. I wanted this to be simple, and I have a feeling whatever's in here isn't going to be."

She squeezed his arm, and the touch settled him. "Life often isn't. Do you need to talk to Sam before you open it?"

"No. I should open it here, in case there's something else in Johnson City to follow up on before we head back. She hasn't wanted anything to do with Lonnie's stuff from the beginning. I'll pass it onto her later." And if it was just something that would hurt his sister, he could make it disappear.

Jonah slid a finger beneath the flap, breaking the seal on the envelope and pulling out the pages inside. The lined yellow sheets were full of his father's angled scrawl, something Jonah had become familiar with as he'd gone through paperwork and the other detritus of Lonnie's life.

Dear Jonah and Samantha,

Please don't rip up and throw away or burn this letter before reading the whole thing. I know that's what you'll want to do, and you have every right. But there are things I need to say. Things I need to explain. After that, you can do whatever you want.

I was a shit father. I acknowledge that. I know my leaving hurt you both, and your mother, too. I wish I'd been able to explain all this years ago, but as you'll see, my options were limited, and I did what I thought was best to protect you.

Jonah felt a furrow dig in between his brows. Protect them from what? With a sense of unease, he kept reading.

Your mother and I both liked people. That had a lot to do with how we landed in our specific professions. Rebecca was always amazing with hair, and I had a fair hand behind a bar. Back in the early days, she'd just hung out her own shingle, and I was bar tending at Elvira's. And the thing about bartenders and beauticians is that people tend to treat us like priests or therapists. They tell us stuff. Your mom and I, we made a game of who had the juiciest bite of the week. It wasn't malicious, just a way to keep ourselves entertained. Part of that small-town life we both loved.

Eventually, if you listen long enough, you overhear things that are so big you feel like you just have to share them immediately. When your mama found out through a client that Cassius Fuller—yeah, of those Fullers—was on the verge of foreclosure, she rushed on over to the tavern to tell me. It was big news because the Fullers had been sitting on some prime mountain land for generations. It was their legacy, and who knew what they'd do if they lost it?

In the end, the property was purchased by Howard Danforth before the foreclosure could go through. Everybody was shocked Cassius had sold, and there was all kinds of speculation. I just shrugged it off. At least until Howard showed up at the bar one night, near closing time, with a check. It turned out he'd been in Elvira's the night your mom shared that little piece of information, and he'd used it to negotiate the sale. As it was so beneficial to the real estate devel-

opment plans he had, he figured we ought to be cut in since we'd provided the insider information he'd needed. I didn't see how we'd done much, and it hadn't been on purpose. Howard said the check was a gesture of good faith. I wish I could say I spit in his face. But I didn't. And when he suggested there was more where that came from, if we could continue to pass on useful tidbits that led to more deals, I didn't see what harm it would do. We could use the money. Your mom's shop was barely staying afloat in those days, and I wanted to save to open my own place. So I said yes, and I didn't tell Rebecca.

Of course he hadn't. Because she'd have pitched a fit and made him give the money back. Rebecca Ferguson was a proud woman who valued making her own way. No way in hell would she have been okay with a deal like that.

It took six months to realize I'd made a deal with the devil. It took another six for me to overcome my own greed and weakness to try to get out of the arrangement. Turns out, that wasn't so easy. When I said I was done, Howard insisted I wasn't. He said if I didn't continue doing exactly what I'd been doing, he'd tell Cassius Fuller exactly who'd outed them. Not even pointing directly at me, but at your mother.

Jonah didn't realize he'd fisted his hand on the papers, until Rachel covered his white knuckles, stroking until his fingers relaxed.

"Do you want to stop?"

He jerked his head. He had to get to the end of this. Smoothing the pages, he shifted them to his other hand, so he could lace his fingers with hers, absorbing the quiet calm through her touch.

You've been around long enough to know the reputation of that family. They've been the Feral as Fuck Fullers since well before I was born, and that reputation is well deserved. I went to school with one of Cassius's sons. When a classmate of mine asked out his ex-girlfriend, he ended up in a body cast. Wouldn't admit who'd put him there. He was too damned afraid. But we all knew. Cassius isn't the kind of guy who verifies the truth of information before acting. If Howard pointed him in our direction, no one in our family would have been safe.

I didn't see any way out. We didn't have the money to move and start over somewhere else. And I confess, I couldn't handle the shame of actually telling your mother the truth. The only answer I could think of was to distance myself from all of you. So that's what I did. I walked away. Cut myself off and made you think I didn't care. All so they wouldn't think I gave a damn, so that you couldn't be used as leverage.

"You stupid, selfish mother fucker."

All these years, I've been forced to be Howard's little pet, and I got a cut from every deal that the information I provided helped to facilitate. I put every penny into an account at the bank where you found this letter. I only touched it when I needed a little help keeping the bar afloat.

If you're reading this, well, then we've never had a chance to make up. I've never had an opportunity to explain or apologize for the poor decisions and mistakes I've made or the hurt I've caused. No amount of "I'm sorry" can make up for that. Neither can money, though I hope you both will put it to good use, making your own dreams come true. And I'm hoping you can bring about the justice I've been after all this time.

I always intended to take Howard down. I've been collecting information for years, waiting for him to cross the line from merely morally gray situations to outright illegal. It took decades, but I've finally got it. All the information is hidden on a flash drive. You'll find it if you take a walk down memory lane and remember the secrets we used to share.

I know it's too little, too late, but I love you both more than life, and I hope knowing why I left will ease a little of the hurt I caused.

Dad

Jonah sat back in his seat, torn between shock and a need to rage.

"What did he say?"

Without a word, he handed the letter to Rachel. His mind continued to reel as she read it. He had no idea how to feel because this up-ended everything he knew about his father.

"He walked away to protect you."

"Seems like." Jonah stared out the windshield without seeing a thing. He'd imagined his dad involved in blackmail, or maybe drug running. He hadn't ever considered that Lonnie might have been a victim himself.

"Is this family—the Fullers—are they still around?"

"Oh, yeah. Still causing problems. Everybody steers clear of them. That's the one part of this I don't have any trouble understanding. You don't fuck with the Fullers. Not for any reason. They take their own vigilante approach to justice with no mind to the actual law."

"They sound like a legitimate threat. What did he mean about this walk down memory lane and the secrets you used to keep?"

He scrubbed a hand over his head, rubbing at his scar. "I don't have a damned clue. But that would imply that the answer was somewhere in all of his stuff, and we don't have any of it anymore. Whatever was left burned to the ground, so we're shit out of luck finding the actual evidence he pulled together."

"Maybe not. We should turn this over to Xander. Maybe there's something he can do."

"There's nothing in here that's proof of anything criminal on Howard's part. Just the implication that he's involved in something."

Rachel's hand curled around his, quieting the turmoil. "One step at a time. We've got the bank records. Between the two, maybe there will be enough grounds for Xander to get a warrant to search for me. Either way, it seems like there's a lot here that your mom and sister need to know. So why don't we head on back to the Ridge to talk to them?"

"Yeah. Okay." He cranked the truck and put it in gear.

"Maybe they'll remember something you didn't about what he means in terms of where the flash drive is hidden."

"Guess we'll see." But Jonah wasn't holding out hope that they'd ever manage to nail the bastard.

18

How could one man cause so much hurt when he wasn't even around anymore?

Helplessness had Rachel wrapping both arms around her middle as she took in the reactions of the rest of the Fergusons to the letter Jonah had just read them.

Tears streamed down Rebecca's cheeks. "Why wouldn't he tell me? We could have done *something*. We could have left. We could've started over somewhere. Yeah, I'd have had to leave my business, but that would've been preferable to losing my marriage and the family we'd built. Why did he think this was the only option?"

What must it be like for her to hear all this? As far as Rachel knew, Rebecca had made peace with her husband's original betrayal. Was it somehow worse finding out that the man she'd married wasn't as bad as everyone had made him out to be, but that they'd lost their marriage, their relationship, over this foolish mistake?

Jonah had locked down his own reactions on the drive home, so his delivery of the news had been more or less deadpan, but the hand he restlessly rubbed against the back of his head betrayed his disquiet. "I guess he didn't trust that the Fullers wouldn't find you. Us."

From the computer screen, Sam scowled. "Is this really true? Or is this just some story he made up to make himself look less awful?"

Rebecca blinked back more tears. "Why wouldn't it be true?"

"I think he believed it was true, anyway," Jonah conceded. "This wasn't some elaborate setup to try to absolve his behavior in our eyes. It was sheer dumb luck that Mom remembered about the compartment in the drawer and found the damned key at all. That we were able to track down to the safe deposit box to get our hands on this letter in the first place."

"What are we even supposed to do with this information?" Sam asked.

"I've already called Xander. He's on his way out, but I don't expect much. This was a lot more personal than any kind of useful evidence."

Recognizing defeat in his posture, Rachel stepped in to remind him of the one potential piece of good news. "Except your dad said he did collect evidence." She looked to Sam and Rebecca. "Do either of you have any idea what he's talking about with that walk down memory lane and the secrets you used to keep?"

Wiping the tears away, Rebecca straightened in her chair. "It could have been almost anything. Lonnie loved secrets. Puzzles. The desk certainly wasn't the only piece with hidden compartments."

For the first time, Sam's face seemed to soften a fraction. "I remember he liked hiding stuff and putting it where we had to go find it. He had the best time setting up Easter egg hunts. But even outside of that, he set up these little challenges with rewards. Like... what was it, Jonah? You had that dinosaur with the compartment in the belly. He used to hide candy there. You used to get so mad because I'd go steal it before you had a chance."

Jonah's face went blank with shock. "I saw that dinosaur. The stegosaurus. He had it. It was in a box of stuff we went through that first day at the house."

Rachel's pulse leapt with excitement. She remembered seeing it, too. "What happened to it?"

He closed his eyes, his expression shuttering in self-condemnation. "I threw it out. It was part of a childhood I didn't want to remember, so I put it in the trash. It went into the bakery dumpster, which has absolutely been emptied since then. There's no way we can track down where it went." Scrubbing both hands over his face, he paced a tight circle. "Fuck. That's it. There's nothing left for us to do. Whatever the hell evidence he found is gone, and we're screwed."

His shoulders bowed with dejection, and Rachel could see the spiral of self-blame cranking up. She stepped into him, forcing him to stop pacing. "We don't know that. Let's talk to Xander first."

He opened his mouth, no doubt to protest again, but the doorbell rang.

She squeezed his shoulders. "I've got it."

Xander stood on the front stoop of Rebecca's house, hat in hand. "Hey, Rachel."

"Come on in. Everybody's in the living room."

He trailed behind her. "Hey y'all." Glancing at the screen, he grinned. "Hey, Sam. How's that little baby of yours?"

Her expression softened. "Growing like a weed. She's down for a nap at the moment."

"Enjoy those hours while you've got them. The days when she won't take one at all are coming, and then you won't know what to do with yourself."

She laughed. "Noted."

He sobered and looked at Jonah. "So, what is it you found?"

"See for yourself." Jonah pointed to the letter on the coffee table.

They all waited while Xander read through, his brows going up with each page. "Wow. That's... a lot."

Rebecca clasped her hands between her knees. "I never imagined our little game could do this kind of damage. I mean, everyone in this town gossips. That's part and parcel of small-town life. I never dreamed it could be used like this."

"Don't you dare take ownership of this," Jonah snapped. "*He* did this. He made this choice. This is not your fault."

Emotion bubbled close to the surface for all of them. They'd all need time to process and sort through their reactions, but now wasn't the moment for that.

"Is there anything in the letter that's actually helpful in terms of the investigation?" Rachel asked.

"Well, it certainly makes it look like Howard's probably involved in something, but since he doesn't spell out what illegalities there may have been, it seems like the only direction we've got is finding where he hid this flash drive. Have y'all figured out what he means?"

Jonah rubbed at the back of his head again. "Yeah. And I fucked up." He explained how the probable hiding place got tossed out. "And even if it was something other than that, everything was thrown away or lost in the fire. So we're SOL. Unless you have news. Did you hear anything from the Johnson City Police about the break-in at the attorney's office?"

"They traced it back to a guy who was trying to replace the copy of his mother's will in order to change his inheritance. He made a mess to cover his tracks, hoping they'd think something was taken rather than changed. It's nothing to do with our cases."

"Damn. What about your dad? Was there anything he remembered about Howard or Lonnie?"

"Nothing specific. Although he mentioned one thing I

found interesting." Xander rocked back on his heels. "Harley Molina is a Fuller. The connection's somewhere on his mother's side. I find it interesting that the Fullers were the threat Howard used against Lonnie, what with Harley working for him at the bar all those years."

Rachel worked her way through the potential implications. "Do you think he was spying on Lonnie or something?"

"Don't know. Might not mean anything at all. Harley never had a whole lot to do with the rest of the clan. On the surface, at least. I don't know if Lonnie was aware of the link. It just adds to the pile of coincidences."

"Could the Fullers be working with Howard?" Rebecca asked.

"Not sure what they'd get out of it or even if they would work with him, since he's the one who bought their land," Sam argued. "Given their reputation, I'd have assumed they'd believe he stole it."

"If there's a connection there, it's not public knowledge. They certainly don't run in the same circles. But there's also no record of the Fullers causing Howard any problems over the years, which is interesting in and of itself," Xander conceded. "There's no telling whether there was some other aspect to the deal Howard and Cassius struck."

Jonah folded his arms. "Is Cassius still around?"

"Far as I know. Cassius would be well into his eighties by now. Stays close to home. I don't think he's mentally capable of being as involved in running the family with the same iron fist he used to. The few Fullers who've been arrested and prose-cuted made some mistakes that never would've happened under his watch, so we've speculated that the running of things has been passed on to younger members of the clan." Xander held up a hand. "To be clear, I'm not speculating there actually is something going on between Howard Danforth and the Fullers. I'm just tossing around ideas at this point. Either way, without the flash drive, I'll need something like a money trail to go further. Were you able to get the rest of those bank records?"

Rachel lifted the packet from the table. "Yes. And we'll start going through those and seeing what kind of timeline we can rebuild." She'd have time for that in the afternoons once she got off work at the inn.

"If it lines up with what Lonnie outlined in his letter, it's not a smoking gun, but it's another piece to the puzzle. And you never know when you'll find the one that unlocks everything."

She could only hope they found the key they were looking for.

RACHEL STABBED another bite of grilled potato salad. "I dug through all the bank statements and managed to recreate a timeline going back several years. It seems to more or less match up with what was laid out in Lonnie's letter, but it's not really evidence of anything other than the longevity of their arrangement."

Around the picnic table, the faces of the rest of the Bad Boy Bakers and their wives showed varying levels of disappointment. They'd gathered for burgers and a brainstorming session after the revelations from Lonnie's safe deposit box letter yesterday. She'd hoped she'd have more to share, but she couldn't pull evidence out of thin air, no matter how much she wanted to, for Jonah's sake.

On the other side of the table, Maddie squirmed in her seat. "May I go play?"

Holt glanced down at her plate. She'd eaten most of her burger and about half the potato salad. He skimmed a hand down her blonde hair in an unmistakable gesture of affection. "Sure. Go ahead, Bumblebee. Don't forget to clear your plate."

"Okay!" Pivoting around, she scrambled off the picnic table

bench and reached back for the plate, carrying it inside with BB trailing after her.

"No potato salad for the dog!" Cayla called. "And don't forget, it's a school night."

"Yes, ma'am!" The screen door slammed behind her.

Cayla crossed her fingers. "I do not want to deal with stomach upset if she doesn't listen."

Holt began to rub at her nape. "Do we want to loop Cash in on this? He has the skills to dig deeper."

Jonah stabbed another bite of potato salad with more force than necessary. "The skills, yeah, but without having some kind of direction, it doesn't seem like a good use of his time. We definitely don't want to abuse his goodwill. If we can come up with something more specific thing for him to look for, then maybe we should call, but for now, I think we should leave that off the table."

Rachel reached over, laying a hand on his thigh. The muscles were tense, his knee bouncing in a steady, restless rhythm. At her touch, he stopped moving, curling his fingers around hers with a squeeze.

They discussed and debated other possible avenues, but half an hour later, they hadn't come up with anything viable.

"I'm gonna go get Maddie in the bath. I expect a fight, so be prepared to tag in, Daddy." Cayla brushed a kiss over Holt's lips that left him grinning.

"Always."

Rachel rose as well, automatically gathering plates. "I'll get started on dishes."

Mia made a stack from the opposite side. "I'll help."

Cayla was waiting for them in the kitchen, her brow creased with concern. "Hey, you okay?"

Rachel forced a smile as she set the plates on the counter. "Yeah. This is just really hard on Jonah. I don't think he's going to settle until we have some sort of resolution. And I don't know how we're going to *get* any resolution under the circumstances."

"I can definitely relate to that. Brax is the same regarding my safety, and so am I." Mia tugged open the dishwasher and began loading plates. "I would *love* confirmation that none of what happened had anything to do with me because I'd like to be able to go back to just living my life."

"Maybe we should have a summit meeting without the guys," Cayla suggested.

"Maybe," Rachel conceded.

"In the meantime, it's a school night. I need to get the munchkin in the bath. Be back."

She strode out of the kitchen and into the living room where Maddie played some sort of game only she knew the rules to. Based on the animated narration she could hear, Rachel suspected the girl's stuffed animals were on some kind of great adventure.

"C'mon, kiddo. Time to start the bedtime routine."

"Awww, do I have to?"

"You do, indeed. We have to get back to a schedule now that school's started."

"I don't like school."

"You like school just fine. You just prefer summer more."

"I want to hang out with Banana Bread. She's way more fun than Miss Carpenter."

"I bet if you give your teacher a chance, she won't be anywhere near as bad as you think." Cayla's voice faded as she ushered her daughter into the bathroom.

Mia shut the dishwasher. "You want to head back out to the boys?"

"Not yet. I'm too restless to sit." Because she needed to move, Rachel headed into the living room and began picking up the aftermath of Maddie's stuffed animal adventure.

Mia fell into motion beside her. "How are you and Jonah doing?"

"I don't know exactly. He seems to support me staying here, but with the fire and this crap with his dad, I don't know if he's given any long-term thought to us. I don't think he's had a chance. So there are still some things up in the air."

Like mentioning their slip of making love without a condom. Rachel hadn't brought it up. With everything else on his mind, the last thing she wanted to do was add to Jonah's worry. She wasn't due for another week, so why borrow trouble? Plus, a part of her wanted things settled between them without the question of a possible pregnancy because Jonah Ferguson was Mr. Responsibility. He'd do what he perceived to be the right thing, no matter what, and she needed him to want her, to love her, for her.

"It's hard when part of what pushes you together is something outside both of your control. There's that wondering about what will happen when that thing is gone." Mia laid a hand on her shoulder. "But I feel pretty confident that you two will figure it out."

Rachel cast a glance toward the back door and the patio outside where the guys were still congregated. "I certainly hope so."

They continued picking up toys.

"Do you and Brax have any sort of timeline on when you'll hear whether you were approved as foster parents?"

"Hopefully, we'll know something soon. We're finished with the classes." Mia's gaze softened as she looked down at a toy in her hand. "Did you go through a dinosaur-crazy phase?"

"Not so much. For me, it was all about the horses." Rachel's gaze dropped to the dinosaur in Mia's hand and the stuffed cat in her own tumbled to the ground.

That figure looked a hell of a lot like the one from Lonnie's things.

Swallowing, she reached out a hand. "Can I see that?"

Brows up, Mia handed it over.

Rachel turned the thing over in her hands. She couldn't be sure. It was probably just a coincidence. But she strode down the hall and knocked on the bathroom door.

Cayla pulled it open and frowned as she caught sight of Rachel's face. "Something wrong?"

"Where did Maddie get this?"

Cayla looked down at the toy, surprise flickering over her features. "I don't recognize it. Let me ask." She took the dinosaur into the bathroom. "Hey, munchkin, where did you get this?"

Maddie's little voice floated out over the sound of splashing. "I found it outside the bakery by the dumpsters."

Cayla squeaked. "I'll be back, baby." She stepped into the hall, shutting the door behind her. "Could this really be it?"

"I don't know. But we're about to find out." Rachel took the toy and all three of them made a beeline for the backyard.

The guys sat around the unlit fire pit, beers in hand, looking morose and serious. At the sight of them, all three men straightened.

"What is it?" Jonah demanded.

Without a word, Rachel crossed to him and handed over the dinosaur.

His eyes went wide, his face blank. "Where did you get this?"

"Maddie found it out by the dumpsters at the bakery. It's been here the whole time."

"Holy shit."

They fell into a weighted silence as he turned the figurine over, poking and prodding and doing some kind of manipulation of the dinosaur's legs. With a little *snick*, the belly of the beast popped open. Rachel's heart thudded in anticipation as he turned it over.

A tiny flash drive fell into his palm.

They all stared at the small device, hardly daring to breathe.

"Somebody get a laptop."

Holt leapt up and raced inside. He came back a minute later, setting the laptop on the picnic table. They all waited with barely leashed patience as the thing booted up. Jonah plugged the drive into one of the USB ports. A folder popped up, full of other folders, each one labeled with a date and names that meant nothing to Rachel. Jonah clicked one open and found video footage and PDFs. There were other files that appeared to be pictures.

"This is it." Without taking his eyes off the screen, Jonah pulled out his phone. Rachel knew without asking that he was calling Xander.

As soon as the other man picked up, Jonah met her gaze and smiled. "We found it."

19

"Have you heard? Howard Danforth was arrested."

Jonah was grateful to be on kitchen duty this morning. He didn't feel much like explaining his mile-wide smile to the public who'd been coming through the bakery in a steady stream all morning. Everyone was talking about the arrest. It had been after five on Friday when Xander showed up at the man's house with a warrant for his arrest. A calculated move on his part, as the judge was already off on a known fishing trip for the weekend, so the bastard had been forced to cool his heels in a jail cell for the past couple of days.

It had been the best sleep Jonah had had in months.

Holt swung back into the kitchen from the front, arching a brow. "That smile gets any bigger, you're gonna be a contender for the Mad Hatter. You're looking a little bit crazed there, man."

"Just enjoying the sweet, sweet sound of justice in the morning."

"Yeah, well, maybe dial it down a notch. You're up for the next wave."

With a brisk salute, Jonah slid a tray of orange cardamom

buns in the oven. He managed to get his face under control before he pushed through the swinging door and went to man the register. The figure standing on the other side of the counter studying the day's offerings had both hands shoved into his pockets. His gray streaked hair hung almost to his shoulders, and his mustache was trying to do an impression of Sam Elliott and failing.

"Well hey, Harley. Welcome to Bad Boy Bakers. What can I get you?"

"I've got a hankering for those chess squares. They remind me of my grandmama's. Get me two."

"Sure thing." Jonah moved to open the display case.

Harley turned a circle, taking in the shiplapped walls and industrial iron accents. "Man, this looks different."

As far as Jonah knew, this was the first time his dad's old bartender had been back since the renovation. "Yeah, we gave it quite the facelift."

"Didn't know the place could look like this."

"Neither did we. My partner Brax's wife had a hell of a vision." He bagged the treats. "Anything else?"

Harley shook his head, and Jonah began to ring him up as more patrons in line behind him spread the gossip.

"—was arrested."

"No! For what?"

"Nobody seems to know that."

"It has to be some mistake. He's a pillar of the community."

"Well, we all thought that about his son when he was mayor, and look how that turned out. In prison for statutory rape. Maybe the apple didn't fall far from the tree."

Shaking his head, Harley handed over some cash. "That's a hell of a thing."

"Yeah. Takes all kinds, I guess. Figure that'll be the talk of town for a while." Jonah counted out his change. "Thanks for coming in. You enjoy."

The older man saluted with his bag and strode out just as Rachel came in.

Everything in Jonah lit up at the sight of her. Because he didn't have to worry about the end of things. He didn't have a countdown clock ticking away the moments in the back of his brain. She was here. With him. Sure, they still had details to sort out. Like getting her stuff moved down here. But they had time, and that was a damned miracle. Now that Howard had been arrested, Jonah felt like he could finally focus on them in a way he hadn't before.

Rachel circled around the end of the counter, rising to her toes to give him a quick kiss.

"Hey, you."

"Hey back. How'd work go this morning?"

"I'll tell you all about it when you get back to the kitchen. Go ahead and see to your customers."

By the time he made it through the line and headed back, he found her giving Brax a hug.

"That is awesome!"

"Hey now. That's my girl. You've got your own." Snagging her around the waist, he tugged her into his arms and nibbled at her neck, making her giggle.

"I was just telling her we landed a contract with Crystal's Diner to develop some custom desserts, and another with the tavern to provide the bread and buns."

"We're moving up in the world," Holt declared. "Slowly but surely."

"It's fantastic progress. And hopefully, with the other situation resolved, you can all focus fully on the business."

"From your mouth to God's ear," Jonah muttered.

As she perched on the edge of one of the worktables and began to tell them about her morning at the inn and the plans she was developing, Jonah saw a new lightness in her. She fairly glowed with enthusiasm. This new life she was putting together seemed to be working for her. And he was the lucky bastard she'd chosen to spend it with.

On that cheerful thought, he swung back out front for his next turn at the register.

"I heard Pamela was planning to divorce him."

"I don't know about that. He made bail this morning."

Jonah's step hitched for just a moment. It wasn't a surprise. Howard had money and connections. It didn't mean he was going to skate out of anything. The majority of his assets were frozen, and Xander and his team were still going through the records they'd seized from the house. Still, the idea that Howard was walking around free, for however little time he might have left, made Jonah uneasy.

He finished serving the latest spate of customers and returned to the kitchen. Rachel wasn't perched on the worktable.

"Where's Rachel?"

"Stepped out back to make a call. I think she was planning to touch base with Audrey," Holt said.

Just a phone call. She'd likely be back in a minute. But Jonah felt the itch to lay eyes on her, just in case. He opened the door and stepped out, expecting to see her pacing by the dumpster.

No Rachel.

He looked up the side of the building along the porch that extended to the front.

No Rachel.

"Rach?

The itch ratcheted up to disquiet when she didn't answer.

Maybe she'd had to walk closer to the parking lot to get a signal. Her cell carrier wasn't exactly popular in this area.

Striding toward the front, he called out again. Still no answer.

She wouldn't have left without saying goodbye and letting

him know what her plans were for the rest of the day. And hell, there was her car, still in the lot. So where the hell was she?

Jonah swung around, intending to make a circle of the entire building. Something flashed in the sun about twenty feet away, beyond the dumpster. Closing the distance, he felt his heart begin to thrum as he realized it was a phone lying face up in the grass. The screen was shattered, but beneath the spider-webbed glass, he recognized his own face staring back from the selfie of the two of them she'd made her wallpaper.

Scanning the ground around it, he spotted two irregular furrows in the grass. Drag marks.

Rachel had been taken.

RACHEL JOLTED AWAKE, her heart slamming against her ribs as she opened her eyes to darkness. Her head swam, and she couldn't seem to latch onto a thought. Was it a nightmare? Instinctively, she tried to reach for Jonah, but her arms wouldn't move and her shoulders screamed with the effort. Pain cleared away the last of the cobwebs, and she realized her wrists were bound behind her back, and a gag was stuffed into her mouth. Flexing her muscles, she attempted to straighten, but her feet hit resistance.

Something seemed to drag her toward one side, and her head swam with nausea. She was moving. What the hell? A car. She must be in the trunk of a car.

Fighting back the urge to vomit, she struggled for calm, trying to piece together what happened. She'd been at the bakery and stepped out to call Audrey. Except she hadn't ever managed to dial. Someone had grabbed her, choking off her air supply. Gasping at the memory, she began to choke on the gag pressed into her mouth.

Calm down. Calm down, or you'll pass out from hyperventilation.

Body shaking, she forced her breathing to slow, sucking in the musty, humid air inside the trunk until the worst of the panic receded.

How long had she been out? Who the hell had grabbed her? Howard Danforth was in jail. Everyone had been talking about it. Had they been wrong about who was behind everything? Where was this guy taking her? It had to have been a man. Whoever had grabbed her was taller than her 5'9" and definitely stronger. What were his plans for her?

Fresh panic began to bubble. Rachel dug her nails into her palms, giving herself something else to focus on. The guys would figure out that she was missing when she didn't come back in from her phone call. They couldn't be far behind. Jonah would move heaven and earth to find her. She just had to survive long enough to give him the chance. How far she'd come from all those days when she'd wished she'd followed after her husband. She wanted to live. Wanted to embrace the life she'd found with Jonah.

John, if there's anything you can do from up there, help him find me. Don't let it end like this.

Struggling to roll over, she groped along what she could reach with her bound hands. A lot of new cars had release latches in the trunk as a safety feature. Maybe if she could find one... But with the restricted range of motion, all she felt was the rough carpet beneath her and the rise of the trunk lip. She couldn't reach either corner. Abandoning the attempt, she searched the space around her for anything that might cut her bindings. But so far as she could tell, there was nothing back here with her. And even if there had been, she wasn't sure she'd be able to use it.

The car stopped, and the engine shut off. A door slammed. Wriggling around so her back was to the front of the vehicle,

Rachel braced herself for a confrontation with her captor, tensing her legs in preparation to kick out. It was a weak defense, but under the circumstances, it was the only one she'd be able to manage. Time stretched out, and the trunk didn't open. Was he just going to leave her in the trunk? Where were they?

She waited and waited, losing all proper sense of time.

What felt like hours later, but might only have been minutes, she heard two faint male voices.

"Were you able to get it?"

"Not exactly."

"What the hell does that mean?"

The trunk latch released, and the lid lifted.

Rachel flailed, striking out with her feet. The dark blurs against the bright glare of light only dodged her ineffectual attempt at defense.

"You dumb son of a bitch. What have you done?"

"Well, it's in police custody. I couldn't get to it. So I brought you leverage instead."

Her eyes began to adjust as the second man let out a creative string of curses. He was older, with silver-shot blond hair and a beard. Even from her poor vantage point, she recognized Howard Danforth from some of the videos they'd spot-checked on the flash drive. What the hell was he doing outside of jail? He must've made bail.

Her gaze swung to the other man, the one who'd grabbed her. He was tall and lanky, with gray-streaked dark hair pulled into a tail and a Sam Elliott mustache. She'd seen him at the bakery when she'd arrived. Who was he? More importantly, what were their plans for her? Obviously, Howard hadn't been in on the kidnapping plot.

"What were you thinking?" he demanded.

Mustache shrugged. "I saw an opportunity, and I took it."

"You know this is why your family doesn't trust you with

their business, right? This impulsive streak of yours is very problematic," Howard lectured.

"You're a smart man. I figure you can come up with something."

Scowling, Howard stared into the trunk at her. Rachel held in a whimper. She'd seen both their faces. Did that mean they were planning to get rid of her as a loose end?

"I don't do business involving a body count. I've explained this before."

Rachel wished that fact were more comforting.

Howard scrubbed a hand down his face, considering. "Okay, maybe this isn't a complete disaster. Your beau is a reasonable and resourceful man."

He knew who she was? Knew about her relationship with Jonah?

"If this idiot couldn't get what I need, I expect he can—and will—in the name of saving your life."

"Now you're thinking."

Ransom? He was going to ask Jonah for some kind of ransom? To retrieve whatever it was the police had confiscated?

"Take her to the cabin. I'll make arrangements and let you know what happens next."

"Yes, sir." With that, her kidnapper slammed the trunk, and she was shut into darkness again.

But this time, as the car began to move again, she had hope. If Howard called Jonah and gave him any sort of in, he'd do whatever he had to in order to outsmart the son of a bitch. She refused to believe that an entitled rich guy who'd built his fortune on the backs of others was smarter than her Navy SEAL.

She just had to wait for him to come get her.

20

"**G**et out of my fucking way," Jonah snarled.

Brax set his stance. "You're not going anywhere like this."

"He fucking took her!" And as soon as Jonah got his hands on Howard, he'd make sure the bastard couldn't ever hurt anyone again. But his friends were currently blocking both exits from the kitchen.

"And do you have any clue *where?*" Holt demanded. "Or are you just planning to drive on up to his house, guns blazing?"

"It would be a start." Even as he said it, he knew it wasn't the way.

"Come on, man. You're a better tactician than this. Think. You'll waste more time running all over the county trying to find her than if you wait and gather more intel."

And where the hell was that supposed to come from? The footage from their security cameras only showed hands reaching out to grab her and yank her behind the dumpster. While they were chasing their own tails, he could be doing anything to her. Jonah's brain was more than happy to fill in the options with a parade of horrors he'd witnessed during his military career. And all that was assuming the bastard wasn't taking her outside the area. The longer they waited, the further he could get, and they didn't have the first damned clue where to look.

Brax stepped closer. "Look, I get it. We both get it. You're scared out of your mind right now. But you've gotta lock it down and be smart about this. You know we've got your back, whatever's needed."

Jonah grunted an acknowledgement. He trusted these two men as much as his former SEAL team. They'd get it done. Whatever it took, they'd help him bring Rachel home. But Brax was right. They needed a plan.

"Xander's on his way. We're civilians now, so no matter what, we need law enforcement on our side for this."

Jonah didn't appreciate Holt's reminder. He had the skills to make this son of a bitch disappear, and he wanted to be able to use them. But potentially going to prison for murder wasn't exactly in line with building that life he so desperately wanted with Rachel. The one he'd been too afraid to reach for. He'd do anything for the chance at that life. And if that meant following the damned rules, so be it.

The bell over the door jangled, and Xander strode into the bakery, trailed by Ty Brooks and Leanne Hammond.

"What do we know?" he demanded.

"That Howard Danforth should never have been granted bail. What time was he released?" Jonah snarled.

"A little before ten. We don't know that he did this."

"I find it a little too convenient that within half an hour of his release, my girlfriend is kidnapped. I found her phone halfway between the backdoor and the parking lot. There are drag marks in the dirt."

Xander's face hardened. "If he's behind it, we'll find out. Kidnapping opens up a whole other set of charges and certainly violates the terms of his bail. How long has she been missing?"

"I found her phone twenty minutes ago. She was outside for no more than fifteen minutes before that."

"What about surveillance footage?" Leanne asked. "You guys wired this place up to hell and back in the spring."

Holt showed them the video.

"He knew where the cameras were," Ty observed.

"See what you two can find." As Ty and Leanne strode outside, Xander continued. "I'll send officers to Danforth's house. If he took her, I doubt she's there, but maybe his wife will know something."

Jonah just growled, impatience nipping at his heels.

Xander clapped a hand on his shoulder. "I swear to you, we're going to find her."

"How?"

Holt crossed his arms. "Does she have one of those fitness tracker watches?"

"I think so. Why?"

"Cayla's got one. She's gotten kind of obsessed with getting her steps to walk off all the baked goods I bring home. Hers has GPS. Maybe Rachel's does, too."

"How would we track that? Doesn't it have to sync with a phone or something?"

"Cash might be able to hack something. It's worth a try." He reached for Rachel's phone, which they'd put into a zip-top bag to protect any evidence. "I'll see if I can find out what kind she's got."

But before he could pick up the device, Jonah's phone began to ring. He didn't recognize the number. Signaling for silence, he answered.

"Mr. Ferguson." The man didn't identify himself. He didn't have to. His call was all the confirmation Jonah needed.

"Danforth." It took everything he had not to demand

Rachel's whereabouts. But that would tip his hand, make him look as desperate as he felt. "What do you want?"

"Well, I'm sure you've heard about my unfortunate... situation."

"You mean your arrest? Yeah, I guess that could be considered unfortunate."

"Yes, well, the fact of the matter is, I am not made for prison."

The men around Jonah shifted. He knew they could hear the conversation because of how loud he had to keep his phone in order to combat his hearing loss. Holt began texting furiously, probably tagging in Cash to trace the call.

"Why is that my problem?"

"Because I have something you want."

Jonah's temper slipped, and his hand clenched around the phone. "What have you done with her, you son of a bitch?"

"Ah, see, I knew you were smarter than your father. You're catching right on. As of now, your lady is perfectly fine. I don't want to hurt her. I'm not interested in racking up a body count. This was not the plan at all. I was supposed to be on a plane to South America to live out my days on a tropical beach. But the problem is that the police confiscated the phone I need to access my golden parachute."

"What exactly are you saying?"

"I'm a businessman. I'm proposing an exchange. You bring me my property, and I give you her location. I get out of town, and we never hear from each other again."

"How do I know you're not lying?"

"Oh, well, you don't. But the alternative is that I let my associate know his attempt at providing more leverage failed, and I'm not responsible for what he does with her after that."

Jonah closed his eyes, taking an iron grip on the fear that had him by the throat. Associate. So Howard wasn't working alone. That wasn't a surprise. He'd hired Abruzzi. He wasn't the sort of man who got his own hands dirty.

"How exactly am I supposed to get ahold of the phone if it's in police lockup?"

"As I recall, you were best friends with the sheriff. I'll leave you to work that out with him. I'm sure you can be... persuasive."

"Where and when?"

"Two hours. Come alone. I'll know if you don't. If you involve anyone else, I'll be instructing my associate to take care of the loose end he's created."

"That's the when. Where?"

"I'll text you the coordinates a half hour before the meet. That'll give you just enough time to get there. Good luck, Mr. Ferguson. I'll be waiting."

The line went dead.

"Damn it. Cash didn't manage a trace."

But Jonah wasn't paying attention to Holt. He looked at Xander, who was already shaking his head.

"I can't turn over evidence, man. Especially evidence that would allow him to flee the country. He's giving us a location. We can arrest him again. He's clearly a flight risk."

"And what if you're wrong? What if he does exactly as he says and sends a message to whoever the hell he's working with to take Rachel out? I'm not risking that. We can't do anything to Danforth. Not until we know where she is."

"Without having a location until half an hour before the drop, we're limited in our ability to plan anything," Brax pointed out.

"Limited, but not completely hamstrung," Holt said. "Cash didn't manage to get a specific location on the phone—it was a burner by the way—but he narrowed it down."

"We don't know that he's calling from anywhere near where

he intends the drop to be. He said half an hour would be just enough time for Jonah to get there from here. That's somewhere within the county, but it still covers a lot of territory," Xander said.

"An airfield." Jonah shared a glance with the rest of the men. "Somewhere a small plane or a helo could get in and out. He wants to get the hell out of Dodge in a hurry. Only way to do that without risking being caught in a roadblock or by other vehicles is to fly. The number of places that fit the bill that are still within half an hour's drive of the Ridge are few. So let's get some maps and make a fucking plan for how we're going to take him down and get her back."

"I haven't agreed to this," Xander pointed out.

Jonah leveled a gaze on his oldest friend. "I'm doing this, with or without you. I'd just as soon do it with you in a way that doesn't get me arrested."

Xander stayed silent for several long moments, a muscle ticking in his jaw. "I need him to come out of this alive so the son of a bitch can be prosecuted. Agree to that, and I'll let you do the rest."

Alive didn't mean uninjured. Jonah could work with that. He offered his hand. "Let's go get this son of a bitch."

RACHEL'S HEAD SWAM. How much longer was he going to keep her in here? The late August sun made the interior of the trunk an oven. Sweat dampened her back and dripped down her face, soaking the gag. Or maybe that was all the moisture from her mouth. The air was heavy and damp, and seemed to take more than a reasonable effort to drag into her lungs. Were trunks airtight? Would she run out of oxygen before they got where they were going?

She was wheezing by the time the car stopped. The trunk

popped open. Her eyes wheeled, trying to focus on her captor, but everything was hazy.

He swore, scooping her out of the trunk and carrying her into a building. She tried to focus on where she was, but all her effort was having to go into breathing. Mustache set her on a threadbare sofa and tugged her gag down. She gasped, sucking in huge lungfuls. The air in the room was musty, too, but nothing like the trunk. With the extra oxygen, her head began to clear.

She licked her lips. "Water? Please." Her voice came out in a croak.

After a moment's hesitation, he retrieved a bottle from somewhere, twisting off the top and holding it to her lips. Could it be drugged? Surely not. This guy didn't seem that organized. Nabbing her had been an impulse. So she sipped at the water, slowly drinking the warm liquid down. When she'd finished, he moved to put the gag back into her mouth.

"No, please. I'll behave. Just let me breathe."

He sat back.

"What's happening?"

"Jonah's going to get the thing I couldn't. He's bringing it to Howard, who's going to trade your location at the drop. We've got a little time yet, but you just sit tight, and you'll be home by dinner."

Rachel didn't know if she could trust this assertion, but he seemed to believe it. Maybe if she got him talking, she'd learn something useful. At the very least, it would give the guys and the police more time to find her. They had to be looking for her by now.

"How did you get into this, anyway? Working for Howard Danforth?"

He folded his arms, positioning himself beside a nearby window. "I didn't."

"I don't understand."

"Lonnie and I were friends. I figured out that he had some kind of gig going with Howard. We worked together for years, and he never would even admit to it, let alone cut me in on it. But I'm not stupid." The defensive tone in his voice made it clear this was an accusation that had been leveled in his direction over a lifetime.

Worked together for years... This must be Harley Molina, Lonnie's old bartender.

"After Lonnie died, I wanted to pick up where he left off. I went to see Howard about it, but he wasn't interested in that. Apparently, Lonnie had been working to screw him over, and all he wanted was the evidence Lonnie had been collecting. He said he had it taken care of. Hired that outsider. Well, that didn't work. That asshole didn't find jack during the renovation, and ended up dead for his trouble. After that, I thought maybe if I could find the information myself, it'd prove I could be a valuable asset, and Howard would cut me in."

"You were the one who broke into the bakery?"

"Yeah."

"And was it you who came back a month ago?"

Harley's mustache twitched, and he ducked his head. "Yeah. Nobody was supposed to be there. I didn't mean for you to get hurt."

He seemed genuinely remorseful about it. That was good, wasn't it? If he didn't want to hurt her then, maybe he wouldn't want to hurt her now.

"So what happened?"

"Nothing was working. I'd already been through most of Lonnie's shit when I was helping pack it up. Didn't find squat. And then when Howard mentioned that there was still stuff to go through and wanted it taken care of, I figured out where Jonah had stashed it all and torched the place. Figured that would destroy any evidence." He frowned. "Nobody was supposed to get hurt from that, either. Don't know why Rebecca went in when the house was on fire. But I guess it worked out all right. Nobody had any lasting damage."

Rachel absorbed the story. This explained the inconsistencies in what the guys had told her. How they'd seemed to be dealing with a trained professional, and then with someone with few to no skills. It hadn't made sense that Howard would've hired a bumbling idiot. And that was because he hadn't. Harley had been acting on his own.

She remembered what Xander had said about how Harley was a Fuller somewhere on his mother's side. "What did Howard mean about you not being allowed to join in the family business?"

Harley scowled. "All my life, I've been accused of being dumb. Nobody thought I had anything of value to offer. But I could see how that whole deal Granddaddy struck with Howard back in the day was gonna blow back on us, eventually."

"Your grandfather is Cassius Fuller?"

He jolted. "Yeah."

"Didn't Howard buy his land?"

"They made a deal. Howard bought the land, took on the debt, and let us keep working, doing what we'd always done. Nobody expected that, so nobody looked for it. Win-win, as they say. But it was only a matter of time. I wanted to get in close to Howard, so I'd know what he planned."

"So you could prove your worth to your family."

"Yeah."

"How's that gonna work if he flees the country?"

"He needs a right hand. I'm going with him."

Rachel was pretty sure Harley was delusional, because it seemed obvious to her that Howard was setting him up to take the fall. But bringing it up could as easily piss Harley off at her as turn him against Howard. She wasn't willing to take that risk. Not yet, anyway.

"So, what are we doing out here? Wherever here is."

Harley gestured out the window. "That's where the drop is gonna happen."

Neck straining, she peered out. She didn't know what she was supposed to see other than a flat, grassy expanse well down a hill. Before she could ask about it, a pulsing noise sounded in the distance.

Harley angled his head. "That'll be our ride."

He turned to the window, peering out, and she spotted a gun tucked in the back of his waistband. He hadn't waved it at her, but that didn't mean he wouldn't use it if he had to.

The thrumming sound got louder.

"Is that a helicopter?"

Harley grunted.

Rachel wriggled, working her way down the sofa, closer to the window. Her shoulders and arms had gone numb from the restraints, and she couldn't feel her feet.

"What are you doing?"

"I just want to watch."

Tucking one arm under her elbow, he lifted her up, nudging her over into a chair beside the window. "Front-row seat."

A small helicopter dropped onto the field, and a couple minutes later, an SUV pulled up the road far below.

"That'll be Howard. Now we've just gotta wait on your boy to make his delivery." Harley turned to face her. "I have to put the gag back in. Sorry."

Rachel didn't fight him. If he'd let her watch from here, she'd have a better idea what was going on when the drop actually happened. Her gaze was fixed on the distant road when Jonah's truck rolled down it. The familiar sight of it kicked her heart into a gallop. He'd get to her. Maybe all this really would be over soon.

At the edge of the field, Jonah stopped, stepping out of the vehicle with both hands up, showing they were empty. No one else was in the truck, but surely he didn't come alone. He was a man accustomed to working in a team. Holt and Brax were probably somewhere nearby, and likely the police, too.

From where he stood maybe twenty feet away from the helicopter, Howard held a gun on him. Jonah moved slowly, pulling something from his pocket and flashing it. Howard made a toss-it gesture, and Jonah complied. The thing landed a little in front of its target. Howard kept his eyes and his gun on Jonah as he came forward and knelt to grab it.

Rachel kept waiting for something to happen. For a shot or a tackle. Something. But Jonah only stood, clearly waiting for the information he'd come for.

The helicopter's blades began to spin. Howard backed toward it, and Jonah lost the relaxed posture, shouting at the other man.

Rachel tried to speak, jerking her head toward the scene below to get Harley to realize Howard was going to make a run for it.

His brows drew together. "That son of a bitch. He can't just leave me here."

He rushed toward the cabin door and opened it. The moment his foot crossed the threshold, there was a *pop* and a *thud*. Rachel could just make out the toe of Harley's scarred boot inside. He wasn't moving.

She jerked her attention back to the field below. Jonah drew a gun from somewhere. And then Howard was falling to the ground, and the helicopter was lifting off.

Holy shit! Holy shit!

At the movement in the cabin doorway, she cringed back in her chair. But it was Brax and Holt, moving in tandem as they cleared the room.

"I'll take care of our friend out here." Holt stepped back outside, presumably to deal with Harley.

Brax closed the distance, pulling out a wicked-looking knife and leaning down to slice through the thick cable ties binding her ankles. "Well, you're a sight for sore eyes." He made short work of the gag and the restraints on her wrists. "You okay?"

Tears streamed down her face as blood and pain rushed into her shoulders and arms. But she nodded, rubbing to get the feeling back into her limbs.

Jonah charged through the door, his gaze moving unerringly to hers. The grim, vicious expression on his face softened as his eyes took her in. Rachel tried to stand, to go to him, but her legs wouldn't hold her.

Then he was there, his big strong arms wrapped around her, and she knew it was over.

She buried her face against his neck. "Is he dead? Are they both dead?"

Jonah pulled back just far enough she could see a grim smile. "No. That was the deal we made with Xander to run this operation. We used tranq guns. They'll be out for a while, and back in jail before they wake up."

So they'd both survive to be prosecuted. Rachel only hoped that the justice system did its job. But she was grateful he had no more bodies on his conscience.

Burrowing closer, she breathed in the familiar scent of him and felt the fear leech away. "I knew you'd come for me."

As the sounds of sirens drew closer, he pressed a kiss to her temple. "Always."

21

Jonah held the bundle in his arms as if it were a bomb that might go off at the slightest jostling. The bundle stared back at him, unblinking, and he had no idea who was gonna win this apparent game of chicken.

Samantha smirked. "She won't break, Uncle Jonah."

He didn't believe his sister. "She's barely bigger than a football."

"With lungs to rival Coach Bates when she's fussy," Griff declared.

Jonah winced. Their old high school football coach had probably been a drill sergeant in a former life. "Good thing she's cute."

"That's part of the genius of biology. They're beyond adorable, so it gives you a Swiss cheese memory for the hard parts." But Sam's smile was soft.

"I can't believe how much she's grown already." Rachel leaned in to press a kiss to Rory's head, lingering with a blissful expression.

Jonah arched a brow. "Did you just sniff the baby?"

"Just getting my fix of that new baby smell. There's nothing like it."

"This is a thing?"

"Totally a thing," Cayla confirmed.

"Since you're looking like you think she's gonna bite you, why don't you hand this little cutie over to me and go check on the grill?"

When Rachel reached for his niece, he gladly relinquished her. She widened her eyes in an exaggerated happy face as she easily scooped the baby into her arms, settling her in the crook as if she'd been doing it for years. She bounced and swayed. "Who's a cute little muffin? You're a cute little muffin."

Jonah felt a mule kick somewhere in the vicinity of his chest.

Turning blindly toward the back door, he nearly plowed into Holt, who offered him a beer and a smirk.

"What?"

"Nothing."

It wasn't nothing, and they both knew it, but Holt wisely kept his mouth shut.

His house was full. In the two weeks since Howard and Harley's arrests—without bail this time, thank God—he and Rachel had moved back in from the cabin. Griff and Sam had come up with the baby, and everybody was hanging out, ostensibly for Labor Day, but really to celebrate the fact that their long ordeal was finally over. He found he liked it that way. Things felt settled in a way they hadn't in years. Maybe not since he'd been a kid. Dr. Graham would no doubt say he'd had a breakthrough. He mostly just felt as if he'd completed his final mission. Maybe that was something he'd needed after his precipitous exit from the Navy.

As the ribs were ready, Jonah pulled them off the grill and carried the tray back inside. "Ribs are done! Let's get the fixins sorted."

Everyone fell into motion, uncovering side dishes, adding in serving spoons. Someone set the table. Somebody else took drink orders. Jonah loved every minute of the cheerful chaos of getting plates filled and butts in seats. When they were all settled, he raised his bottle. "I'd like to propose a toast."

Always game, his friends and family lifted their own beverages.

"To the justice system. May it continue to operate smoothly and effectively."

"Cheers to that," Rebecca muttered.

"So, is everything really over?" Sam wanted to know.

"Yeah. It's over. Howard Danforth's got a boatload of additional charges pending. Harley, too, though not as extensive, since he gave Xander enough information to track down the Fullers' current meth operation. Turns out, Xander was part of a DEA task force that took that whole thing down earlier this week. He called me about it this morning."

Rebecca shook her head. "I can't believe they were holed up on Howard's land this whole time."

"It was a smart play. Howard looked like a pillar of the community. Nobody was expecting him to allow something like that on his property. Evidently, it was part of how he made up for the debts he took on when he bought the land in the first place. He'd been getting a cut of the Fullers' profits for years."

"So all that stuff that happened back at the beginning of the year—" Mia began.

"Didn't have a damned thing to do with you. We've got confirmation. Howard's been singing like a canary, hoping to make some kind of deal that will land him in a different prison from where the Fullers are going. It was always about finding the information Lonnie had collected on him."

Her shoulders slumped in relief, finally shedding the burden she'd been carrying for months. "I'll drink to that."

Everyone lifted their glasses in another toast.

"So we're safe to go on back to normal life?" Brax prompted.

"Looks like we all can," Jonah confirmed.

"Well, that's a damned good thing." His grin spread wide. "Because we just got our approval to be foster parents yesterday."

"That's fantastic!" Cayla immediately popped out of her seat to run around the table and hug Mia.

More congratulations, handshakes, and backslaps were passed.

"You two are going to make great parents," Rachel declared.

Mia sucked in a bracing breath. "We sure hope so. We know what it is to grow up in the foster system, so we've got a better idea what we're getting into than most."

Rebecca beamed. "Those kids are gonna be lucky to have you."

Brax wrapped an arm around his wife. "We were hoping you'd be honorary grandma."

"Oh!" Her eyes began to glisten. "I'd love that."

Discussion turned to plans for the fall, now that the threat hanging over their heads had been resolved. Jonah let the conversations flow around him, content with the fact that all his people were here, safe, and happy. As they moved on to dessert, he brought up one lingering issue.

"There's still the matter of the money Lonnie saved over the years."

Sam wrinkled her nose. "I don't want it. I know he apparently wasn't as bad a guy as we thought. I just... don't really want to touch anything that came from that whole mess that led to him leaving."

"Fair enough. But I was thinking maybe we should earmark it for Rory's college fund. And that of any other kids you might have. I mean, it's not like school's getting any cheaper."

"You make a valid point. And it would be one less stress to

know that was squared away." She looked at Griff. "What do you think?"

"I think it's probably a nice gesture to know that at least something good will have come out of his sacrifice."

"Then I'm happy with that plan. But what about your half, Jonah? By rights, half that inheritance is yours."

It was beyond tempting to say he'd earmark it for his own kids' college someday. But he wasn't yet sure he'd be having any. He still needed to work on taking care of that. Rachel had come out of everything physically no worse for wear. But the past six weeks had been a hell of a lot. He needed to know she still wanted him. Still wanted the future she'd talked about.

"I'll figure it out. There's time."

At the end of the meal, they broke apart. Sam went to feed the baby. Those who hadn't cooked turned their attention to cleanup. Spotting Rachel on the back deck, searching for any stray dishes, Jonah stepped out to join her.

"Will you take a drive with me?"

She glanced back at the house. "And leave our guests?"

He liked that she thought of them as theirs.

"They aren't guests, they're family. And they're all gonna be in a coma from that Italian cream cake you made for dessert, so it's not like they're gonna miss us." He held out a hand, reaching for the woman he wanted more than anything in the world.

Rachel smiled, her blue eyes sparkling as she placed her hand in his. "Let's go."

RACHEL HAD no idea where Jonah was taking her. He stayed quiet, eyes focused ahead, his hand linked with hers across the console. Maybe he really just needed some space from all the people in the house. She did, too. The aftermath of her ordeal hadn't been bad, but she still got easily overwhelmed. She hadn't had nightmares, and a big part of that was because she went to sleep every night wrapped up in Jonah. They hadn't talked about the future, but she no longer felt the pressure now. The ticking time clock was gone, and the thing that had been sucking up a big portion of his attention was over. They were in a good place. There were still endless logistics of figuring out how to dismantle her life in Syracuse and fully settling here, but there was time. And that was, perhaps, the greatest gift of all.

She'd woken this morning to confirmation that she wasn't pregnant. In all the chaos of her kidnapping, she'd straight up forgotten about the possibility. There'd been a twin sense of relief and grief. But Jonah was still here. They still had plenty of time to figure them out, and certainly it was better to do that together and on purpose.

Was he even interested in kids? Thinking about the almost panic in his eyes as he'd held Rory earlier, she wasn't sure. Before him, she'd made peace with the idea of giving up on the dream of family. If she'd started thinking about it again, it was only natural. Her biological clock was ticking. But if it wasn't something he wanted, well, in finding another good man to love her, she was already getting more than she'd expected to find after John died. She wouldn't be greedy.

Eventually, she realized he'd worked his way around to where his Nanna's house had been. The truck rolled down the rutted drive, coming to a stop in front of the charred rubble that was all that remained. Rachel's gut clenched, remembering the fear of knowing he was inside. Her hand tightened on his, reminding herself that he was here. He was whole. She soaked in the gratitude of that until he squeezed her fingers and slid out of the driver's seat.

She followed, circling around the front to join him as he looked over the blackened mess. There wasn't much left. The concrete footings. Some pieces of what might once have been appliances. A lot of the stink had faded, courtesy of thunderstorms that had rolled through in the past few weeks. But the sight was still a punch.

Because Jonah hadn't moved, she stepped in close, slipping her hand back into his. "It wasn't your fault. None of it was your fault."

He glanced her way, his eyes serious. "Yeah, I know. There were things I could've done differently. But no, at the end of the day, it wasn't my fault. My dad was weak and selfish."

No matter what they'd uncovered, that would probably always be his perception of Lonnie. But Rachel saw a different picture. "Not entirely weak. It took an enormous amount of strength to walk away from all of you in the name of protecting you. Maybe it was the right thing. Maybe it wasn't. But it wasn't an easy thing."

He tipped his head in concession to the point. "True enough."

"And if he hadn't been who he was, you wouldn't have become who you are. And who you are is a pretty amazing man."

His lips curved, and he bent to brush a kiss to her brow. But his attention remained focused on the empty space.

She couldn't peg where his head was. "Does it feel over to you?" Maybe it wouldn't until Howard was actually behind bars.

Jonah twitched his shoulders. "It'll probably be awhile before that sinks in. We've been on high alert since the beginning of the year. That kind of hyper-vigilance doesn't just turn off like a switch. But yeah, I'll get there." He shifted to face her, those sharp green eyes searching her face. "A lot has happened in the last six weeks."

"Yeah." She barely even recognized her life.

"You were hurt. Kidnapped."

He hadn't talked about it. Not really. Maybe that's what this was about. Bracing herself to battle with his demons yet again, she stepped closer. "And I survived in both cases because you rescued me. Don't start blaming yourself."

"I'm not. I'm just acknowledging that it's a lot for somebody to handle."

Narrowing her gaze, she studied him. "Are you talking about me or you?"

"Both."

What the hell did that mean? When anxiety threatened to take root, she reminded herself that he hadn't let her go. Hadn't attempted to push her away. He was working his way around to something in his careful, deliberate way. So she waited to see where he was going with this.

Turning away again, he surveyed the land beyond the perimeter of the fire. "You know, we've had this property in our family my whole life. We've never done anything with it because the house wasn't in good enough shape to salvage, and it costs money to demo things. I mean, in this particular sense, Harley kind of did us a favor. Now the lot is more or less cleared to do something with."

"What kind of something?"

"It's a good spot for a house. Quiet. Big yard. It needs work, but it could be a hell of a property. A good place to raise kids."

Her heart stuttered as he turned back to her.

"You had plans for your life that didn't come to fruition. Married a good man who died too soon, and had to give all those plans up. But maybe you could consider building new ones with me. Is that something you might be interested in? Sticking around here and starting that life with me? Starting a family with me?"

Her throat closed up, and tears gathered in her eyes. She'd resigned herself to giving those dreams up, and here he was offering her everything. How had she gotten so very lucky?

Swallowing past the knot, she nodded. "Yeah. Yeah, I'd love that."

The corner of his mouth tipped up, and he dropped to one knee.

"Oh my God."

The other corner lifted, but his eyes remained serious as he looked up at her. "I don't know how many good years I'm gonna get. But I love you, and I swear I'll give you my all for every single one of them. Marry me, Rachel."

The tears spilled over as she framed his face in her hands. "Yes."

He surged up, wrapping her in his arms and pressing his mouth to hers. And as she kissed the man she was going to marry on the site of the house and the life they were going to build, she knew nothing would ever top this second chance at a new beginning.

EPILOGUE

C ash Grantham opened his eyes, fully alert and awake. That quick snap to awareness had been baked in early and well, thanks to a childhood that had included fists and feet and daily reminders of exactly how much his existence had fucked up his mother's life. The Army had honed that edge still more, forging the skills he'd learned to survive into weapons. But he wasn't in the Army anymore, and he was eons away from childhood. A very tangible reminder of that fact lay sprawled in the bed beside him.

Hadley slept in a half-starfish position, turned away from him. A strip of early morning light snuck through a crack in the curtains to highlight her gorgeously toned back and the profusion of color inked into her skin in the form of a phoenix spreading its wings across her shoulders, the long plumes of its flaming tail streaming down her spine to wrap around her right hip. He knew every line of that tattoo and all of her others. Had traced them with his mouth, tasted all the secrets they hid. She held many, and he considered it a privilege that he'd been granted access.

His fingers itched to stroke down that spine, to tease her to waking. She'd be more than willing to start the day with another round of the mind-blowing sex they'd been having for the past six months. It was, by far, his favorite way to start the day. But he could no longer feel good about it. Because he was keeping this secret from one of his best friends. They were sneaking around, and Cash hated that.

It had seemed like a perfectly fine idea in the beginning. They'd thought they were scratching an itch. That the passion would burn bright for a few weeks, and they'd get each other out of their systems, satisfy a curiosity that had been lingering for longer than either of them cared to admit. But that wasn't what had happened.

He'd gone and fallen in love with his best friend's little sister, and he was tired of hiding everything.

Careful not to disturb her, he slipped out of bed and tugged on some sweatpants.

In his office, he stabbed a button on the espresso machine he'd paid a small fortune for. Good caffeine was worth its weight in gold, in his opinion. As the coffee brewed, he settled into what Hadley had dubbed his cockpit. The six stacked monitors wrapped around the crescent-shaped desk, giving him views into all the different aspects of his business. Normally, he'd fall instantly into the work, checking on the status of his myriad of projects. But the code didn't call to him this morning.

Instead, he picked up his cup of espresso and turned his gaming chair away from the screens to stare out the wide windows of his penthouse loft, mulling over what to do. He was a man who understood the concept of course correction. It wasn't too late to go back and do this the right way. Not that a guy like him, who'd grown up the way he had, had a lot of first-hand experience with observing the right way to do anything. But he knew that sneaking around and hiding this from his best friend was not it.

Cash had spent his life searching for legitimacy. A bastard son, who'd been told every day of his life that he was a burden, a problem, worth less than nothing, he'd ridden on the high octane of spite and fuck-you to make something of himself. He'd saved lives. Helped stop wars. He'd broken countless rules in the name of protecting other people, and he'd built an extremely successful business from the ground up. He no longer had a problem knowing his worth. He only hoped he'd done enough that Holt would believe he was good enough for Hadley.

A whisper of footsteps had him turning.

Hadley shuffled across the floor with bare feet. She'd snagged one of his shirts, buttoning it so that it covered the essentials, but left those long, lovely legs exposed. Her purple-streaked brown hair was mussed, and her eyes were heavy with sleep. She was sexy as hell, and just the sight of her had him stirring.

"I woke up, and you weren't there." The rasp of her voice held a hint of accusation.

"I figured you needed the rest." God knew, they hadn't gotten to sleep until well past midnight.

"Maybe, but you know how I like to start the day." She hooked a hand behind his neck, skimming her nails down his nape in a move that had both his dick and the hair on his arms coming erect.

Not missing that fact, her lips curved in an impish smile. She stepped close, moving to straddle him where he sat.

Cash hurried to set the coffee aside and gripped her hips, holding her off.

She blinked, confusion swirling in those pretty gray eyes. "Is something wrong?"

Knowing this was going to go over like a lead balloon, Cash braced himself. "We can't do this."

He watched the shutters go down and hated it.

She stepped back. "Excuse me?"

"I need to take a break."

"A break. I didn't realize your name was Ross Geller."

He couldn't quite stop the smile because he could see her temper kindling. "I don't want to stop doing this. I just want to do it the right way. We have to stop hiding from your brother."

That temper ratcheted up another notch. "Who I'm sleeping with is none of Holt's business."

"Had, he's one of my best friends. He trusts me. He's gonna see this as a betrayal."

"Only if he finds out about it."

Deciding to take another tack, he angled his head. "Do you want to stop this?"

"No."

"So you'd be content to sneak around for the rest of who knows how long?"

The question actually set her back a step. She dropped onto the edge of the desk. "Well, no. But—"

Cash held up a hand. "I think we need to table this until I can talk to Holt. I need to square things with him before we continue."

A muscle jumped in her jaw. "So let me get this straight. You're breaking up with me until you can get my brother's permission?"

"I'm putting things on pause until he can be informed."

On a scoffing noise, she whirled away. "Sounds like the same difference to me. I'm not someone's property, Cash. I am my own person, who makes my own decisions."

She didn't understand. How could she? He'd been another brother to her growing up. Someone who'd looked out for her and bailed her out of an array of youthful indiscretions. That was still who he was, as far as Holt knew. If this just got sprung on him, he was going to lose his shit. Hadley was his only family, other than his new wife and daughter.

"This is not about permission. You have every right to make your own choices. But I have the right to do what I think is necessary to protect my friendship with him. He's a brother to me, too."

Her face was twisted in disgust as she stepped back out of the bedroom, dressed now. "You let me know when you get all that worked out. I'm gonna head back to my place."

He could've gone after her. Could have tumbled her into bed and placated her until she was limp and sated. But she needed to feel what she felt, and he needed to do this. He was confident he could woo her all over again when it was done.

As the door to his loft shut behind her, he opened a browser to make travel plans to Tennessee.

EPILOGUE 2

C aptain Mitchell Greyson rolled through the sleepy streets of Eden's Ridge, Tennessee, eyes scanning, assessing, searching as he followed the directions of his GPS. Logic dictated he find his lodging first, make his way to The Misfit Inn. But something else had driven him to wait, to head to the bakery for the first part of this mission. Perhaps it was foolish to think about this as an op, but after more than thirty years in the Navy, he couldn't just switch that mindset off. He was here to check on one of the men who'd been under his command. If that wasn't his entire purpose for making this trip, well, he wasn't quite ready to face the rest of it yet.

Bad Boy Bakers was set atop a little hill, nestled in a copse of trees that trailed on up the mountain. He pulled into the partly full gravel parking lot in front of the building, taking in how the dark green siding and tin roof made it look as if it had been here for years. A hand-painted sign hung on the front showed a military-style insignia, with a whisk and a rolling pin crossed like swords on a shield. It suited a business that had been built by a trio of former military men, though he wondered if the Navy SEAL he'd come to see was satisfied with this life.

God, he hoped so, since he'd been directly responsible for seeing the man had landed in that experimental therapy program after a mission gone awry had ended his SEAL career.

Mitchell slid out of the Jeep and strode inside. Business looked good, with more than half the tables filled and a line three-deep at the counter. He used the wait as an opportunity to watch the men behind the counter. Neither of them was the man he'd come to see, but he could tell they were military from the way they moved and how their gazes continued to scan the room in automatic assessment.

Sharp blue eyes met his. "Welcome to Bad Boy Bakers. What can I get you?"

Mitchell studied the contents in the case, his mouth already salivating from the assortment of delicious smells wafting out of the kitchen. "What do you recommend?"

"Today we've got fresh cinnamon rolls, pain au chocolat, bagels—whole wheat and everything—pear muffins, and cheddar and chive scones. And, of course, we've got an array of breads if that's your fancy." The guy waved a hand at the baskets of bread lining the shelves behind him.

After the long drive, Mitchell thought he could eat one of everything. But he put a pin in that. "Actually, I'm looking for someone. Is Jonah Ferguson here?"

The kitchen door swung open, and the man himself came through, wiping his hands on a towel. "Hey, are we nearly out of something up here? Because I've got some—" His eyes landed on Mitchell, and he dropped the towel, snapping to immediate attention and lifting his hand in a salute. "Sir."

You can take the SEAL out of the Navy... His lips twitched. "At ease, Sailor."

Jonah came out from behind the counter, leading with a

hand to shake. Mitchell took it, pulling him in for a back-slapping hug.

Jonah rocked back on his heels, a look of surprise on his face. "Not that it isn't good to see you, Captain. But what are you doing here?"

"Well, you're not the only one who retired. I heard what you'd been up to and wanted to come check on you." It was the truth, if not the total truth.

A flicker of bafflement crossed Jonah's face before he managed to hide it. That was entirely fair. The man had no idea he'd been playing guardian angel all these years. Mitchell had been compelled to for reasons he hadn't felt at liberty to explain. Reasons he hadn't been able to face. Until now.

Realizing the silence had stretched into awkward territory, he shoved his hands into the pockets of his leather jacket. "How are you doing?"

Jonah's smile spread wide. "I'm great. I'm getting married."

"That's wonderful." And it was. Jonah was young enough to build a full and rich life with a wife. He more than deserved that.

"Actually, where are you staying?"

"At The Misfit Inn. Although I haven't checked in just yet." Maybe a part of him had been braced to leave in case a retreat became necessary.

"My fiancée, Rachel, is the in-house baker there. You'll be enjoying her breakfast."

Seeing Jonah's pride and pleasure in her, some of the worry Mitchell had harbored for him since the injury that ended his career in the Navy was assuaged. He was moving on with his life, clearly doing well for himself.

Mitchell smiled, and the expression felt rusty. "I'll look forward to it."

"How long are you staying?"

"Well, that's a little up in the air. I have some personal business to attend to while I'm here."

The bell over the door jangled, and a woman's voice rang out. "Hey, Baby. Do you have my order ready?"

That voice took him back more than thirty years, to a whole other lifetime.

Jonah lifted his chin in acknowledgement. "Sure, Mom. It's in the back. I'll get it in just a minute."

Bracing himself, Mitchell turned. And there she was. Rebecca Ferguson. The woman who'd haunted his dreams. The years had been kind to her, even if some of life had not. Her thick dark hair hung just past her shoulders, with only a hint of the waves he knew would go wild in the summer humidity. She was every bit as beautiful as the last time he'd seen her all those years ago.

At the sight of him, she froze, her jaw going slack, those gorgeous green eyes going wide, proving she knew exactly who he was. And though they'd parted on harsh words, he couldn't stop the grin or the hint of East Tennessee that crept into his voice as he took a step toward her. "Hey, Rebel. It's good to see you."

He'd imagined this moment countless times over the decades, wondering what she'd say and do if they saw each other again. There'd been silence. Slaps. More of the angry words that had followed him out of town when he'd been just eighteen. With years and distance and longing, those had morphed to indifference or strained politeness. But in the moment, the bloom of her actual smile—the one that had taken her all the way to Miss Tennessee—lit him up like a sunrise.

She broke her paralysis, closing the distance to wrap him in one of the hugs that had once been second nature. "Oh, my God. What are you doing here?"

It took every ounce of his control not to twine around her

and bury his face in her hair. He'd never expected to feel this easy affection again. Never thought to have her in his arms after how they'd parted. And surely, if she was this easy with him, he was wrong about his suspicions?

Returning her hug as the friend he'd once been, he kicked his brain into gear. "I came to check on your boy, to see how he's doing now that he's retired."

She pulled back, blinking in surprise. "You know my son?"

Mitchell pressed his lips together. So she didn't know.

"I was his commanding officer for a number of years."

Some of the color left her cheeks at that. "How did you know he was mine?"

He couldn't stop the laugh. "It was impossible not to. You stamped yourself all over his face. And, of course, he's a Ferguson." He'd wondered about that. About why Jonah hadn't carried Lonnie's last name.

A throat cleared behind them.

Mitchell turned and nearly laughed again at the look on Jonah's face. He was so clearly torn between his conditioned respect for a commanding officer and a desire to protect his mother.

"I'm sorry. What the hell is happening here? You two know each other?"

Rebecca laid a hand on Mitchell's shoulder. "This is Grey."

Grey. The name he'd gone by all those years before he joined the Navy. The man he wondered if he could become again.

Apparently, it meant something to Jonah. His brows drew together in disbelief, his eyes—exactly like his mother's—skimming him from head to toe. "You? You used to be skinny as a rail and have a *ponytail?*"

"He saw some of the pictures of us from back in high school recently," Rebecca explained.

"I did have a life before the Navy."

Beside him, she stiffened, and her hand fell away.

Shit.

Reminding her of the thing that had split them up in the first place was hardly his best move. But none of this was going how he'd expected. Nothing with her ever had.

"Baby, if you can get my order. I really need to get going. I'm gonna be late."

After a moment's hesitation, Jonah jerked a nod and disappeared into the back.

This time, the smile she turned on him didn't reach her eyes. "Well, it's been great to see you, Grey. I'm glad to see you're doing well."

He could easily read the subtext. *And now get the hell out of town and don't let the door hit you on your way out.*

"I'm retired, actually."

"Oh?" There was so much to that single syllable he couldn't decipher.

"Yeah."

Something flickered in her eyes at that. But it had been too many years, and he couldn't read her anymore.

Jonah came back out, handing his mother a box. "Here you go."

She bussed his cheek. "Thanks, sweetie." With one last glance at Mitchell, she lifted the box, as if it were a toast and headed for the door. "I've gotta go. You take care."

"Will do. And I'll be seeing you around, Rebel."

Her step hitched.

"I figure it's high time I looked at moving home."

～

Choose Your Next Romance

THANK you for reading *Stirred Up By a SEAL!* I hope you enjoyed the conclusion of the primary trilogy about the bakers we've all grown to know and love. As you can see, there's MORE STORY AFOOT with bonus novellas featuring both Cash and Hadley (*Hung Up on the Hacker*) and Grey and Rebecca (*Caught Up with the Captain*). Be on the lookout for both of those in October.

While you're waiting, if you're in the mood for more small town military romance, you can hop on over to check out the Rescue My Heart series, which kicks off with *Baby It's Cold Outside,* a grumpy soft for sunshine, forced proximity, opposites attract, snowed in together romance, also set in Eden's Ridge. Keep turning the pages for a sneak peek.

SNEAK PEEK BABY, IT'S COLD OUTSIDE
RESCUE MY HEART, BOOK #1

A grumpy lumberjack

Former Army Ranger Harrison Wilkes isn't actually a lumberjack, but he's doing his best impression while hiding out in the mountains of East Tennessee. He needs to rest, recharge, and stay the hell away from people, while he wrestles with ghosts from his past and figures out his future. Neither includes a snowbound rescue of his favorite author.

A runaway writer

Ivy Blake is on a deadline. Her hero is MIA, and she's desperate to find some peace, quiet, and inspiration to get her book—and her life—back on track. She doesn't plan on driving off a mountain. Or the mysterious stranger who shows up to save her.

Who's rescuing who?

When Winter Stormageddon traps them together, Ivy finds the inspiration she didn't know she needed in her real-life hero. As more than the fireplace heats up his one-man cabin, they both find far more than they bargained for. This intuitive author just might have the answers Harrison's looking for, but will their newfound connection survive past the storm?

~

"Where are your pages, Ivy?"

Ivy Blake winced at the snap of her agent's voice on the other end of the phone. Marianne was pulling out her stern, mom-of-three tone. That was never good. "They're coming."

At some theoretical, future time that was actually true.

"You've been saying that for weeks. And you've been avoiding me. You only do that when the words aren't flowing."

You have no idea.

"The book's been giving me a smidge of trouble." Understatement of the century. "But I promise, I'm nearly done." Flagrant lie. Ivy wondered if Marianne's Momdar was sounding an alarm. Ivy's own mama had an Eyebrow of Doom that could be heard over the phone when engaged.

"You have to give me something to give to Wally. I can't hold him off much longer."

Walter Caine—who inexplicably went by Wally, a fact that made it utterly impossible to take him seriously—was currently at the top of Ivy's avoid-at-all-costs list. Her editor was brilliant but a bit like a banty rooster when he got angry. He had deadlines. Of course, Ivy understood that. Everything about publishing involved deadlines. He'd absolutely blow a gasket if he knew she was still on Chapter One. The thirteenth version.

It was probably a sign.

"Next week." Was this what it felt like to be in debt to a

bookie? Making absurd promises in hopes of avoiding broken kneecaps or cement shoes? Except in this case it was Ivy's career, not her actual life, in danger.

"Ivy." Marianne drew her name out to four syllables, which was tantamount to being middle-named by her mama.

Ivy hunched her shoulders. "I swear I'm finishing up the book. In fact, I'm taking a special trip for the express purpose of focusing on nothing but that until it's done."

Where the hell had that come from? She had no such plans. Apparently in lieu of offering up reasonable plot, her brain had decided to just spew spontaneous, bald-faced lies.

Her agent sighed. "Fine. How can I reach you?"

In for a penny...

"Oh, well, you can't. There's no internet up there, and I was warned that cell service is spotty. The cabin has absolute privacy and no distractions. It's perfect."

Actually, something like that *did* sound perfect. If she went totally off the grid, Marianne and Wally wouldn't know where to send the hitman when she missed her deadline. The one that had already been pushed back once.

You've never missed a final deadline, and you're not going to start now.

Marianne offered another beleaguered sigh. "Find an internet connection and check in on Monday or I'm hunting you down, understand?"

"Yes, ma'am." Ivy had no doubt she meant it. Despite her trio of children and the stable of other writers she managed, Marianne would absolutely get herself on a plane and show up on Ivy's doorstep if she thought it would get results.

"I'll do what I can to hold off Wally. This morning's starred review at Kirkus for *Hollow Point Ridge* should appease him for a little while. You know he loves nothing more than seeing you rack up acclaim."

"Because acclaim means dollar signs for us all," Ivy recited.

As if she could forget that it was more than just her depending on income from her books.

"Damn straight. I forwarded the review to you. Check your email before you go," Marianne ordered.

She'd already seen the review this morning. Somebody had posted it in her fan group, which had generated a discussion thread that was already twenty pages deep about where she planned to go with the series next. But bringing that up would only prolong this conversation.

"Will do."

"Happy writing."

For just a moment, Ivy considered coming clean and telling Marianne the stark, unvarnished truth. Her agent was, ultimately, meant to be her advocate. But right now, she was only more pressure. So Ivy held in her snort of derision as she hung up the phone and tossed it on her desk.

It had been a long damned time since she'd been happy writing. The truth was, she had a raging case of writer's block, and she was already weeks past her initial deadline. That wasn't like her at all. She was a machine. Her first three books had poured out of her. The next three were each successively bigger, deeper, harder. And with each had come more success and higher expectations from her publisher, who wanted to capitalize on momentum to maximize sales. That was a business decision on their part. She was a commodity. Ivy understood that. And up to now, she'd been able to work with it.

But along with the professional pressures had come the rabid excitement of her fans. They loved the world she created, the characters she'd given them, and not a day went by when she didn't get emails and messages on social media demanding to know when the next book was coming because OMG they needed it yesterday! They had no idea the months, sometimes years of work that went into each book. What ate up her entire life occupied theirs for mere hours or days. And their insatiable enthusiasm was just one more stone piling on and crushing her with stress.

This book wasn't like the other six in her best-selling series, and she just hadn't found the right hook yet.

She would. Of course, she would. She just needed some more time and less pressure.

"Why don't you ask for world peace, while you're at it?"

Dropping into her office chair, Ivy shoved back from the desk and rolled across her office to the massive whiteboard occupying one wall. At this stage, the whole surface should've been covered with color-coded sticky notes detailing the assorted character arcs and how they drove and were driven by the action of the external plot. But it was empty other than the scrawl of "Michael" at the top in red marker. Below it a bright yellow note read, *You are a stubborn, taciturn asshole, who won't talk to me.* In a fit of pique and stress cleaning earlier in the week, she'd stripped away version number twelve of her plot. Now she couldn't face the blank space.

Page fright was so much a real thing.

Maybe she *should* get away. Find one of those out-of-the-way cabins to rent, with no phone, no internet, no way to be crushed under the weight of other people's expectations. Maybe then she could hear herself think.

Rolling back to her computer, she opened a browser, compulsively clicking on the little envelope that told her she had seventy-nine unread messages.

She'd cleared her inbox this morning.

"Why do I do this to myself?"

She started to close it out when a subject line caught her attention.

Come visit the brand new spa at The Misfit Inn!

She'd forgotten about The Misfit Inn. Last summer, she and several girlfriends had taken a weekend trip up there in sponta-neous celebration of Deanna's divorce. The owners had mentioned they were considering adding a spa. Ivy had signed up for the mailing list and promptly forgotten about it. She opened the email, feeling the first hints of excitement as she read it. Okay, maybe that was desperation. But really? A spa? One set right in the gorgeous Smoky Mountains, just four short hours away? She desperately needed to relax. It had to be a sign from the Universe.

Someone answered on the second ring. "Thank you for calling The Misfit Inn. This is Pru. How can I help you?"

Ivy remembered Pru, the kind-hearted woman who'd done everything possible to make the inn feel like home.

"This is Ivy Blake. I don't know if you remember me, but a bunch of girlfriends and I stayed with y'all last summer for a Thank God I'm Divorced party weekend—"

"Deanna's group! Yes, certainly we remember y'all."

"Well, I got the email about the opening of the spa, and it did say call to ask about booking specials that covered the inn and spa, so here I am."

"Wonderful!" The genuine warmth in Pru's voice had some of the knots relaxing. "How many?"

"Just me."

"In need of some pampering?"

"You have no idea."

"Okay then. When were you wanting to come?"

The sooner the better. "Um...today?"

"Today! Good gracious. Y'all are all about the spontaneity aren't you?"

Sure, let's call it that. "I know it's last-minute, but I was hoping to book two weeks."

"We can certainly accommodate that. But you should know before you make the drive that we're supposed to be having some really serious winter weather. Full-on snow and ice. The drive is liable to be pretty nasty and there's a really good chance you could get snowed in."

Snowed in at an inn and spa for two weeks, far away from everyone who knew her? "That sounds absolutely perfect. I'll see you in a few hours."

GRIEF SMELLED OF ONIONS, cheese, and cream of something soup. Multiple tables groaned under the weight of death casseroles along one wall of the church fellowship hall. The scent of it wafted over as Harrison Wilkes walked in, simultaneously curdling his stomach and making it growl. A quick scan of the room told him the widow hadn't made it over from the cemetery yet, but he spotted the man he'd come to support hovering near the dessert table. Careful not to make eye contact with the other mourners, Harrison wove his way through the crowd.

If possible, Ty looked worse than he had during the service. But then, he was here against medical advice and had served as a pall bearer. Sweat beaded along his brow. His shoulder had to be hurting like a son of a bitch from over-exertion.

"Sit your ass down before you fall down, Brooks."

Ty lifted bloodshot eyes to Harrison's. "You're not my CO."

"I'm still your friend." He took a step closer and lowered his voice. "You did your duty to Garrett. Don't you go blowing all the work you've done in PT by pushing yourself too far."

Ty's pale face turned mulish, but before he could pop off, another familiar voice interrupted.

"Step aside, y'all. I've got food to add to the table."

Sebastian Donnelly muscled his way past, a casserole dish in hand. Its contents smelled both familiar and noxious.

"Tell me that's not what I think it is," Harrison said.

Sebastian plunked the dish down on the table and took off the foil. "My famous barbeque beef casserole."

"More like infamous," Ty said. "Only you would try to make a casserole out of MREs."

"I tried to talk him out of it." Porter Ingram joined the group. "We all know how much Garrett hated that shit."

Sebastian straightened, suddenly sober. "Yeah, but he'd hate this damned wake even more."

They all lapsed into silence, aware of the dubious privilege of standing here able to bitch and moan about the wake. A privilege Garrett didn't have.

Everything about this sucked. Funerals sucked to begin with, no matter who they were for. They sucked worse when it was a friend. Someone you'd fought alongside, who'd saved your ass, who should've made it home. And they sucked most when they brought up old shit you were still trying to move past. There were too many ghosts stirred up for anybody to be comfortable.

"Come on. Let's either make plates or go sit down." Porter's voice interrupted Harrison's thoughts.

"I'm not hungry," Ty insisted.

"Then let's get out of the way for the people who are." Porter smoothly managed to nudge him toward a table.

"Always the peacemaker," Harrison murmured.

"Yeah, he's good at that." Sebastian picked up a paper plate and began filling it from the assortment of dishes, skipping his own offering to the spread.

Not knowing what else to do, Harrison fell in behind him.

"How are you doing with all this?" Sebastian asked.

It was instinct to deflect. "Better than Ty."

They both looked across the room, where he'd finally sat, shoulders bowed, head bent as if he couldn't hold it up anymore. Porter had a chair pulled up, talking to him in a low voice, one hand on his arm.

Sebastian scooped up some kind of hash brown casserole. "You think he'll come back from this?"

"You never come back from this. Not really." Harrison twitched his shoulders inside the jacket of his suit, wishing the thing didn't feel like a straitjacket.

Glancing at Ty, seeing the clench of his jaw, the lines of strain fanning out from his eyes, Harrison knew exactly the kind of shit going through his buddy's head. He'd been there. It was the reason he'd left the Army. It didn't feel like three years. Not when so many familiar faces filled the room. Men he'd fought with, bled with. Many were still fighting the fight. In his own way, so was he. But he couldn't do what they did. Not anymore.

Harrison trailed Sebastian across the room, nodding acknowledgments to those who greeted him, but not stopping until he reached Ty's table. Ty went silent, straightening in his chair with a Styrofoam cup he no doubt wished held something stronger than sweet tea, as they all realized Bethany Reeves had just arrived.

Ty hadn't spoken to her at the funeral. He hadn't even been able to go near her. He blamed himself for Garrett's death. Wrongly. But none of them could talk him out of that at this stage. So the three of them ranged around him, buffers between their friend and everybody else here. They shoveled in food and talked football and other stupid, civilian shit because he needed distraction and it was all they could do here. But they each tracked Bethany's progress around the room and braced themselves when she made her way to Ty.

He didn't bolt. Ty was no coward and his mother had raised him better than that. But Harrison knew he wanted to.

Bethany's face was ravaged by grief as she reached out for Ty's hand. "Ty."

"Ma'am."

Her expression twisted. "Don't you ma'am me, Tyson Brooks. You were the closest thing Garrett had to a brother, and that makes you family."

Ty's Adam's apple bobbed. "I loved him like a brother."

"I know you did." She tried to smile, but tears streamed down her face. "He got out because of you. You're a hero for that."

Ty shoved to his feet so fast his chair tipped over, the metal clattering against the industrial tile floor as he jerked his hand from Bethany's. In the sudden silence, his words sounded too loud. "I'm no hero."

He walked out without another word. With apologetic looks at Bethany, Sebastian and Porter followed, no doubt to make sure he didn't do something stupid. That left Harrison to find the right thing to say to the poor woman to smooth things over. Fuck.

He didn't know how much Bethany knew about the details of her husband's death. Some of the details were classified, as Ranger missions often were. There were things he didn't know himself, but could easily fill in from experience. And he knew those things wouldn't bring comfort to Garrett's widow. In truth, he had no idea how to comfort those left behind. Standing beside her, looking into her stricken face, he felt all the old impotence rise up, strong enough to choke him.

Harrison didn't know what he said to Bethany. His head was too full of the visits he'd had to make to the significant others of his own men. But he said something, taking a moment to squeeze her hand because even he could tell she needed human connection. The grasp of her cold, clammy fingers sent him back, until his head echoed with tears and recriminations. Needing to get the hell out, he made his excuses and all but ran for the exit.

Outside the fellowship hall, he braced his hands against the trunk of a car and sucked in big, cleansing lungfuls of the cold, winter air. It was so cold it hurt, colder than it should be in north Georgia this time of year. But the pain was good. The pain brought him back to the now.

"Hey."

Harrison straightened and turned to Porter. "Where's Ty?"

"Sebastian took him home. He's gonna stick around a while, keep an eye on him."

"Good." Ty didn't need to be left alone right now. He had a long, dark road ahead.

Porter angled his head, studying Harrison with eyes that saw too much. "You're not looking so great."

Because it was Porter, because he'd see through the bullshit, Harrison admitted the truth. "I need to get the hell out of here."

"I've got a cabin nobody's using. It's a chunk out from town, away from everything and everybody. It's yours if you want it. Peace and quiet and a chance to get your head screwed on straight. And Eden's Ridge is closer than you driving all the way home."

The whole idea of being in the middle of nowhere in the mountains of Tennessee, away from people and pressures, where he could *think* was beyond appealing. He had some decisions to make. It would be easier to make them without all the reminders of the past.

"Lead the way."

∼

GRAB your copy of *Baby It's Cold Outside* today!

OTHER BOOKS BY KAIT NOLAN

A complete and up-to-date list of all my books can be found at https://kaitnolan.com.

~

THE MISFIT INN SERIES
SMALL TOWN FAMILY ROMANCE

- *When You Got A Good Thing* (Kennedy and Xander)
- *Til There Was You* (Misty and Denver)
- *Those Sweet Words* (Pru and Flynn)
- *Stay A Little Longer* (Athena and Logan)
- *Bring It On Home* (Maggie and Porter)

RESCUE MY HEART SERIES
SMALL TOWN MILITARY ROMANCE

- *Baby It's Cold Outside* (Ivy and Harrison)
- *What I Like About You* (Laurel and Sebastian)
- *Bad Case of Loving You* (Paisley and Ty prequel)

- *Made For Loving You* (Paisley and Ty)

MEN OF THE MISFIT INN
SMALL TOWN SOUTHERN ROMANCE

- *Let It Be Me* (Emerson and Caleb)
- *Our Kind of Love* (Abbey and Kyle)
- *Don't You Wanna Stay* (Deanna and Wyatt)
- *Until We Meet Again* (Samantha and Griffin prequel)
- *Come A Little Closer* (Samantha and Griffin)

BAD BOY BAKERS
SMALL TOWN MILITARY ROMANCE

- *Rescued By a Bad Boy* (Brax and Mia prequel)
- *Mixed Up With a Marine* (Brax and Mia)
- *Wrapped Up with a Ranger* (Holt and Cayla)
- *Stirred Up by a SEAL* (Jonah and Rachel)
- *Hung Up on the Hacker* (Cash and Hadley)
- *Caught Up with the Captain* (Grey and Rebecca)

WISHFUL ROMANCE SERIES
SMALL TOWN SOUTHERN ROMANCE

- *Once Upon A Coffee* (Avery and Dillon)
- *To Get Me To You* (Cam and Norah)
- *Know Me Well* (Liam and Riley)
- *Be Careful, It's My Heart* (Brody and Tyler)
- *Just For This Moment* (Myles and Piper)
- *Wish I Might* (Reed and Cecily)
- *Turn My World Around* (Tucker and Corinne)
- *Dance Me A Dream* (Jace and Tara)
- *See You Again* (Trey and Sandy)
- *The Christmas Fountain* (Chad and Mary Alice)

- *You Were Meant For Me* (Mitch and Tess)
- *A Lot Like Christmas* (Ryan and Hannah)
- *Dancing Away With My Heart* (Zach and Lexi)

WISHING FOR A HERO SERIES (A WISHFUL SPINOFF SERIES)
SMALL TOWN ROMANTIC SUSPENSE

- *Make You Feel My Love* (Judd and Autumn)
- *Watch Over Me* (Nash and Rowan)
- *Can't Take My Eyes Off You* (Ethan and Miranda)
- *Burn For You* (Sean and Delaney)

MEET CUTE ROMANCE
SMALL TOWN SHORT ROMANCE

- *Once Upon A Snow Day*
- *Once Upon A New Year's Eve*
- *Once Upon An Heirloom*
- *Once Upon A Coffee*
- *Once Upon A Campfire*
- *Once Upon A Rescue*

SUMMER CAMP
CONTEMPORARY ROMANCE

- *Once Upon A Campfire*
- *Second Chance Summer*

ABOUT KAIT

Kait is a Mississippi native, who often swears like a sailor, calls everyone sugar, honey, or darlin', and can wield a bless your heart like a saber or a Snuggie, depending on requirements.

You can find more information on this RITA ® Award-winning author and her books on her website http://kaitnolan.com.

Do you need more small town sass and spark? Sign up for her newsletter to hear about new releases, book deals, and exclusive content!